W9-BRF-937

NOT JUST A PRETTY FACE

As Athena began to grow from child to woman, she resented it every step of the way. The older she grew, the more circumscribed her life became. She also, to her horror, became beautiful. Her body was lithe and muscular, but it acquired breasts that made it hard to shoot a bow. Shooting a bow was an unwomanly skill, Nurse informed her, and it came of running around with that boy from the forge, getting all sooty.

Athena despairingly studied her face in her polished silver mirror. She had just met her uncle Poseidon in the corridor, and he swatted her backside with a genial air and looked down the neck of her gown.

"He's a beast," Athena said to Polumetis, her best friend. "He sleeps with everyone's wife, just because he can. He gives them presents or they're afraid of him because he's the king's brother."

Athena knew that her father and mother had already begun to fight over her own marriage. Father wanted to marry her to Uncle Poseidon to cement his brother's claim to kingship. If she had to marry him, Athena said, she would kill him in their bed on their wedding night. . . .

Don't miss the previous *Goddesses* books. . . .

Love Underground
Persephone's Tale

Fatal Attraction
Aphrodite's Tale

THE GODDESSES

ALL'S FAIR IN
LOVE AND WAR

Athena's Tale

Alicia Fields

A SIGNET ECLIPSE BOOK

SIGNET ECLIPSE
Published by New American Library, a division of
Penguin Group (USA) Inc., 375 Hudson Street,
New York, New York 10014, USA
Penguin Group (Canada), 90 Eglinton Avenue East, Suite 700, Toronto,
Ontario M4P 2Y3, Canada (a division of Pearson Penguin Canada Inc.)
Penguin Books Ltd., 80 Strand, London WC2R 0RL, England
Penguin Ireland, 25 St. Stephen's Green, Dublin 2,
Ireland (a division of Penguin Books Ltd.)
Penguin Group (Australia), 250 Camberwell Road, Camberwell, Victoria 3124,
Australia (a division of Pearson Australia Group Pty. Ltd.)
Penguin Books India Pvt. Ltd., 11 Community Centre, Panchsheel Park,
New Delhi - 110 017, India
Penguin Group (NZ), cnr Airborne and Rosedale Roads, Albany,
Auckland 1310, New Zealand (a division of Pearson New Zealand Ltd.)
Penguin Books (South Africa) (Pty.) Ltd., 24 Sturdee Avenue,
Rosebank, Johannesburg 2196, South Africa

Penguin Books Ltd., Registered Offices:
80 Strand, London WC2R 0RL, England

First published by Signet Eclipse, an imprint of New American Library,
a division of Penguin Group (USA) Inc.

First Printing, January 2006
10 9 8 7 6 5 4 3 2 1

PUBLISHER'S NOTE
This is a work of fiction. Names, characters, places, and incidents either are
the product of the author's imagination or are used fictitiously, and any
resemblance to actual persons, living or dead, business establishments,
events, or locales is entirely coincidental.
    The publisher does not have any control over and does not assume any
responsibility for author or third-party Web sites or their content.

For Marian

AUTHOR'S NOTE

She is tall, frozen in painted marble, forbidding as the stone from which she was carved. Her gaze is stern, as befits the tutelary goddess of a city as great as Athens. The citizens come, bringing offerings to her temple on the Acropolis beneath her marble gaze. Poets and philosophers argue the meaning of life while sitting on her steps. Despite her patronage, it is men who run her city: the lawmakers, the soldiers, the gentleman farmers. Respectable women stay at home, minding the servants and the children, venturing outside their houses only for festivals. Only occasionally the hetairai, the elegant, well-educated courtesans, come to see her, painted faces a mark of their freedom from domestic tyranny.

This is the classical age, the golden age of Greece and of Athens, the proudest of its city-states, its economy fueled by the source that feeds and lights the whole Aegean—the olive.

Once it was not like this. Once there was a village of stone and mud huts. Once there were only flocks of goats; tallow to burn in smoky lamps; a bloodstained stone altar to the older gods. The olive is old, but not as old as Athens. Once there was a real woman inside the marble shell.

Her name was Athena.

I

❧

The Owl

Metis lay gasping with the new baby, bloody and squalling, clutched to her breast.

The midwife clucked her tongue sadly. "Pity it's a girl," she said to Kosmetas. "She may not carry another one. It was a hard labor and she's done herself damage."

"Get out!" Metis shrieked at her.

"I was just saying I was sorry," the midwife said. "They're often like that," she added to Kosmetas. "After a long labor. Especially the first ones. They get a little mad in the head."

"I am not mad in the head."

Kosmetas looked as if he wasn't sure. He had not been allowed in until after the baby had come, and from the sound of it, his wife had been trying to kill the midwife. Now she lay on the bed, her hair a wet, dark tangle about her face, and glared at the midwife in the smoky light of the tallow lamps.

"That baby needs to be washed," the midwife said briskly, and held out her hands for it.

Metis looked at her suspiciously.

"Let her have it," Kosmetas said. "There's a good girl."

Metis's eyes narrowed and she glared at him too, but she held out the baby. The midwife took her and dipped her in a pot of warm water on the stone floor. The cut end of the umbilical cord stuck out like a twig from her navel. The baby stopped crying when she felt the warm water. "There, now," the midwife cooed at her. She lifted her out, washed her face with a wet cloth, and wrapped her up in blankets. She laid the baby in the wooden cradle beside the bed.

"Go away again," the midwife said to Kosmetas, "while I bathe my lady. Then you can come back in."

Kosmetas looked relieved, and disappeared into the hallway outside.

Metis lay back resignedly and let the midwife bathe her and change the bandages that absorbed the seeping blood between her legs. The afterbirth, a translucent mass that had once sheltered the baby, lay in another pot beside the cradle. Metis looked at it pointedly. It had magical properties, and the midwife had been instructed to burn it in the proper fashion, according to the customs of Metis's people. The midwife had snorted in annoyance, but Metis had instructed her maids to follow her and make sure she did it. If the after-birth wasn't given to the Goddess, she would have no reason to look after the child as she grew.

"I'm sure I'm sorry if I insulted my lady," the midwife said, gathering her kit of rags and knives and picking up the pot with the afterbirth. "I only meant it's a shame for the king not to have a son to come after him and all. If you don't have a boy, I suppose it will be that brother of his."

"Certainly not!" Metis said.

The midwife handed her the baby and Metis closed her eyes, snuggling the child against her breast. A daughter was fine. Old ways were the best ways.

Metis named the baby Athena, which was a name from her own language, mostly given up in her public speech now that she had married the king, but spoken with her maids, and in the times when she wanted to be easy in her speech and not hunt for words. Kosmetas argued that it was a name he couldn't get his tongue around, but he let her have her way, since the child was a girl.

"I hear she's not likely to have another," his brother Poseidon said cheerfully, slapping Kosmetas on the back.

"You never know with women," Kosmetas said. "Don't measure your head for my crown just yet."

Poseidon laughed, a cheerful bellow. "Early days yet indeed." He stretched his long legs out in front of him and grinned at his older brother.

Kosmetas chuckled and shook his head. Poseidon was nearly twenty years his junior, barely fifteen this winter, but already a better horseman than anyone else in Attica. He would make a good king if it came to it. But Kosmetas wasn't old yet. He might make another baby, on Metis or someone else, the way his father had done. He couldn't divorce Metis, of course, he thought ruefully. He had married her in the first place to cement his rule over the Pelasgians, the people who had held the land before the Achaeans, Kosmetas's father's people, had come. She had been an unsatisfactory wife, never quite refusing him or going against his wishes, but always managing somehow to do the things she wanted to. She was thick as thieves with the priestesses of the Pelasgians' Goddess as well. One of them had told her what to name the child. It was necessary to show regard for the Pelasgians' Goddess, who was represented by a crude stone that they anointed with tallow and fed on festival days, but Kosmetas's ancestors had worshiped the Goddess in her Achaean form and she had done well by them.

Metis knew what he was thinking. She generally found her husband transparent enough to interpret without asking, a talent that she knew irritated him enough that he might change his mind on an issue just to prove her wrong. She also knew that she was regarded with suspicion by the Areopagus, the council of nobles named for the rock where they met with the king to decide matters of state. The Areopagus had decided on her marriage, for instance, but they had expected her to be a subservient wife, and they had gotten a surprise. The Achaeans didn't pay attention. It was necessary to pay attention. Metis paid attention to everything, as the priestesses had taught her.

As her daughter grew up, Metis saw that Athena learned to pay attention too. She was given a nurse to follow her, and the run of the palace, a limewashed stone building two stories high that sat beside the temple of the Achaean Goddess at the top of the Acropolis. The city spread down the slopes below, a collection of tile-roofed stone houses and temples giving way to mud and thatch huts on the lower slopes. Beyond were wheatfields, vineyards, and goat pastures, and the blue harbor to the south. Athena's room in the palace had fish painted on its plastered walls, but the houses of most of the citizens were rough stone.

When Athena was old enough, her mother taught her to count, and to do small sums in her head, which her father couldn't do. She taught her the names of the birds that flocked along the shoreline or nested in the meadows or flew overhead in their twice-yearly migrations to distant lands. She spoke to her in the Pelasgian tongue so that the child grew up with two languages in her head. She taught her to weave fine cloth and tapestries with pictures in them, from the wool of the goats that also gave Attica milk and leather and meat for sacrifices. What her mother didn't teach her, Athena paid attention to herself at the smith's forge or the carpenter's bench or the smelly confines of the fishmonger's stall. When she was five she burned her fingers on a sword blade in the forge when the smith turned his back.

"Child, you oughtn't to be in there," her nurse said, when she saw the burn. "What was Smith thinking of?"

"Amoni goes in there," Athena said. Amoni was the smith's son, a year older than Athena.

"And he is a boy," Nurse said, "if I recall correctly."

"That does not make any difference," Athena said, sucking her burned fingers. "Ask Mother."

Nurse sighed. She didn't need to ask Athena's mother; she knew what the queen would say. Metis was raising the girl like a boy, and no good would come of it, but Metis wouldn't listen.

When Athena was six, she was allowed to explore the city, safe in the knowledge that everyone knew who she was. Beside the palace was the temple of the Achaean Goddess, where Kosmetas and the Areopagus went each spring and fall to kill two goats and a boar and burn the bones on the altar. Behind the altar was a statue of the Goddess, a fierce figure with great bird wings, and snakes in her hands, brightly painted. The temple was stone, with four stone pillars holding up the tile roof. The temple of the Pelasgian Goddess, where Athena's mother went to worship, was older, and smaller, but Athena thought it held more magic. The statue of the Goddess there was just a stone, dark with old blood and smears of tallow from the sacrifices, but when Athena looked at it, she was sure she could see a face. The Goddess in her father's temple was just a carved lady, but somebody was *in* the stone.

Outside the new temple was the agora, the market square, where Cook shopped among the butchers and fishmongers and greengrocers every morning. Athena investigated the peddlers hawking amber, ivory combs, clay jugs painted with octopi, bronze lamps, goatskins, songbirds in tiny cages made of twigs, necklaces of amethyst and lapis lazuli, pots of rouge and green paint for ladies' eyelids, and the wine merchants with their wares in brown clay jars. She made faces at her father's soldiers stationed on the palace steps, hoping to make them laugh, and bought sweets and fresh goat milk from an old woman with a tray around her neck. She made friends with Pallas, whose father was Kosmetas's captain of the guard, and Nike, whose father was the vintner and whose large, noisy family Athena sometimes pretended was her own when she was feeling lonely. Pallas lived with her mother and father and baby brother in a small, elegant house near the palace, and her equally elegant mother let Athena practice her weaving along with Pallas on a little loom. Farther down the hillside, past the old temple, was Nike's house, where there was almost always a fight going on between two or three of her brothers and sisters, or a loud, rowdy game of horse-and-chariot in the street outside. Nike's house was a mud-brick hut with a thatched roof, and it always seemed to be exploding at the seams with Nike's family.

If it wasn't raining, which it hardly ever did, the three took picnics out into the barley fields or walked south to climb along the rocky coast to look down on the harbor with the white-sailed boats coming and going on the blue sea. Sometimes they went the other way toward the goat pastures, where the goat boys herded their flocks out to graze in the morning, and back to the city at night for fear of lions and wolves. Athena and Pallas and Nike were careful not to go too far into the hills because of them. Outside the city was wild land where anything might be lurking. At least, that was what Nurse said.

In early spring, when the land turned green, they picked anemones and helped Nike's mother whitewash her mud-brick walls so they looked nicer. In summer, when the sun was hot and the sky was a clear brilliant blue like the sea, they went out to watch the grain harvest and got in the way. In the fall, they watched the boys and young women trample the wine grapes in the press, and waited impatiently to be old enough to do it themselves. In winter, when it got cold, they stayed indoors by the hearth and played draughts or drew pictures on the floor with charcoal. Whatever they did, they did together.

When Athena was seven, she found an owlet fallen from its nest, a fluff of feathers not yet fledged. She scooped it up even though it bit her, and brought it home.

"You can't keep that," Nurse said.

"It's mine."

"Nasty, dirty thing. And it won't live."

"It will." Athena stood with her chin up. The owlet looked out from the cloth Athena had wrapped it in, regarding Nurse with baleful yellow eyes. Athena's gray ones snapped little sparks. Her dark hair had bits of twigs and leaves in it, and her bare knees were scraped and dirty.

"Did you climb a tree after that thing?" Nurse demanded.

"No! It fell." She had been in the tree, but she hadn't known the owl's nest was there. It had climbed out of its hole in the tree to watch her, and fallen. Everyone knew their mothers wouldn't take them back if you had handled them.

"You've broken your sandal strap, too," Nurse said.

Athena nodded and disappeared, the broken strap flapping, before Nurse thought of something else she'd done wrong. She put the owlet in a wooden box, after she evicted her dolls, and took it into the kitchen garden, along with a spoon stolen from Cook's stores. Athena sat down next to a row of beans and began to dig. The owlet watched her from its box, opening its beak hopefully.

"Here!" Athena produced a worm from the dark earth and held it, dangling pink and squirming, over the owlet. It opened its beak again and the worm disappeared. Athena dug the spoon back into the dirt.

It was a lot of work, hunting for an owl, she discovered.

"Mice," said Amoni, when she went to the forge to see if she could make a cage for it. "That's what it eats."

"I think it's too little yet."

"Have you taken a good look at that beak?" Amoni asked her.

"Well, I'll try it on them. Nurse is always setting traps."

"What have you named it?"

"I think I'll call her Polumetis. She looks like she's thinking all the time."

"How do you know it's a she?"

"I don't, I suppose. She just looks like a girl to me."

"I suppose you'll know if she lays an egg," Amoni said.

"I need a cage. Have you got some wire your father isn't using?"

"There's no such thing as something Father isn't using." Amoni's black hair stuck up on end, and his face was sooty where he had rubbed his nose when it itched.

"I'll pay for it. I have a silver piece." Athena was aware that her position as the king's daughter gave her certain responsibilities. Not taking things from people just because she could was one of them.

"I'll ask Father."

They were sitting on a bench in the shadows

where Smith's tools hung from hooks in the roof beams, when Smith came back with Athena's Uncle Poseidon behind him.

"Little one, you aren't supposed to be here," Poseidon said. "This is no place for little girls."

"I want some copper wire."

"And I want to sprout wings. Go play with dolls." Poseidon turned to Smith. "I need a new head on my hunting spear. I'm to hunt with the fellows tomorrow, and the blade is nicked where I drove it into a stone."

"How did you do that?"

"Temper mostly." Poseidon grinned. "I missed my kill."

"Bring it down then. But I can't do it today."

"I need it tonight."

Smith and Poseidon looked at each other for a long moment, and then Smith shrugged. "I'll see what I can do."

"*He* won't pay," Amoni whispered to Athena.

Athena showed Smith her owl, and he found her a flat piece of wood to use for the cage bottom, and a roll of copper wire. "I'll drill some holes in the bottom to take the wire, but it's not going to be as easy as you think. I could make you one if you'll give me a few days."

"I can do it," Athena said. She handed him her silver. She nodded at Amoni. "You can help me."

"Why do you think the gods made bugs?" Athena asked. "I think it's so frogs will have something to eat." She flicked a large beetle away from the wire she was twisting into a row of spirals. The owl watched its trajectory with interest.

"Owls too, maybe," Amoni said, noting it.

"They didn't have to give them so many legs," Pallas said with distaste. She and Nike had come to see the owl.

"My brother Akakios ate one," Nike said. "A beetle, I mean. Theios bet him he wouldn't." Theios was her next-to-oldest brother.

"What was it like?" Athena asked.

"It sounded crunchy."

Pallas shuddered.

"There." Athena laid the pincers down and twisted the copper spirals around the framework she had built up from the wooden base. "I don't think she can get through that, do you?"

"Not if you fasten it down good," Amoni said. "That's nice. I like the way that looks."

Athena nodded. She found spirals very satisfactory, the way they just kept going, enclosing something at their heart and flowing on to the next thing at the same time. Spirals were very old, and connected to the Goddess and the moon and the tides, Mother said. The spiral was the baby in the womb and the old moon in the new moon's arms. "I'm going to put twists of wire here and here, to keep it from wobbling." She showed Amoni the anchor points, and he nodded approvingly. The cage leaned a little to the left, and she had nearly used up the wire, which was expensive because it was tedious to make, but she liked the way it had turned out. It was big enough for a grown owl to live in, although she intended to tame this one to sit on her shoulder so it didn't have to live in a cage all the time.

"She needs a perch." Athena stood up, with the owl in its box under one arm, and the cage in the other, and they followed her. Wherever Athena was going always seemed important, something you would want to be in on.

At the woodworker's shop, she begged a short length of branch left over from a chair leg, and fastened it across the cage.

"She needs water," Pallas suggested.

"Mmm." Mother had lots of pots for her face paint. Surely she could spare one. Athena had already offered the owl some water in a spoon and it hadn't seemed interested. Did owls drink? That was something else she needed to find out. There was always something that needed finding out.

Metis was in her sunroom, spinning wool with the palace maids. She set the spindle down to inspect the owl. The gaggle of children was clustered in the doorway, afraid to come in. Metis nodded as if she found the owl extremely satisfactory. Athena was relieved. You never knew with Mother.

"I think I have something it can have," she told Athena in Pelasgian. "And you three," she added in Achaean, "may see it later. I expect it's tired." They darted away down the corridor, and Metis took Athena's hand. "Come."

Metis sat down on the bed in her chamber, which had walls painted with leaping dolphins. The bed was ebony, with a summer mattress of sweetgrass mixed with rosemary and lavender, and a coverlet of soft blue wool. She patted the place beside her. "I have an ivory pot that you can have for it to drink out of," she said.

Athena looked startled. "That's your good one."

Metis smiled. She had dressed her hair so that two dark curls fell in front of her ears, and the back hair was pulled into a knot from which a few curls descended. It smelled of lavender water, and a gold diadem with a poppy at its center encircled her head. "Owls are lucky. They belong to the Lady. It's a good sign that this one has come to you."

"Well, it didn't exactly come to me," Athena admitted. "I picked it up."

Metis looked at the owl, apparently asleep now in its fluff of feathers. "All the same. When it is your turn to rule Attica, people will remember that you tamed an owl."

"My turn?"

"Listen to me, child." Metis took her by the shoulders and looked into her eyes. "You have the blood of the Old Ones in you. My people will follow you if you ask them to."

"Follow me where?" Athena envisioned a crowd trailing after her as Nike and Pallas and Amoni had. Would Mother let them all in the palace?

"They will make you queen when your father dies."

Athena's eyes widened. Was Father dying? She rarely saw him, as he made it plain he had no time for small girl children, but he had looked healthy enough this morning. He had roared at her and smacked her for being underfoot while the stewards were talking about taxes, and for leaving a wooden horse where he had stepped on it.

"When you are grown, of course," Metis said, relieving her mind about that.

"Uncle Poseidon says he is going to be king because I don't have a brother," Athena informed her.

Metis's mouth compressed into a tight line. "That is his opinion of the situation," she said. "He will try. Listen to me, child. If you will take my people back to the old ways, when the queen held the power, they will follow you, and Poseidon will have nothing, unless you decide to marry him."

Athena screwed her face up at that thought. "Then he would be king," she said practically.

"In the old days," Metis said, "the king went to the Goddess every seven years. And then there was a new king."

"Went to the Goddess?"

"Married her. In the Underworld."

"Oh." Athena didn't quite understand that, but she wanted to think about it by herself.

"This is not something to discuss with your father, you understand," Metis said.

Athena nodded.

"But it will do no harm to sit quietly by him when he talks with his councilors, and listen."

"Will he let me?" He hadn't seemed glad to see her this morning.

"If you are quiet and respectful. I will bring you with me. You are old enough now."

"Mmm." It didn't sound as much fun as playing with Nike and Pallas and Amoni.

"You have responsibilities," Metis said.

The next morning, Metis sent Nurse to rouse Athena and dress her in a good gown, with her leather girdle with the seashells on it.

"Where are we going?"

"Your mother wants you." Nurse pursed her lips disapprovingly at the owl dozing on its perch.

"I need some mice," Athena said.

"You may see about the traps when your mother is through with you."

"Do you think I ought to cut them up for it?"

"Ugh! Certainly not!"

Athena pondered that question while she sat beside Mother in the throne room and listened to Father decide things, like whether Aglaia from the fishmonger's had put a curse on Eleni from the tavern and made a boil come out on the end of her nose; and the claim of a merchant from Crete that Nikolaos the unguent maker owed him for a sack of pepper that was moldy. The chairs in the throne room were carved stone, with goatskins over them, and they were very old. They had belonged to the kings and queens of the Pelasgians, and you couldn't be king if you didn't sit on them.

There were two smaller chairs beside the thrones, also stone but with no goatskin. Athena shifted her bottom uncomfortably in hers while Eleni displayed the boil and Kosmetas peered at it. Metis leaned forward and touched it with the tip of her finger while the merchant patted his foot impatiently.

"It seems an ordinary boil to me," Kosmetas said. "Had them myself. No respecter of kings."

"She bewitched me!" Eleni said. "It wasn't there yesterday!"

"And why would she bewitch you?"

Eleni glared at Aglaia. "I don't know."

"Come now. She doesn't bewitch just everyone, or there would be boils all over the city. She must have had a reason."

"I can't help it if her man won't stay home," Eleni said.

"Out running around all night, and then he won't get up in the morning when the boats come in," Aglaia said.

"It isn't my fault men come to the tavern," Eleni retorted. "I'm not going to turn custom away, and me a poor widow with no husband."

"You might get one if you didn't have boils on your nose."

The merchant from Crete looked aggravated, but Kosmetas considered all this carefully, Athena noted. Eleni and Aglaia were both Pelasgian, if you didn't count Eleni's late husband, and Kosmetas listened as Metis whispered in his ear. Athena thought that sometimes Father was annoyed when Mother gave him good advice, but he listened to it. Now he said to Eleni, "If it's a magical boil it won't go away. Real boils take a ten-day to go away as a rule, unless you lance them. We'll have a physician lance it, the sooner to see which kind it is."

Eleni put her hand over her nose. Athena tried not to giggle. "I won't serve him anymore, if that's what you want," Eleni said grudgingly.

Kosmetas looked at Aglaia. "Does that satisfy you?"

Aglaia nodded.

"I'm the one brought the complaint against *her!*" Eleni said.

"You brought the complaint against the boil, as I understand it," Kosmetas said. "I expect it will go away now, and there is to be no more talk of witches, understood?"

They both nodded grudgingly. Athena looked at the boil as Eleni left, trying to decide if it was a magical one or not. She thought it wasn't, and Father had been clever. Or Mother had.

The foreign merchant and Nikolaos were next, and Athena saw Poseidon slip in while they were talking, and Kosmetas give him an annoyed look. Poseidon was supposed to be at these councils, learning things. The things that Mother wanted her to learn, Athena supposed. Poseidon would usually rather be hunting or chasing girls.

Nikolaos had spilled the contents of the pepper sack out on the throne room floor in front of Kosmetas's chair. Kosmetas looked further annoyed as peppercorns skittered across the tiles. Most of them stayed in a clump by the king's feet. They were indeed moldy. "Just look at that!" Nikolaos said. "And he wants good money for them."

"I believe that the seller has brought the complaint against you," Kosmetas said. "Complaint first, if you please. Then defense."

"I am Celeus of Knossos, Basileus," the merchant said, giving Kosmetas his most respectful title. "Come to your fair city with a cargo of pottery lamps, fine carpets, purple dye, ivory, pepper, and juniper berries, and this fellow owes me three obols of silver."

"The pepper does appear to be moldy," Kosmetas said.

"It wasn't when I gave it to him. The fool leaves it in a damp cellar and does the Bull knows what else with it, what does he expect? Mold comes to damp; that is an elementary fact of natural philosophy."

"It was moldy when I got it," Nikolaos said.

"It was not." The Cretan prodded the pile accusingly with the toe of his boot.

"I turned it out right away to see, and it was spoiled." Nikolaos's gray beard jutted out emphatically. He spread his hands out toward Kosmetas, an honest man seeking justice.

"Then why did you wait five days to come and complain about it?"

"I didn't. I said I wouldn't pay, and you've been hounding me for five days. Take it back then, if it's not moldy."

"It's moldy now! What did you do to it?"

"Stop!" Kosmetas raised his voice just a little, and they were silent, watching him apprehensively.

"That cellar of Nikolaos's is always damp," Poseidon said lazily from Kosmetas's side.

"And how would you know?" Kosmetas asked him.

Poseidon leaned toward him. "Been in it," he said softly. "Don't ask me."

Athena could just hear him. She thought Nikolaos could too. She saw him stiffen. Poseidon was always sniffing around after any pretty woman, and Nikolaos had a young, pretty wife. She let Athena put dabs of perfume behind her ears when Athena went to Nikolaos's shop.

Kosmetas sighed. "You'll get in trouble one day, sticking it where it doesn't belong," he told Poseidon under his breath. "I expect better of you." To the petitioners he said, "Half of that looks usable. Sweep it up off my floor and pay him one obol."

"Basileus!" The merchant looked aggrieved.

"I have decided." Kosmetas gave him a look that suggested he not argue. "Go away before I look into whether you have paid your port taxes."

"But a whole obol!" Nikolaos protested.

"It should be one and a half. I have it on good authority that your cellar is damp."

Athena thought her father might have deducted

that extra half an obol on account of its being
Poseidon who had been in the cellar. She fidgeted
in her chair while a stream of other citizens
brought their pleas for justice or protests over
taxes or blocked drains to her father. As they kept
coming, she lost interest and began to slide down
in the chair, until her legs stuck straight out and
her tunic had hiked itself up over her waist. Metis
reached down and smacked her knee and she sat
back up. When the last citizen had departed, Kosmetas rose and settled his state cloak about his
shoulders. It was fine wool lined in goatskin, with
a border of the expensive red-purple dye that
came from Crete or from Tyre and was made, so
the cloth dyer's daughter, Arachne, had told
Athena, from sea snails. Athena had wanted to
know if the snails themselves were purple or just
their insides, but Arachne didn't know.

After the citizens' petitions came the council
meeting. Kosmetas strode down the palace steps
with the queen beside him, towing Athena, and
the members of the Areopagus fell in behind
them. Athena didn't know why they couldn't
meet in the throne room, but they couldn't. It had
always been done this way, Metis said. The Areopagus, the hill from which the council took its
name, was a rocky promontory not quite so tall
as the Acropolis upon which the palace and the
temples perched. The top of the Areopagus had
been leveled to make a flat spot, and a half ring
of stone seats occupied the middle, with the king's
high throne at the open end. There were no seats

beside him here, and Metis had told Athena that in the old days, which Athena had finally figured out were so old that her mother hadn't actually been there, the queen sat in the high seat. Now she took a seat at the end of the ring, and beckoned Athena to her. "Stand beside me and listen," she whispered. "And don't fidget."

The Areopagus, which consisted of seven men with long gray beards and one young one, and Uncle Poseidon, took their places in the seats. Gelon, the eldest of them, rose from his seat almost immediately and began a long story that Athena couldn't follow, about the practice of young men in the city of playing lewd songs on the lyre, which was an instrument of refinement and played by men of learning, and how it had happened to him sitting in the agora and spoiled his morning's thought on important matters, and therefore these young men were a disgrace and a law should be passed.

The Areopagus argued that among themselves while Kosmetas kept silent. In the Areopagus the king was only the highest of equals, and his councilors must be listened to. Athena leaned on her mother's chair and yawned. Uncle Poseidon saw her and winked at her. He didn't take any part in the argument until the elder councilors had wound themselves down. Then he stood up and said, "How will we define what is bawdy?"

There was a general muttering. "Unrefined."

"Frivolous."

"Love songs?"

When they couldn't agree on a definition of songs to banish, they gave up and went on to the matter of taxes on vineyards, which was more important to everyone except Gelon, who had had his morning disturbed and was still brooding about it. Athena found that even more boring than the question about bawdy songs, but Metis pinched her and said, "This is important. Listen to this," so she tried to.

The Areopagus met until noon. When the sun was a blazing bronze disk overhead and everyone's shadows were squat dwarves under their chairs, Kosmetas stood and lifted his hand, which stopped the debate. By this time, Athena was drooping over her mother's shoulder, playing with Metis's hair.

"Is this enough responsibilities for this morning?" she asked plaintively as the Areopagus rose.

Metis chuckled. "I expect so. But remember, these matters are important to the citizens and the council, and so they are important to you. Don't forget that."

Then Metis let her go back to see her owl and check whether there were any mice in the traps. There were two. Athena carried them by their tails, swinging them, and offered them to the owl, who grabbed one in a claw and tried to eat it whole. It turned out that whole mice were too big, and Athena had to fight Polumetis to get it away from her again. When she had, her hands were scratched bloody. She took the mice to the kitchen and got a bronze knife that she knew she wasn't supposed to touch, and cut them both in half, while Cook was in the garden. The owlet gulped each of the three pieces down in one bite and rubbed her beak against Athena's battered hand.

"She ate a mouse and a half," she reported to Amoni, Pallas, and Nike, when she had put Polumetis back in her cage and taken her down to Nike's house. Athena suspected that Pallas's mother might not care for owls, but Nike's mother never cared what you brought in the house. Her brothers had a pet badger and a lynx cub.

"What did you do with the other half?" Pallas asked her.

"I gave it to a cat from the granary," Athena said. "I don't think they keep." The cat, a scruffy tom, had taken it and run off. The granary cats weren't tame; they were just tolerated because they caught mice.

"I'm going to teach her to perch on my hand." Athena lifted Polumetis out of the cage and held her other arm out. The owlet gripped her wrist with talons like needles. "Ow!" Athena detached her and wrung the injured hand, spraying drops of blood. "She already clawed me when I tried to take the mouse and cut it up. You would have choked, silly," she told the owl.

"You need a glove," Amoni said. "Father has heavy gloves he uses at the forge."

"I could put my whole head in one of your father's gloves," Athena said. "Rhoecus can make me something." Rhoecus made saddles and sandals and anything else from leather. "Let's go see him!"

They picked up the cage and flew out of Nike's house in a cloud of scurrying feet, darting up the steep streets and through the afternoon crowd in the market square, dodging the soldiers changing the watch and a laundrywoman with a basket of wet clothes on her head.

Metis watched them from the balcony of the palace, her arms resting on the warm plaster wall. Athena was always in front, she had noticed, with the other three spread out behind like chicks behind a hen. Even Amoni followed Athena's lead. Metis put her hand over her belly. She had thought twice since Athena's birth that she was pregnant again, but both had miscarried. The midwife had been right. Below her in the agora she saw Poseidon coming out of the tavern, wiping his mouth with the back of his hand. His blond head gleamed in the sunlight, and he walked with a swagger that was charming and dangerous at the same time. Metis stood watching both of them, the child and the young man, their shadows rippling long across the agora now, lapping at the walls of the palace and the temple.

Rhoecus made Athena a strap to go around her wrist for Polumetis to perch on, a glove to wear with it just in case, and a padded perch on a baldric to wear on one shoulder.

"Owls don't know how hard they're gripping

you," Rhoecus said. "Those talons are made to carry off dinner; that's why they have such sharp points."

Athena nodded. It wasn't Polumetis's fault. And for now Polumetis seemed quite content to sit on Athena's hand or shoulder and eat the mice Athena pulled from the traps in the palace. She ate them messily, tearing them apart herself with her sharp beak as she grew bigger. In a month she was nearly fledged, and quite tame. She flapped her wings occasionally but showed no sign of trying to fly with them.

"How am I going to teach an owl to fly?" Athena asked Amoni.

"Set her an example," Amoni said lazily. "Flap your arms."

"Don't be stupid." Athena frowned at him and tried to interest Polumetis in watching the shearwater wheeling across the sky.

"I think maybe if you drop her she'll fly," Amoni said. "Just from your arm."

Athena detached Polumetis and held her out in one hand. Polumetis looked at her with annoyed gold eyes. "You're a bird, silly," Athena said. "Just try it." She let go and Polumetis fell flapping to the paving stones.

"There! See? She nearly did it," Amoni said. Polumetis gave him a baleful look and walked over to Athena's foot. Her plumage was pale brown now, spotted with white dots. Her feathers grew all the way down to her sharp toes so that she looked as if she wore fluffy leggings.

Athena held her hand down, and Polumetis walked onto the wristband, sinking her talons into it firmly. "She's just not ready," Athena said. "She'll learn."

They both felt a good deal of sympathy for an owl unready for its lessons. Amoni had been sent to school, and spent most of his days learning to recite poetry and play the lyre and count things, making the strange marks on clay that the merchants used to tally cargo. Afterward his father taught him to use the hammer and tongs at the forge, and Pallas's father taught him and other small boys the use of the spear and the bow. Athena was learning to weave, which she liked, and to spin, which she loathed, as well as attending to her mother's lengthy lessons in diplomacy and government. Nike and Pallas were learning to spin and weave as well, and Nike's mother was teaching her to make cheese. Pelasgian girls were also allowed to practice at the bow and spear along with their brothers, but none of it was as much fun as running wild in the hills had been, and when their lessons were ended the four of them darted through the streets and out of the city gates, before someone could think of something else that they ought to be doing.

Polumetis learned to fly on one of their late-afternoon excursions. She saw a shrew in the tufts of grass beside the road that wound out of the city and headed west toward Eleusis. (In the other direction it ran to the sea and mysterious places in Phrygia and Thrace.) Polumetis beat her wings once and dove off Athena's shoulder. She soared silently toward the shrew and at the last moment pulled her head back and dropped her talons, driving them into its back. It shrieked and was silent. Polumetis flew into a pine tree and ate it while they watched, fascinated. When she had swallowed most of it she sailed proudly to Athena's shoulder with the tail hanging from her beak.

"What a good girl you are!" Athena said. Polumetis gulped down the tail and began to preen her feathers. Later, Athena knew, the indigestible parts of the shrew would come back up, neatly wrapped in its fur, in a little pellet. Generally Polumetis waited until she was in her cage. Then she would develop a pained expression, as if she had a stomachache, and her eyes would close. She would stretch her neck up and out and the pellet would drop from her beak. Athena wondered how owls did that, but no one seemed to know. Athena had picked one apart and found mouse bones and tiny perfect teeth and claws.

After that Polumetis began to hunt for herself. She always came back, so Athena began to leave her cage door open. At night Polumetis would disappear on silent wings into the dark and return before dawn. Metis said that a magical inner light gave Polumetis her night vision. Nurse said she would bewitch Athena some night and she would wake up with feathers. Athena, looking into those round gold eyes, could believe both.

II

※

Cicadas

Polumetis, Athena's constant childhood companion, became later her comfort and adviser as she began to grow from child to woman, resenting it every step of the way. The older she grew, the more circumscribed her life became, even with Metis's loose hand on her reins. She also, to her horror, became beautiful. Her dark hair was a lustrous black-brown, and her gray eyes held flecks of amber. Her face was a perfect oval, her lips full, her brows arched. Her body was lithe and muscular, but to her resentment it acquired breasts that made it hard to shoot a bow. Shooting a bow was an unwomanly skill, Nurse informed her, and it came of running around with that boy from the forge, getting all sooty.

Athena despairingly studied her face in her polished silver mirror, a gift from her mother on her fourteenth birthday. She had just met Uncle Posei-

don in the corridor, and he had swatted her backside with a genial air and looked down the neck
of her gown. "Nice ones!" he had said, and Athena's face had burned red.

"If I were ugly, I wouldn't mind at all," she
said to Polumetis, who sat on her shoulder,
grooming her. Having finished preening her own
feathers, the owl was giving Athena's hair little
swipes with the side of her beak. She made a soft
"keew keew" sound, which Athena took for
sympathy.

"He's a beast. He sleeps with everyone's wife,
just because he can. He gives them presents, or
they're afraid of him because he's the king's
brother." Athena refastened the bronze pins that
held the shoulders of her woolen gown together,
so that the neckline sat higher on her chest.

Nike and Pallas were growing too, and there
was talk of a marriage for Pallas in the next year.
Pallas told them about it as they sat on the promontory above the harbor, eating figs and sharing
a flask of fresh goat's milk.

"I wish someone would want to marry me,"
Nike said. "I'll probably spend my whole life
making cheese."

"No, you don't," Pallas said darkly. "I saw him.
He's old and he has a goiter."

"Ugh. Well, someone young then. Without a
goiter. It can't be worse than making cheese. I
don't see why I can't learn to do Father's job, and
tend the wine jars, but he says that's for my
brothers."

"I'd rather make cheese," Athena said firmly. "When you marry, your husband has all the power. He has everything you used to have; it all goes over to him. Look at my mother. She had land of her own and money, and Father controls all of it." Athena knew that her father and mother had already begun to fight over her own marriage. Father wanted to marry her to Uncle Poseidon to cement his brother's claim to the kingship with Metis's people, and Metis's eyes had blazed as yellow as the owl's, and she had refused to agree. Her agreement counted for a lot, because she came of the old royalty. So there the matter rested for the moment, to Athena's relief. If she had to marry Uncle Poseidon, she would kill him in their bed on their wedding night. She had said so to Father, and he had smacked her and told Mother that she needed discipline.

"It might not be so bad," Amoni said the next day when she complained to him about Pallas's dilemma. "She might like him, no matter what he looks like." He sounded wistful, but she thought he meant to comfort her.

Athena made a face. She had meant to show him her idea for altering the frame of her loom, even though she knew Nurse didn't approve of him, particularly not in Athena's chambers. When they were small it had been another matter, but lately whenever she was with Amoni she was acutely aware of Nurse hovering just within earshot.

He bent down and watched her fingers moving

over the threads, and cocked his ear to the click
of the shuttles. "I see what you mean. If you tilt
the angle here . . . yes." He rocked the frame a
little to see what would happen.

Amoni had grown too, and now he was a good
handspan taller than Athena was, with dark curly
hair, and a beard beginning to show. His eyes
were light blue, like the seawater, and his hands
were long-fingered and graceful despite the cal-
luses and scars of old burns. One brushed against
hers as he studied the loom. If she had to marry
someone, she thought, she could maybe stand to
marry Amoni, and then she wondered where on
earth that notion had come from. She was suddenly aware of his breath on her cheek.

She slid her eyes toward him and caught him
looking back at her. Amoni stood perfectly still
for a moment, frozen, leaning over her shoulder,
seeming to sense what she was thinking, she decided uneasily. Then, without warning, he kissed
her neck and ran from the room.

Athena stared after him, heart abruptly thud-
ding in her chest. He had gone mad. Plainly that
was it. And if so, why was her heart pounding?
She could sense Nurse just outside the door, radi-
ating disapproval. Athena took a deep breath and
let her fingers slide back to the shuttles and the
thread. Slowly she picked up their rhythm again,
fumbling at first while odd, disturbing thoughts
bounced about in her head, then settling to the
task. Despite weaving being a womanly chore,

and approved of by both Nurse and Father, Athena liked it. It was soothing, and she could turn things over in her mind while her hands worked the shuttles and the picture she had designed gradually grew in front of her, like a window opening very slowly.

The design of her life gave her more trouble. Amoni's kiss had opened some door of which she had been only dimly aware. Now she had a mad urge to run after him, kiss him on the mouth, keep him by her. What if Pallas did learn to love her husband? What if Mother actually loved Father? Was that why women put up with the rules of marriage, because they wanted to? Because, maybe, it was lonely outside it? Was that it? Did you marry and give some man the power to control you, or did you spend your life alone, your own person, and maybe lonely? Could you be happy with just your friends? Certainly Athena had been happy that way until now. Why did that change when you grew older?

"What did you do that for?" she demanded of Amoni the next day. He hadn't come anywhere near her, and she had tracked him down at the forge. His father eyed them with some interest over his anvil, but he didn't say anything.

Amoni looked hunted. "I don't know!" he blurted. "I just . . . You were talking about getting married, and I know they'll never let me marry for years now; men have to be older. . . ."

Athena knew that. Girls got married at fourteen or so, but a man was supposed to be at least twenty-five, and ready to support a family.

"And I realized I'm too young for you," Amoni said miserably.

"Well, you needn't worry," Athena said. She patted his hand in a sisterly fashion. "I'm not going to marry anyone. So we can just go on the way we are."

Amoni knew that the way they were would drive him mad in short order, now that he had kissed her neck, but he didn't say it.

There, I've settled that, Athena thought, but on her way back to the palace in the dusk she saw Polumetis with another owl. The two of them were flying about the balcony outside Athena's chamber where Polumetis perched in the evenings looking for dinner. They swooped and soared, first one ahead and then the other, a windborne dance of flirtatious catch-me-if-you-can, oddly undignified and silly for a normally solemn owl. Athena knew that owls mated after their first year or so, and when Polumetis stayed a spinster, Athena had assumed that life in the palace offered contentment enough. Now it seemed that, late in owl life, she was wrong, and Polumetis wanted romance. When Athena went to bed that night, the other owl was still on the balcony, and in the corner against the wall fallen leaves and twigs had been raked into what looked suspiciously like the beginnings of a nest.

*   *   *

Amoni's father said what Amoni hadn't, when Athena had gone and the two of them were alone in the forge, banking the coals and latching the shutters and doors. Amoni had always been a co-operative child, despite a curiosity that led him to dismantle things to see how they worked. He had done well enough at his studies and could use a spear and a bow, but Amoni gave his true attention to the things his father taught him at the forge, which pleased the smith. That as a child he had spent his free time playing with girls didn't trouble the smith. Whatever the boy's proclivities, he would marry when the time came; that was what a man did. It came as a mild surprise to him now that he had misjudged the lad, and he felt unsettled. "That's the king's daughter, you young fool," the smith said. He poked at the coals. "I should have known better than to let you run wild with her and those girls."

"Why did you then?" Amoni demanded grumpily.

"What was I supposed to do, with your mother dead? I'm no nursemaid. I thought it would do you no harm to be friends with the king's child. And I thought if you were playing with the girls when you were little, it meant you'd not likely be chasing after the big ones when you got older."

"I didn't think about her as a girl!" Amoni said. "Not till lately, I mean. She thinks about things; she likes to make things. You saw the cage she made for that owl when she was just little. She's like me."

"Too much like you for her own good."

"And I do like girls!" Amoni said, coming back to his father's assessment.

"Aye, that's clear enough now," the smith said.

The encounter made Amoni and Athena both jumpy when they were together after that, as if something hadn't happened that ought to have, or ought not to and was going to anyway. Athena felt like that more and more now, uneasy in her skin, despite the seductive warmth of the spring air that was like bathing in perfume. She did her best to avoid Uncle Poseidon, who had begun to act proprietary, although she didn't think Father would allow a marriage that Mother was so adamantly against.

"I don't want to get married!" she said fretfully to Metis, as Metis combed her hair by lamplight. The shutters were open to let in the scent of the sea and the rosemary growing in its pot outside the window, where Polumetis had her nest. There were eggs in it now.

"Not yet," Metis said. The ivory comb fanned the dark strands out across Athena's shoulders like a raven's wing. "It isn't time. When it is, then it will be different. Trust me."

"Mother, what are you plotting?" Athena held the mirror up to look at her, and Metis's face looked back over Athena's shoulder, dark and smiling and mysterious.

"When my people ruled Attica, it was the queen

who held the power," Metis said, letting her daughter's hair slide through her fingers like dark water. "Don't you forget that. A queen gives a land nourishment; a queen mothers it."

"Then why does Father own all of your land and money?" Athena demanded.

"Your father's people are new to this place, and they brought new ways with them. But the old ways are still there, and they need a queen to set them free again."

Athena put the mirror down and cocked her head at her mother. "I do know what you are hoping for. It's what you have raised me for. But I don't think there is the faintest chance that Father will make me his heir. And no one wants the old ways back." Athena had finally figured out how the old kings of Attica married the Goddess. They were killed to make the crops grow.

"Don't be too sure," Metis said. She set the comb down and fidgeted with a red clay pot full of the rouge that Athena declined to wear, spinning it between her white fingers. "My people have roots that go very deep in this soil, and the Lady has not left us."

"Aren't they the same? I mean, the Goddess in your temple and the Goddess in Father's?"

"They are and they aren't. She inhabits more than one body."

Athena thought of the priestesses in her mother's temple, old women with black veils and mysterious eyes. Their rituals were less elaborate than the priestesses in the new temple, and the old temple was dark and smoky with centuries of incense and sacrifices.

"And you expect me to become queen and sacrifice my husband every seven years? Maybe I will marry Uncle Poseidon then. Do I have to wait seven years?"

"Don't make a joke of it," Metis said.

Athena hadn't been, not entirely. She was fifteen and old enough to see things that she hadn't noticed as a child. Uncle Poseidon was a bully, for a start. Athena considered that that alone meant that he would make a bad king. But she also saw—and this was a newer revelation—how the Pelasgians in the city, her mother's people, followed her with their eyes when she went out; how they made small gestures of respect as she passed, and accorded her an odd kind of devotion, touching the hem of her gown surreptitiously, giving her small tokens, a flower, a smooth polished stone, things of the earth that they thought she might like. Offerings. It made Athena uneasy, as if they thought she was one of those people whom the Goddess inhabited.

At the vernal equinox, when the city made its sacrifices to the goddess of the plowed fields, she began to see just how deep the old ways ran under the newly paved streets and the Achaean conquerors' new temple. The old Goddess in her blood-smeared stone had her feet in the rocks that were the bones of the hillside. It was only her head that they saw, Athena thought. The rest of her was in the earth. The rest of her *was* the earth.

The spring festival was still a women's festival, despite new ways. When seed was put in the earth, that was women's business. Athena walked in the procession along with Metis, and Nurse, and Pallas and Nike, and all the other women of the village, from the old grandmother of Eleni from the tavern to the youngest baby girl in her mother's arms. Everyone was crowned with flowers, and Metis carried a bowl of milk and eggs for the sacred serpent who lived in the old temple. Behind her, a girl followed with a goat on a lead.

Pallas looked reasonably cheerful, and confided to Athena that her elderly suitor with the goiter had a congestion in his lungs that the physician didn't like the sound of, and her father had changed his mind and was looking around again.

Nike reported that her eldest brother was getting married and building his own house. "I was afraid he was going to move her in with us," she whispered as the procession wound through the narrow streets to the old temple. "I like her, although why she wants my brother I don't know, but it's like trying to sleep in the agora as it is. I wonder if the priestesses at the temple get to have their own rooms," she added when the procession halted.

"Those women scare me to death," Pallas said. "And anyway, you have to be dedicated to the Goddess when you're little."

"I like your house," Athena said. "There's always something going on there."

"That's the trouble with it," Nike retorted. "Akakios and Theios had a fight in the kitchen over whose turn it was to take the slop bucket to the pig, and broke Mother's oven. They knocked it over; they might as well be bears. And they spilled the slop bucket. Father was making them clean it up when we left."

"Well, it's not boring," Athena said. Akakios and Theios were always fighting over something, when they weren't stealing figs off someone's tree or riding their father's old shield down the steep, rutted street from the Acropolis to the bottom, overturning old ladies as they went.

"Sssst!" Metis turned and fixed the three of them with a firm stare, and they subsided. The queen went into the temple bearing the gold bowl of milk and eggs. The women in the procession began to chant the Spring Hymn, the notes rising and falling like the slow swell of the tides. In spring things were born, and that which had died rose up again.

From the temple steps, Athena saw the dark priestesses come out from their cave at the rear of the temple, bearing the sacred serpent in his box. Metis set the bowl before him on the altar, and his head came out of the box to lap at it. Slowly the rest of him followed, smooth, dark, undulating coils that flowed across the altar and wrapped themselves around the bowl.

The child with the goat, prompted by her

mother, led it forward and handed the lead over
to the priestesses. The mother beamed proudly.
The girl who led the goat was chosen every year
for her beauty, as a suitable suppliant to the Goddess. This one had a cloud of rose-gold curls fram-
ing her face and huge blue eyes like cornflowers.

The goat disappeared among the black-
shrouded women. Athena heard it bleat once frantically and then it was silent. Once the sacrifices
had been humans, Athena thought; not just kings,
but probably also the small girl who was chosen
for her beauty. That would have been a long time
ago, when people were not civilized. Athena saw
her mother at the altar, her pale gown surrounded
by the black-robed priestesses, and wondered just
how long ago that had been. If Athena was queen,
what would they expect of her? The smell of blood
filled her nostrils, and she saw her mother lift red
hands and put them on the stone that was the
old Goddess.

A little wind stirred the air, carrying the salt
scent of the harbor and a faint odor of fish, over-
laid with the sweet smell of the flowers, almost
but not quite masking the blood. The notes of the
Spring Hymn quivered in the air, an eldritch hum
in her ears. The hymn was as old as the Goddess,
and some of the words had lost their meaning,
so that it was a mystery, sung in the faith that
the Goddess understood, even if her worshipers
didn't. *What are we saying?* Athena wondered
suddenly.

Metis came down the steps from the altar, and

for a moment Athena saw the old Goddess in her stone, like a bird inside its egg, or a seed in the shell. Then the procession reversed its path, leaving them at its end, following the bearers of sacrifice to the Goddess in her new temple. At the other end, Arachne, who was a cousin of Gelon, the chief of the Areopagus, led a spotted sow for the Achaean Goddess. The sow was garlanded with flowers.

As queen, Metis played a part in the next sacrifice as well, and the procession stood aside to let her pass from the rear of the line to the front, but her presence was ceremonial, and Athena saw the Achaean women give her the respect that was due their king's wife and no more. This new Goddess was theirs, and Athena knew that, unlike Metis, they considered her a different—and better—deity altogether. Her statue was of marble, remarkably lifelike, and painted with bright colors so that her fierce blue eyes were ringed with kohl and green paint, and her wings were feathered red and blue and gold. The snakes in her hands were green with gold tongues. She was beautiful, but she didn't frighten and attract Athena the way the old Goddess did. Maybe, Athena thought, she was too new. Maybe you had to worship the Goddess in a thing for a long time for her to actually come and live in it.

A ten-day later, after the men had made their own sacrifice to the Goddess, Polumetis had a new owlet in her nest. Athena saw it from her window, a bald red head peeking out from under Polumetis's wing. Athena crept out onto the balcony to look. It was still wet, its pinfeathers plastered to its red skin, and thoroughly ugly, but Polumetis looked extremely proud. The male owl arrived with a grasshopper in his beak, and he beat his wings and shrieked at Athena.

Athena backed off. There were two eggs left. One of them already had a crack all the way around it, and she could hear the owlet inside peeping as it worked. The hatched one was already sitting with its beak open. The male owl bit off a piece of the grasshopper and dropped it into the open beak.

"I'll bring you some mice," Athena said placatingly. The male glared at her with huge yellow eyes. Polumetis didn't look particularly welcoming either, and Athena knew that owls were defensive about their nests. She had long ago realized that Polumetis's mother must have been dead or she would have driven Athena away from hers. "I'll just leave them on the balcony," she said. She missed Polumetis, who had been sitting on her eggs for a month, and would be raising her owlets for the rest of the spring, until they fledged. Then she would probably drive them off. Owls were maternal only in the short term.

Athena had been thinking about the things her mother had said about the Goddess, and about being queen, and they all seemed to her to be tied into the owls in some way. Owls were sacred to the Goddess, who was the goddess of birth, but also of sex and death. The things that made up the wheel of life, the planting and the reaping, of people and of plants, those were the Goddess's. Somewhere in there lay the notion of the king, or the queen, and how the ruler's shadow lay along the land, shaping the rocky hillside to its own contours, and bringing corn out of the ground. Or blighting it into black stubble. That happened, Mother said, if the ruler was not fit. Not only could a maimed king not rule—Athena's grandfather had stepped down and handed the kingship to Kosmetas because he had lost an eye in a battle—but a king who was damaged inside, in the soul (which lived in the lungs), Mother said, would bring ruin to the land as well. Athena knew Mother was talking about Uncle Poseidon. That, Mother said, was why Athena needed to rule Attica, because the land wanted her and not him.

The notion of what the land wanted made Athena uneasy. It seemed to want too much. Either her marriage or her spinsterhood. Or the blood of her husband. All of those choices seemed untenable. It began to seem impossible to live in your body and your mind at the same time.

She leaned her arms on the windowsill for a long while, watching the owls. The rough plaster of the sill was warm against her skin, and the spring air made her feel as if she were floating in a bowl of water with the fish on her walls. They leaped and cavorted in blue-green light, their fins flashing in the rays of some invisible sun shining just above the corner of her room. Outside, Polumetis was feeding the other half of the grasshopper to her owlet. Her mate had disappeared to find more food, and Polumetis preened the chick with her beak when it had eaten the grasshopper. The second egg rocked and split. A chick's wet, bald head emerged, followed by the body, raw and red and repulsive. It flopped down on its shell in apparent exhaustion. It was hard work, Athena supposed, pecking your way out of a shell. The first-hatched chick was nearly dry now, the feathers that had seemed so thin and bedraggled fluffed out so that it looked like a feather ball with beak and eyes. The egg tooth gave its beak a strange humped look.

The male came back, and Athena turned away from the window reluctantly, because he seemed so annoyed by her watching. She wondered wistfully if he would stay around after the chicks had fledged, and if Polumetis would ever come sit on her shoulder again. At a loose end, she wandered into the corridor and down the stone stairs to the lower level, where the kitchen was. Heat billowed from the clay oven in the center, where Cook, red-faced, was taking out bread.

"Oh, give me a loaf of that," Athena said. Mother would be looking for her any minute to come and sit in the throne room, and then to spin with the maids, or else count the number of wine jars in the cellar and mark them down on wet clay tablets to practice her sums and marks. Father could do neither of the latter, but Metis had made it clear that women needed to know more than men did. This morning Athena felt that she knew far too much already.

She begged a cheese from Cook as well, to go along with the bread; a wineskin full of last season's vintage; a few small, slightly withered apples from the cellar; and cold, cooked sausages wrapped in cloth.

"Your Mother is going to be looking for you," Cook warned her.

"And you don't know where I am!" Athena said. She packed her thieved goods into a basket and patted Cook on the cheek. She slipped through the kitchen doors, through the walled garden, and out through its gate into the street unseen. She felt giddy suddenly, as if she might abruptly take flight like the owls. Amoni was at the forge but he wouldn't come with her.

"Father is ill," he said. "I have to stay here and work."

Athena wondered whether that was true or not, or if he was just afraid to be near her. Ever since he had kissed her neck, she had found herself wanting to experiment with this new feeling, do other, more dangerous things, and she suspected he felt the same.

"Very well then, stick-in-the-mud," she said, because she didn't want to go near the other question. "I'll just get Pallas and Nike."

"A safer choice," he murmured.

Fine, she thought, *let him stick to his hammering*. She banged her fist on Pallas's door and burst through it before a servant could open it for her.

Pallas was sitting at her loom, her mother nowhere in sight.

"Pallas! Come on! We're going to take a picnic up onto the cliff the way we used to. I've run away from home, and you're going to, too!"

Pallas chuckled. "You're like a whirlwind. What if I have to finish this rug?"

"Bah! It's spring. No one needs rugs. Your mother has already pulled them up and put rushes down. No one needs your silly rug until fall."

"What has gotten into you today?"

"Spring!"

"All right, then. It may be my last chance, so all right. Father has found another suitor for me."

Athena groaned.

"This one is young," Pallas confided with a grin. "He's nice. I actually got to meet him, and he was very nice."

Athena felt suddenly envious. "Well, come on, then; let's go find Nike and rescue her from the cheese."

Pallas pulled her goatskin cloak from its hook and bundled it under her arm. "We can sit on this. Mother will be furious if I spoil my dress, and I haven't got time to change; she's just gone to the fishmonger and she'll be back any moment."

"Then run!" Athena grabbed Pallas's hand, and they flew out the door. They skittered down the steep street, dodged behind the barber's house to avoid the fishmonger, the basket flying from Athena's arm, and raced down the steps past the unguent boiler's shop, laughing like fiends, while older women shot them disapproving looks.

The street outside Nike's house was littered with the pieces of a broken wagon, and they found Nike struggling with the goat that had been pulling it, while her baby sister sat in the dirt and howled. Athena picked the child up as Nike detached the goat from the ruins of its harness.

"Theios let her hitch it to the cart," Nike said furiously.

"Where is Theios?" Athena asked, as the little girl snuffled against the front of her gown.

"Gone down to the vineyard, where he was supposed to be in the first place, I expect," Nike's mother said, coming through the door, wiping her hands on her apron. She took the girl from Athena. "Now, there's no harm done. You're not even wounded, are you then? Come along; I'll give you a drink of milk. Next time don't ask Theios if you can do things. You know he always says yes."

"That's why I asked him," the girl said, rubbing the back of her head.

"Well? You see how that turned out?"

When the door closed behind her mother, Athena beckoned Nike into the shadow of the next-door house, out of earshot.

"We're going up on the headland. I have bread and a good cheese and some wine. Come on."

"If Theios ever has any children, they won't live to grow up," Nike said disgustedly. "I don't see why I should be the only one who stays home and minds Mother. She'll be mad, though."

"Father's found me a husband," Pallas said. "It's our last chance."

"All right, then."

It was a long walk south to the sea, and the sun grew hotter and the warm buzz of cicadas in the trees rattled the air as they climbed the headland.

"Imagine living underground and only coming up after seventeen years," Pallas said.

"I expect the world would seem miraculous after that," Athena said. "You'd be giddy with it. Like us." She danced along the dusty track.

"They come up to mate," Nike said with a grin.

"And then they die," Athena said. "But I suppose they have a satisfactory life until then. Maybe a summer is a long time if you're a bug."

"Pallas is our cicada," Nike said. "Seventeen years—well, sixteen—underground, and now she's going to fly off with her mate."

"Ugh," Pallas said. "He's nicer than that."

They settled on a flat stone along the headland, where they could look out over the harbor and see the fishing boats with their red and white sails, and the water shading from green to bright dazzling blue. The wind whisked their hair into tangles and carried the cries of shorebirds on its currents. Athena flicked a few drops of wine on the ground for the gods of the place, and broke off a piece of the bread, scattering the crumbs to the breeze. A gull swooped down from the sky and snatched up the biggest one, followed by four more, squawking and fighting for the rest. Whatever you gave the gods, something else always ate it. It was the gesture that mattered, Athena thought, and maybe that was how the Goddess's creatures were fed. She gave another bit to the wind, and then broke off pieces for the three of them. Pallas had spread her goatskin out, and they sat on it, sharing the cheese, which was warm and runny, and the apples and wine.

"This will be our last summer," Athena said dolefully. "Nike, you know they'll marry you off too, and Mother will have me penned up listening to old men drone on for days at a time. We should do something special and wonderful to remember this summer by."

"What?" Nike was almost always ready to do anything, but she counted on Athena to think the things up.

"We could play pirates," Pallas said. "Or is that too babyish?"

"We could go hunting," Nike said. "While they'll still let us. Only I didn't bring my spear."

While women did not hunt, Pelasgian girl children were allowed to play with spears along with their brothers. Nike had a good arm, and generally could bring home something for the pot that fed her large and ravenous family.

"We could make spears, the way the first people did," Athena said. They occasionally found the chipped stone spear points that Metis said were the leavings of the oldest inhabitants of the place, the Stone Men who hadn't had bronze or copper. (Metis could throw a spear, and she had seen to it that Athena learned too.)

"We could sleep out here tonight," Pallas said. "We haven't eaten the sausages, and there's enough of that cheese to go around for supper as well, and you know there's a spring just up the track. And berries. We could be like the Stone Men—Stone Women—and sleep under the stars."

The other two stared at her, grinning. Pallas rarely suggested anything very adventurous, but this was a brilliant notion.

Athena clapped her hands. "Yes! We'll make a brush hut and light a fire—Amoni's father showed me how to make a fire drill, in case I ever need one. We can cook the sausages over it."

They set about being Stone Women. Pallas and Nike cut myrtle saplings, hacking at them with Nike's belt knife, and Athena gathered stones for a fire pit. When she had them arranged to her liking, in a cleared space from which she had dug and swept any dry grass that might catch fire, she sawed through the woody stems of tamarisks with her own knife, and crumbled twigs and leaves between her hands for tinder. It wouldn't burn very long, but they could keep feeding it. There was plenty of brush on the headland.

Pallas and Nike bent the saplings into a crude hut frame and began to weave smaller green branches into it, while Athena made her fire drill from two sticks and some threads unwound from the hem of her gown. They worked with happy purpose, expending far more energy on their play than they ever gave willingly to their duties at home. The fire drill was a simple contraption, as old as the Stone Men: A round stick, its end braced against a flat one, and driven by a third stick and string, would rotate and grow hot at the end, spilling charred sawdust into a pile of tinder. So said Amoni's father. Athena had never actually done it. She was still trying to get it to light when Nike and Pallas finished the hut and settled down to watch her and give advice.

"You need to spin it faster, I think," Pallas said.

"You need drier wood," Nike said.

"Bah! You two do it then."

"No, you seem to be getting there. I think I see smoke."

"Where?" Pallas peered at it.

"I thought I did."

"If you two were Stone Women you'd have to eat your kill raw," Athena said, twisting the drill harder. Her hands were beginning to ache, and she could feel a blister coming.

"Well, the only kill we have is sausages," Pallas said.

"It's the principle of the thing," Athena said. But there definitely was smoke coming from the drill now. Pallas leaned down and blew on it gently. A larger wisp of smoke began to coil from the tinder. Pallas blew again a little harder, and they saw a tiny flame.

"That's it! You've got it! Keep going!" Nike bent

and poked the tinder with a twig, prodding the little flame. It licked at the twig and the twig caught.

"Get something bigger!" Athena said. Pallas grabbed a stick with a bit of dry leaf at the end. They poked it into the fire, and the tinder blazed up. Athena laid more sticks on the flames. The larger sticks caught and they danced about it, whooping.

"Quick, get the sausages before it goes out." Pallas and Nike stuck the abandoned sticks of Athena's fire drill through the sausage ends and held them over the flames. The sun was beginning to sink, and Athena scooped up as much dry wood as she could find and stacked it in the fire pit. The hot sausage smell filled the air. Athena looked at the fire and at Pallas's cloak, which was the only one they had brought. It would get cold after darkness fell, and they would end up going back before morning or someone would be looking for them. But it was fun to eat half-burned sausages and pretend they wouldn't. When the sausages were hot, the three retreated to the brush hut, which Pallas and Nike had woven of myrtle branches and juniper. The wind whistled through the green boughs with a merry sound like a kettle singing. The sun was falling in a molten puddle into the sea, and a flock of white birds erupted from the cliffs below them in a flurry of feathers.

"Wouldn't it be wonderful if we could stay like this always?" Nike said wistfully, munching on a sausage. "The three of us together? Just us?"

No husbands, no children, no aged councilors, Athena thought.

"We should take a vow," Pallas said. "Not to forget what it was like when we were young." She had leaves in her hair, and the dress she had worried about had a tear in the hem.

"I know; we'll be blood sisters," Athena said. She unsheathed her belt knife and held it out. "We'll prick our thumbs and mix the blood and be true sisters."

"You go first," Pallas said, eyeing the knife dubiously. "I want to, but I think you'll have to cut my finger for me."

"Here, give it to me," Nike said. She wiped her greasy hands on her rough woolen skirt and pricked her thumb swiftly and efficiently. She handed the knife back to Athena, who dug the tip into the soft pad of her own thumb until a drop of blood welled up, scarlet as wine.

"I can't do it," Pallas said, watching them. "I'm such a coward. You'll have to."

Athena took Pallas's hand, and Pallas closed her eyes while Athena pricked her pale thumb with the tip of the bronze blade. She set the knife down in her lap and they solemnly held their thumbs together, rubbing them back and forth to mix the blood.

"Now we are sisters," Athena said, sucking on the tip of her thumb. The blood left a hot metallic taste in her mouth.

They ate the rest of the sausages and apples and drank the wine while the stars came out overhead.

Athena drew her knees up and rested her arms on them, chewing the last bite of apple. She flung the core out in a long arc over the cliff. *I will remember tonight*, she thought. *Nothing will be the same later, but I will remember this and what it was like to sit here and eat sausage and apples with my sisters. Whatever happens next, I will remember that.*

They sat in the brush hut while the cicadas vibrated in the evening air, not yet distracted from their purpose by nightfall. Finally it grew cold enough that even Pallas's cloak, wrapped around the three of them, wasn't enough, and the cicadas stilled. "It's no good," Nike said, grumbling, as Athena had known she would. "We'll have to go back. I'm so cold my backside is frozen."

Athena and Pallas stood up. "We're frozen too," Pallas said. "We just didn't want to be the first to say so."

"It doesn't matter," Athena said. "We were Stone Women. We made a fire and a hut. And I want to see if Polumetis's third egg has hatched."

Athena slung the empty wineskin over her shoulder, and Nike scooped up the empty bag. They looked at the fire.

"We'd better put that out properly," Pallas said. Wildfire would run through the dry brush on the headland in a heartbeat. "Give me the wineskin. I'll get some water from the spring."

"We'll come with you," Athena said. "To keep the cyclopes away."

"I don't believe in cyclopes," Pallas said, starting up the track.

"Oh, yes, you do. They're huge and they have one great big eye in the middle of their foreheads and they *eat girls!*" Athena darted up behind her and grabbed her by the waist.

"Stop that!" Pallas shrieked, laughing. She began to run, with Athena and Nike behind her.

It was nearly dark-of-the-moon, and the headland was black as onyx, but they had run wild over the land since they could walk. None of them slowed down. "Can't catch me!" Pallas called in the darkness, and they followed her trail, yelping like hounds and laughing, stopping to catch their breath and plunging on. The sounds of the waves below them masked her footsteps.

Athena heard the gurgle of the spring when they were nearly on it, and stopped, panting. "You're faster than you used to be," she gasped.

No one answered.

Nike came up behind her and laid a hand on her shoulder. "Where is she?"

"She's hiding."

"Pallas! You have the wineskin. We need to put the fire out!"

They peered into the darkness. "Pallas?"

There was no one at the spring.

The spring bubbled from the rocks under a grove of stunted trees, but between it and the promontory where they had made their camp, the track ran perilously near the cliff edge. If you missed your way and your footing there was nothing below but a circle of fanged rock along a sliver of beach that was covered at high tide.

Athena felt her stomach contract. She turned and made her way back down the trail, creeping as close as she dared to the edge, looking down. The tide was out, and below her, on the dark rocks that ringed the silver beach, she saw a splash of white.

III

The Cloak of the Lady

They found Pallas on the rocks, her blood a dark blotch in the faint light, pooling under her body. Athena sat beside her, holding her hand, willing her to breathe, while Nike ran back through the night to the city. Pallas never stirred.

Pallas's mother and father and what seemed half the city followed Nike back to the shore, on foot and by wagon, and by the time they came it was clear that Pallas was dead. Her mother wailed, tearing at her hair while Athena and Nike stared blindly, dumbstruck, frozen. Death had never come so close to them before. Two of Nike's small brothers had died shortly after birth, hardly in the world at all. And Athena remembered her grandfather, the old man with one eye who had sat her on his lap and fed her sweets beside the fire. But Pallas was different. Pallas had been part of their charmed circle since they could walk.

Nike sank down in the sand, exhausted from her run. She howled as Pallas's father picked up her body and started along the sand with it, toward the harbor steps. It was an anguished wail that cut through the cold night like a knife. Athena sat still frozen, silent misery washing over her. She saw in the crowd her father and mother, who had come from the city, faces washed pale in the torchlight as people made way for them. Metis put her hand on her daughter's shoulder, and Athena felt it tremble. She knew what her mother was thinking: It could have been her—and a wave of guilt flowed over her, congealing into bone-deep sorrow.

In the morning she saw that Polumetis's third egg had indeed hatched, a tiny sprig of new life, one small bird to offset all that loss. Athena walked back up to the headland alone and sat in the abandoned brush hut, its green branches wilted, the limp leaves already turning brown. She stared out at the sea, a rough gray this morning with dark clouds rolling in from the west, and huddled inside Pallas's goatskin cloak, trying to feel Pallas inside it with her. Sometimes she thought she did; sometimes she thought it was her sorrow that sat beside her, and Pallas was far gone, a seabird soaring over the cliffs that had pulled her to her death. Finally she folded the cloak under her arm and took it back to Pallas's mother, and asked if she could keep it.

"I don't care," Pallas's mother said, red eyed. "It's just a cloak. Take it if it makes you feel better. It will do me no good."

Athena ran home and stuffed the cloak in the bottom of her clothes chest, slamming the lid down on it, as if death might get back out. Her mother came to fetch her to pay their respects at Pallas's house, where Pallas's body was on display on a bed in the front of the house. Athena stood a long time staring at it, at the pale face and the rouge and white lead powder meant to mask the look of death. All they did was make it worse, she thought. Pallas's mother had laid out a funeral feast that Athena knew must have cost them more money than they could afford, but it was important to Pallas's family to maintain their standing. And now there would be no bride price, of course. Pallas's suitor was there, drinking wine and eating the meat of the goat sacrificed that morning, and already looking about him, Athena thought, for a replacement.

She saw Amoni among the crowd, and he made his way through the mourners to her. "Father's worse," he said. "I can't stay."

Not another one, she thought. Death came in threes, according to Nurse.

"He can barely breathe," Amoni said. "The physician put mustard poultices on his chest and gave him arum in honey, and hellebore, but nothing helps. The hellebore makes him throw up, but the trouble is in his lungs, not his stomach."

"Doctors always think it's your stomach,"

Athena said, remembering certain unpleasant potions.

"That's because they don't actually know anything about any other part," Amoni said. "In my opinion. Are you all right? You look dreadful."

Athena turned red-rimmed eyes up to his. "It was my fault that she fell."

"No, it wasn't."

"Amoni, I chased her. We were running and it was dark. I killed her."

"No, you didn't," he said gently, firmly.

"You weren't there. Ask Nike what happened."

"I did. And it wasn't your fault."

"Pallas's mother thinks so."

"I doubt that. But if you are determined that it was your fault, then you'll think so no matter what anyone else says," Amoni told her. "I have to go and see to Father. I shouldn't have left him this long."

Athena watched him shoulder his way through the crowd. Maybe the smith would die too, and that would be her fault as well for having drawn death near him. She wished she could cry like Nike, but the tears stayed inside, making her eyes itch so that she rubbed them red.

They buried Pallas the next morning, in a grave on the Hill of Tombs to the north where her grandparents and two uncles already lay. The fresh-dug earth looked sad and raw in an early-morning drizzle, as the funeral procession set out just before dawn. They carried Pallas through the city on her bed, lying on a red cloth, with her hands folded on her chest and her gold fillet in her hair, the one she would have worn at her wedding. The place where her head had struck the rocks was mottled dark, and not even the white lead could hide it.

Outside the city, past the road that went to Eleusis, were the vineyards that Nike's father tended, and beyond them the hill on whose slopes the city buried its dead. A path branched off the main road there, and they followed it past terraces of grapevines, wheatfields turning golden and nearly ready for harvest, and the leafy groves of apple trees; past the long valley where the goats and sheep were driven to pasture; up the rocky trail that led to the city of the dead.

The hillside was pocked with graves, the long barrows of the Achaean families, some with marble marking stones, and the round mounds of the Pelasgians, who burned their dead and buried them in urns. The procession threaded its way among them, the women in the front, carrying the offerings: jars of wine and meal, and a second goat trotting at the end of its lead. There would be another feast after the funeral, with Pallas's house full of mourners once again, eating and drinking them dry. Nike and Athena were at the front of the procession, just behind Pallas's mother, because Pallas's mother had asked them. Athena felt like an impostor, a murderer pretending to mourn her victim. Nike carried Pallas's woolen shawl, and Athena the miniature clay horse Pallas had prized and the wooden dolls she had barely outgrown.

At the grave they laid Pallas in the hole that had been dug already, just as the rising sun was burning off the drizzle and mist. The grave was lined with stones and cushioned at the bottom by a mattress of straw. Her father and an uncle lifted her off the bier and set her in it, folding her hands again and putting a silver piece in her mouth for the journey. Athena laid her toys beside her, and Nike spread the shawl over her so that she looked as if she had gone to bed in the ground. Her mother was weeping again, brief, noisy gusts stifled with the end of her mantle. Her father was grim-faced but he didn't weep now. That would be an unbecoming emotion in a man. Metis came to the grave after them and tucked a small gold pot of honey into it beside Pallas. Then she put her arm about Athena's shoulders and pulled her close to her side.

The priestesses of the Goddess began to chant, a long, low, sad sound, like a wind far off in stones. Amoni came up to Athena's other side, and although Metis gave him a disapproving look, he stayed. When the chanting was finished and the hole filled in; the goat killed and its bones burned beside the grave on the marble slab that Pallas's father had bought to mark it; when there was nothing left to do, they all turned around again and walked back to the city, scattered now in twos and threes, the women comforting Pallas's mother, the men, the soldiers of his guard, marching straight as a spear shaft behind her father. Amoni walked beside Athena. Her mother beckoned her toward the chariot that had come behind them with a driver to take the queen back to the city, but Athena shook her head. Metis shrugged her shoulders and climbed up beside the driver, settling her cloak about her and gripping the sides tight with both hands because the chariots bounced like grasshoppers on the rutted track. The driver shook the reins out. The horses snorted and they rattled off, the wheels churning up clouds of dust.

Amoni studied Athena, who walked with her head down, watching the puffs of dust her sandals kicked up. "You might as well cry," he said. "Grief heals."

"It won't," she said, certain of that.

"It must," he said. "Otherwise how do we stand life?"

"I don't know." Athena stopped and bent down to the scattered stones in their path. She picked up a shed snakeskin, a gleaming opalescent yellow-green, each scale perfectly delineated, translucent as a cicada's shell. She cradled it in both hands. "Like a soul," she said.

"No, that's backward," Amoni said. "It's a body. Or it was."

"It's a skin. The snake grows out of it."

"Are you supposing Pallas grew out of hers?"

"She was driven out," Athena said bitterly.

"I suppose." Maybe she had found another skin. He thought of all the stories about maidens turned to trees and flowers, shepherd boys transformed into birds. They were like fauns and chimeras. No one they knew had actually seen one, but everyone knew of someone who knew someone who had a sister whom it had happened to. It would be nice to think of Pallas as a laurel tree.

Athena didn't say anything else until they had reached the city again. In the agora, she turned to him and said, in an oddly formal voice, "Thank you for walking with me. I hope your father is better."

Amoni watched her trudge up the street and vanish into Pallas's house. Her misery followed her like a dark aura. He hesitated, wanting to follow her, comfort her, tell her again that it wasn't her fault. Hold her and let her cry. Perhaps not a good idea, that, and he couldn't leave his father alone any longer. Eleni from the tavern had said she would sit by him while Amoni went to the burial. "You've known that child since the two of you were babes. You go. I'll sit by the smith. We'll be all right. Get along."

Amoni had hesitated all the same, and now when he pushed his way through the doors from the smithy into the house behind it, he found his father asleep, the breath rattling and gurgling in his chest.

"He's no better," Eleni said, standing up. She folded the bit of embroidery she had been working on, sticking the bronze needle through its corner. "But he's sleeping. A blessing that, maybe. I'll leave a handful of corn at the Lady's feet for him."

Eleni was Pelasgian and made her worship at the feet of the old Goddess, who made Amoni uncomfortable, but he thanked her anyway. His father sighed and twitched at the bedclothes in his sleep. Amoni sat down in the chair beside him to wait.

Amoni's father died four days later, and they buried him on the same hill where Pallas lay. Athena walked grimly beside Amoni, convinced that she had caused this death, too, and that a third was bound to follow. "Superstitious nonsense," Metis had said briskly when Athena had whispered her fear to her mother, but Athena didn't believe her, not when she saw her mother go to the temple of the old Goddess and prick her finger twice, rubbing the blood into the stone. Metis looked stern when she saw Athena and lectured her on prying into other people's prayers.

The funeral for Amoni's father was less elaborate than Pallas's had been, but grief was not factored by wealth nor by the age of the lost one. Amoni's blue eyes were as red-rimmed as Pallas's mother's. He bought a goat for the sacrifice and a jar of wine from the tavern and sat stoically in the mud-brick house behind the forge while the neighbors came to bring him their commiserations.

Afterward, Amoni went to work at the forge,

finishing the chariot wheels and pruning knives, the breastplates and bridle bits, that his father had left in his illness. It was said that the young smith did good work, a credit to his father's teaching; you could trust him to make a sword blade that wouldn't shatter. There was no time now to run free in the hills.

Nike too was put to work, as her mother considered it the best tonic for grief and, like the queen, went in fear of the paths along the headlands where their children used to wander.

Athena went with Metis to hear the deliberations of the Areopagus, and the judicial decrees of her father, and waited for the third death.

"High time the girl was married," Kosmetas announced. "That will put a stop to her running wild."

They were at their breakfast, an oddly familial group, as they rarely sat down together. Athena and Metis were used to taking their morning meal together most days in the walled courtyard at the center of the palace. This morning Kosmetas had joined his wife and daughter, eliciting suspicious looks from both of them.

Metis laid down the fig she had been about to bite into, and her back stiffened. "She is too young."

Kosmetas turned to Athena. "How old are you, girl? Fifteen?" His eyes ran over her form, inspecting her.

"Fifteen," Athena said. "I don't want to get married."

"Who gave you a choice in the matter?" Kosmetas fixed his daughter with a thunderous glare.

"If you are talking about Uncle Poseidon, I won't do it," Athena said stubbornly.

Kosmetas swatted the back of her head with the palm of his hand, and her ears rang. "You'll marry whoever I give you to!"

"Not Poseidon," Metis said clearly. Her eyes snapped.

"Best man for her," Kosmetas said. "Fix his claim, after me. And he'll keep her in line." He poured his cup full of wine and cracked a boiled egg on the table.

"No," Metis said.

"I'll stab him while he's sleeping," Athena said.

"The Pelasgians won't stand for it," Metis said. "He bullies them."

Kosmetas glared at them both. "And who is to come after me, then? Where are my sons?" He pointed a finger in Metis's face.

"You have a daughter."

"Bah! And what good is she?" He seemed to feel that perhaps that had been untactful, and tried another approach. He put the egg down and cupped Athena's chin in his hand. "And what's the matter with Poseidon, then? He's a good-looking fellow, beats all the other young men in the festival games."

Athena didn't answer. Her ears still rang.

"She is too young." Metis stared at Kosmetas until he took his hand away from his daughter's chin.

"You were fifteen," Kosmetas said.

"I was married for the good of the land," Metis retorted. "No marriage to Poseidon will bring good here. The Pelasgians won't stand for him."

"They won't have a choice." Kosmetas folded his arms across his chest. The gold diadem glinted in his graying hair, and his cloak was fastened with a gold pin in the form of a bull's head with eyes of lapis lazuli. The ring on his right hand bore the thunderbolt seal of the Achaean kings.

"There is always a choice. Always the possibility that the dance will turn away from you. Ask the Lady and she will tell you that." Metis gave him a long look that Kosmetas found uncomfortable. In theory he could divorce her, lock her up, even kill her. In practice, he knew what he wasn't willing to admit: that his people's kingship was new here in relation to the tenure of the Pelasgians and their goddess on the land, and revolt was always possible if the Pelasgians felt pushed too far.

"You are young still," Metis told him soothingly. "No need to be thinking of an heir just yet." And he let the matter drop for that morning.

Athena tried to find comfort in her father's grudging acquiescence. Pallas might be dead, but at least Athena wasn't married to Uncle Poseidon. She wistfully watched Polumetis with her growing owlets and her protective mate, a thing forever to be denied to her. At night she took out Pallas's goatskin cloak and wrapped it around her own shoulders.

Finally, when no death came, she began to think

that her mother's bloody thumbprint had averted
it, and began to consider how to thank the Goddess for that. She had saved the snakeskin she had
found the day they buried Pallas, tucking it into
the chest with Pallas's cloak and other things she
began to pick up on her now solitary walks: a
crow's wing; a cicada's empty case; half a bird's
egg, brilliant blue with a small green splotch; another snakeskin, this one a viper's, a silky gray
with a zigzag pattern like arrowheads on its back;
a kestrel's barred tail feather. Polumetis's chicks
fledged and flew away, and the male went with
them. Athena found one of his feathers in the nest
and added it to her trove. The day he left, Polumetis landed lightly on Athena's shoulder and
preened her ear, and then resumed her life in
Athena's chamber. That was a comfort, but it
didn't still the grief that stabbed her as she woke
each morning with Pallas still alive in her head in
that tiny moment between sleep and conscious-
ness; before bitter memory flooded back.

One night she dreamed of Pallas. Pallas stood
beside her bed, wrapped in the cloak, which was
now adorned with birds and snakes. On her forehead was a great black bruise. She held out her
arms, and live snakes twined from them and her
back sprouted great bronze wings.

In the morning Athena rose and took out her
silver needle and a small knife to cut her threads
with, and began to stitch the things she had saved
to the cloak, sitting cross-legged on the bed in
her nightdress.

"Is that a nasty old snakeskin?" Nurse asked her. Nurse set down a cup of watered wine and a bowl of apples and figs on the three-legged table beside Athena's bed. "Your mother wants you in her chamber. And whatever are you doing?"

"Making something," Athena said, punching the needle through the crow's wing and the supple goathide.

"It will have mites," Nurse said disapprovingly.

Athena stroked the shiny fan of ebony feathers. "It's something I dreamed," she said. Nurse looked alarmed at that.

She must have said something to Metis, because the queen, when Athena finally appeared before her, demanded to see it. Athena fetched the cloak and spread it out. The feathers made a collar around the shoulders, with the crow's wing at the center in the back. Below she had stitched the snakeskins around the hem, the grass snake's and the viper's and more that she had collected. She had slit them and pressed them flat, and they gleamed with an odd opalescence, their patterns barely visible, ghosts of otherworldly serpents.

Metis studied it a long time. "These things carry power in them; you know that," she said finally.

"Maybe," Athena said. "It makes me think of Pallas." *It's how I remember what I did to her.* She didn't say that. She put the cloak about her shoulders, and Polumetis flew down from the tree outside Metis's window and perched by her ear.

"It will make people think of other things," Metis said. "But maybe that is not bad. Sometimes that is how power comes to a thing; it is believed into it."

Athena remembered what she had thought about the statue of the old Goddess and the new one. "I dreamed about her," she said. "Pallas. She was wearing it." At least, it had been Pallas to start with. Later Athena hadn't been sure. It had had wings. She thought of the statues again.

"You dreamed about her because she was you," Metis said. "She is still you. You will carry her with you. Don't be afraid of her."

"I'm not." Athena wasn't entirely sure of that either, now, but it was a comfort to feel Pallas settle about her shoulders with the cloak, even if it frightened her a little.

IV

❧

The Thing with a Horn on Its Nose

The cloak carried some power. Athena had only to go about in the city wearing it to know that. She had added another band of snakeskins, this one from snakes she had caught live while they hunted for rats in the granary, and killed and skinned herself, pegging the skins out on the warm balcony outside her chamber and forbidding Polumetis, who was allowed to eat the rest of the kill, to touch them. On these the patterns showed clearly, and several of them were vipers.

"You look like one of those old goddesses who lived in the hills and ate travelers," Amoni said with a smile. "I saw an old lady make the evil eye *and* give you a bow as you passed. She couldn't figure out what to do, but she covered all the possibilities."

"People always do that to me," Athena said.

"The Old Ones, anyway, the Pelasgians. It's because I'm Mother's daughter."

"They do it more when you wear that cloak." Amoni set his hammer down on the bench beside his anvil, pleased that she had come to see him. Polumetis was riding on her shoulder, her talons sunk into the goatskin. Amoni offered her a crumb of sausage from his midday meal, and she took it delicately in her beak. "My mother was Pelasgian, too. She used to tell me it's good luck if an owl favors you and spits up its pellet by your door."

Athena chuckled. She scratched Polumetis between her wing bones. "She's very private about that. She likes to go home and do it in her cage. She always looks as if she has a stomachache, and then up it comes. I wonder how they do that."

"That's why they're so mystical," Amoni said. "They're the only creature that can eat its dinner bones and all and then wrap them up in the hide and chuck them neatly back out. You know I have missed you."

"And owl pellets make you think of me?" Athena grinned. It felt good to do that, unaccustomed now and startling. She smiled at him again in gratitude.

"Everything makes me think of you," Amoni said seriously.

"We had better not go down that path," Athena said.

Amoni picked up a pot he had been mending for the unguent boiler and fiddled with it morosely. "Father left me some gold," he muttered, his voice so low she could barely hear him.

"It isn't gold," Athena said. "It wouldn't matter if your anvil was made of it. Father wants me to marry Uncle Poseidon."

Amoni looked horrified.

"Well, I won't do it, and he can't make me. Mother won't let him."

"Can she stop him?" He had seen the king's brother that morning, with one of the girls who worked in the tavern. The girl had been crying.

"Father says she can't. He roars and stomps around and smacks me, but the truth is he's afraid of her in some deep way. But he *will* insist I marry someone who will have some claim to rule after him. *If* I marry. But I'm not going to, because if I do, my husband will have all the power, not me."

Amoni, seeing her in the cloak with the snake-skins stitched to it, felt the thought cross his mind that Athena's husband too might have cause to be afraid of her in some deep way. He remembered what the Pelasgians said of the Lady, which was what they called their Goddess:

> She danced, and as she danced, she stirred up behind her the north wind, which formed itself into the Great Serpent. The dance of the Lady aroused the passion of the serpent, who wound himself around the goddess and copulated with her. Pregnant, the Lady took the form of a dove and laid the universal egg, which the serpent

wrapped in his coils until it hatched. The egg released all other things in the universe, and so the world was born.

The Lady would make an uncomfortable wife. Maybe Athena could hold her own even if they gave her to Poseidon. He could comfort himself with that hope.

"It wouldn't be so bad if it were you," Athena went on, oblivious to his thoughts, "but it can't be you, and I don't trust anyone else. So I'm not going to marry. And I *can't* love you. I absolutely refuse."

You refuse, he thought. *I haven't been given a choice.* Aloud, he said, "There is a ship just in, at the harbor, with a beast no one has ever seen before. Do you want to see it?"

"What sort of a beast?"

"Rhoecus says it has a horn in the middle of its face."

"So do deer," Athena said suspiciously.

"No, one horn, where its nose should be."

"Hmmph. It will be some poor bear with a goat's horn strapped to its snout, like the 'monster' that fellow was leading around last year and charging a silver piece to see."

"You'll never know unless you come with me," Amoni said. "Rhoecus says it's the oddest thing he's ever seen. He went down to see to a load of hides from Mycenae and came back full of the tale."

"Oh, very well." Athena wouldn't admit it, but

she secretly hoped the monster would be just that—a creature out of fable, a chimera or some such, some actual proof that there were things in the world that not even her father knew about, things that couldn't be predicted by the rule of threes or the entrails of a goose.

They set out down the track to the harbor, and it began to appear as if a lot of other people had heard about the monster too. The road was thick with children and lie-abouts from the tavern, and people selling them boiled eggs and goat's milk. The cobbler and his wife had closed up their shop for the afternoon on Rhoecus's report. Polumetis clung to Athena's shoulder, talons embedded in the goatskin cloak, and those on the road gave her a wide berth and many gestures of respect.

At the harbor it was easy to find which ship had brought the monster. It was docked at the wharf where goods bound for the city were off-loaded, and an already sizable crowd had gathered about a wooden cage behind whose slats a large gray animal glowered. It was as tall as a horse and much broader, with stumpy gray legs and a wrinkled gray hide. It had a tufted tail like a cow's, small, annoyed eyes, and, in the middle of its nose, a wicked-looking horn as long as Athena's forearm. A second, smaller horn grew behind it. Every so often it charged the sides of the cage, head lowered, and rattled the slats, and everyone backed up just a little bit more. When Athena arrived, they made way for the king's daughter, opening up a path for her. Amoni followed in her wake and they stood staring at the beast. It stared back and snorted, shifting from foot to foot.

"What is it?" Athena asked the fishmonger, who was standing next to her.

"It's a Thing with a Horn on Its Nose, and it has a very bad temper."

"Where is it from?"

"The south, so they say, in the country of the Aethiopians, on the other side of the sea."

The ship's captain approached her, beaming proudly, as if she had come to interview some particularly talented child. He held a long club in one hand, however. He wore a fine wool tunic and a red belt. A Phrygian peaked cap covered most of his gray hair.

"Welcome, my lady." He sketched an elaborate bow, sweeping the cap from his head.

"Did you catch it yourself?" Athena asked him.

"Not me, my lady. I'm a seaman. I bought him from a fellow on Cyprus. I thought to sell him to the king of this country for a curiosity."

"I'm not sure the king would like him," Athena said. "But you never know." Uncle Poseidon would probably try to hunt it. Maybe it would kill him.

"We will give the king a report of your beast," Amoni said. "Perhaps you might like to present it to him as a gift."

"Not going to do anything of the sort," the captain retorted. "I bought the thing for twenty obols of silver, a good horse, and two slave girls. I have to get my investment back. Kings have more than is good for them anyway; let him pay for the beast. No one else will have anything like it. Why should I give it away?"

"We'll let him know," Amoni said solemnly, while Athena stuffed her knuckles in her mouth to keep from laughing. The crowd parted for them again.

"Very well then, you were right," she said to Amoni as they walked back along the harborside. "It is a monster. You don't suppose Father would actually buy it, do you? Where on earth would he keep it?"

"He could sacrifice it."

"If he can find anyone willing to get close enough to it. Did you see that hide? It would stomp you flat before you could cut its throat. Anyway, if it's the only one there is, it would be a shame to kill it. I don't imagine the Goddess would like it much, rummaging around in the Underworld, charging at people with that thing on its nose."

It struck Amoni as exactly the sort of beast the Goddess might like, dark and unpredictable.

"Why would anyone buy a thing like that?" Athena asked. "And drag it around in a crate?"

"It is rumored that in Phrygia they all have ass's ears," Amoni said. "That's why they wear those peaked caps, to hide them."

The crowd still thronged around them, as if it were a festival day. A few enterprising souls had set up stalls and were selling roasted birds and wine in little clay cups. The smell of the cooking birds hung over the dock. Above them gulls squawked and fluttered, looking for scraps.

A rattle of chariot wheels and shouts to make way drew their attention to the road. A procession of chariots thundered past, kicking up clouds of dust in the dry roadbed, and scattering the populace. The king himself alighted from the first one, while the horses, possibly scenting the monster, snorted and reared. He was accompanied by the queen and, in procession behind him, by all the councilors of the Areopagus. Athena and Amoni followed them to see what would happen.

The elders of the Areopagus made a circle about the cage, a solemn procession of learned men come to scientifically examine the beast, except for Uncle Poseidon, who was poking it with a stick.

"Plainly a supernatural creature," Gelon said. He peered at it nearsightedly and it pawed the ground at him. "Related to the Minotaur. It will eat human flesh."

"It eats grass so far," the ship's captain said.

"I'll hunt it," Poseidon said, confirming Athena's prediction. He poked at the beast again with his stick and it snorted and charged him, shaking the cage. The horn stuck out between the slats and the crowd backed up.

Kosmetas shook his head. "Don't be a fool. I'm not going to pay for the thing for you to hunt it. Run wild through my fields like as not, trampling everything, and then get away from you. Then where would we be?"

Poseidon looked disappointed. "That's what

you do with monsters," he argued. "You hunt them to keep the populace safe."

"The populace is safe as long as you don't set the thing loose in the first place," Kosmetas said.

To Athena's relief he could not be persuaded, even though Poseidon sulked and argued. It seemed a shame to kill a thing like that when it was the only one of its kind maybe. She had never understood the hunter's urge to kill something just to kill it. To eat it, yes. That made sense. Athena had hunted for deer and rabbits in the hills herself, with Nike and Amoni. The meat went into the pot at Nike's house, or to Amoni's father or Cook at the palace. She was absolutely certain that you couldn't eat this beast.

By the cage, Poseidon was still arguing that you could.

"I would love to see him drag that thing to the kitchen and tell Cook to boil it," she whispered to Amoni.

"Your father seems to have made up his mind. Have you seen enough of the monster?"

"I suppose I have," Athena said. "I'm beginning to feel a little sorry for it. If he really wants to sell it, he ought to take it to one of the great cities. Mycenae or Knossos. I wish I could go with him," she added wistfully. "I'll never be able to see anything of the world."

Amoni thought of saying that they could run away together, that he could show her the world, the marvels of the court at Knossos, of which he had heard from travelers, even the wonders of the

Aethiopians. He bit his tongue. She was tied to Attica. She was as much a creature in a cage as the Thing with the Horn on Its Nose, and as she got older he doubted she would be any happier in her confinement.

Instead he bought her a roasted bird and they shared it, walking homeward, with a cup of wine. It wasn't very good wine, thoroughly watered and sour, but they drank it contentedly, pulling pieces from the bird as they went. The day was one of the hot, dusty days that came in summer, when the sky was a bright, brilliant azure and the sun so fierce it looked like molten bronze. The light radiated off the outcropping stones on the hillside and off the limestone walls atop the Acropolis until you thought it might blind you. The road was still thick with sightseers hurrying to the dock in case the monster went away before they could see it. "Is it real?" they asked Athena and Amoni. "Does it really have a horn on its forehead? Is it as splendid as they say?"

"It has a horn on its nose," Athena said. "It's real. I don't think you would call it splendid. It doesn't like being caged either."

"It's very fierce," Amoni said. "Frightening."

They hurried on, reassured. Frightening was as good as splendid.

Athena's mouth turned down. Amoni thought she was brooding over the creature, feeling perhaps too close a kinship to it. "Come and see what I have been making," he said as they climbed the steps to the Acropolis from the harbor road.

In the smithy Athena folded her cloak on a bench, and Polumetis, who seemed to know that her talons hurt, settled on Athena's head instead, hooking her talons into the knot of hair at the back.

Amoni chuckled. "You have no idea how silly you look with an owl on your head."

"I shall set a new fashion," Athena said. She struck a haughty pose. "In a ten-day everyone will want an owl. All the wives of the Areopagus will wear one."

"And a cloak of snakes."

"Probably not." The cloak felt more alive to Athena every time she wore it. She was never sure whether it was the snakes or Pallas who inhabited it, but something did. She was growing used to it, but the one time she had offered it to Nike to wear when Nike had left her mantle at home, Nike had taken it back off in a heartbeat and shoved it at Athena. "Ugh!" she had said. "You wear it. It makes my skin crawl."

"This is supposed to be for your uncle," Amoni told her, taking something out of a box. "He asked me to make an amulet, and he gave me gold to make it with too, but I can't get it to come right. It's dreadfully fiddly stuff to work."

Athena looked at the brooch in the palm of his hand. She could see that it was supposed to be a snake, of coiled gold as thick as her little finger, and she could see what he had wanted to do, to make it lifelike, like the gold skin of a real snake, but the metal was rigid and uncooperative.

"I made it in clay, just to have something to copy," he said, annoyed. He showed her the little clay serpent, each sinuous coil piled on the next, alive as if it might flow off his hand and slide away. "But you can't do that with gold."

Athena took the clay model from his hand and stroked its coils. He had even incised the scales into it with a pick, so that they followed the frozen undulations of its form. Much too nice for Uncle Poseidon. A bee buzzed by her nose, a wanderer from the blooms that covered the pomegranate tree in the palace courtyard, and she swatted at it. Her hand froze. She looked at the little coiled snake and the bee now bumbling about the eaves of the forge, and the idea came into her head all at once, perfect, irresistible, utterly possible and new.

"We need some wax," she said.

"Wax?" Amoni looked at her, puzzled. Wax was good for lubricating things that needed to slide smoothly, like latches and hinges. You could put a wick in it and burn it for light, but it was expensive because you had to steal it from bees in the first place.

"Honeycomb," she said impatiently. "Cook will have some. Come on."

Amoni followed her. She began to run, darting through the agora as she had when she was small, with Polumetis swooping above her on silent wings. Cook had bought a honeycomb only that morning, from a boy who had robbed a bee tree. Athena had seen the boy bring it in, with red welts on his nose and more on his arms. Cook had it hanging over a bowl on a stick, letting the honey drip out.

He flapped his apron at Athena and Amoni as they burst through the door. Polumetis flew around his head and he swatted at her too. "Take yourselves out of here with that cursed owl, before you upset something."

"We need that honeycomb; can't it drain any faster?"

"I'll give you a bite of it to chew when it has," Cook said indulgently. "I thought you'd outgrown that for sure."

"I don't want to chew it," Athena said. "We're going to make something of it, and I'll even bring you back the wax when we're done. Please?"

"And what are you going to make that doesn't use up the wax, hmmm?"

"I have no idea," Amoni said. "It's her notion."

Cook shook his head. Athena had always been full of notions, and some of them worked out better than others. He also knew she wouldn't go away until she had what she wanted. "I suppose I could give you this bit from the top. It's near empty." He lifted the stick and tore off a corner of the comb with his fingers. "It's not clean, mind. Take it and wash it at the well or whatever your grand project is will be covered in ants."

Athena took it gingerly and carried it out to the well in the kitchen garden. She dipped up a bucket of water and swished the comb in it. "Honey is dreadfully sticky, isn't it?" she muttered, licking her fingers. Polumetis watched her from the branches of an apple tree, and Amoni sat on the edge of the well, looking at his reflection. Athena would tell him what she was up to when she was ready. You never could rush her. He thought that sometimes she had a vision of a thing and then thought out the details as she went. Right now she seemed to be seeing them in the honeycomb. She inspected its minute chambers and delicate walls. The cold well water took a long time to rinse the honey away, but she didn't seem to mind. She watched the water flow in and out of the chambers and the way they bent and breathed with its flow. Finally she drew it out and seemed satisfied. She swung the comb in the air to shake the liquid out, and beamed at Amoni. "This is brilliant. You'll see." It didn't matter if it was for Uncle Poseidon. It was brilliant anyway.

He followed her back to the forge, where she pulled the comb apart and set the shreds of it to dry in the sun. "We don't want any water in it, I think."

"I suppose you know," Amoni murmured. It annoyed him when she was secretive, but he thought she enjoyed it.

"And we want some clay," she said happily. She seemed to be bursting with her notion, unable to hold it in any longer if he wasn't going to ask her. "We're going to make a mold!"

"Molds work very well for flat things," Amoni said, balancing the little clay snake in his hand. "I've used them. But you can't get it off again in one piece when you mold something that has three directions. And wax is no good for a mold anyway. It will melt."

"The wax isn't the mold," Athena said, her eyes shining. "The wax is the model. You melt it out of the mold and then pour the gold in."

Amoni set the snake down and cocked his head at it and at the honeycomb. Athena was already working the comb in her hands, warming it, compressing it into a lump. You would have to break the mold to get it off the finished piece, of course, but that wouldn't matter. If you made an amulet for the king's brother, you didn't make duplicates for other people. And you could carve even finer detail in wax than in clay.

"You leave a channel at the top to pour the molten gold in," Athena said. "And several, I think, at the bottom for the wax to run out. When you break the mold off it there will be little dribbles of gold where the channels were, and you can smooth them off."

Amoni held out his hand and she gave him the wax. He grinned at her. "I wouldn't be surprised if it worked," he said.

"I will be very surprised if it doesn't." Athena sat down on a bench behind the forge fire and Polumetis lit on the anvil. They sat and looked at him.

"What? I'm to try it right now?"

"Of course."

"It will take a while to carve the snake in the wax, and I can't do it while the two of you sit and look at me like you were waiting for lunch."

"Polumetis is waiting for lunch. We'll go hunt up a shrew, and come back in a while."

"Fine. Just go away." He balanced the lump of wax in his hand, studying it.

Athena wandered out to the agora. Her parents would both be still at the harbor looking at the monster, and no one in particular would be looking for her to weave or spin or listen to long, boring debates, because all the boring debaters were at the harbor too. Everyone was. She had even seen Cook, his kitchen abandoned, bustling past the forge on his way. Nike's brothers had all been in the crowd at the dock, but she hadn't seen Nike. Athena started down the steep streets to the mud-brick houses at the bottom of the hill.

Nike was at home, with a clean cloth tied over her hair. "I have cheese to make," Nike said. "It's just some poor beast from foreign parts, all caged up. I'd only feel sorry for it."

"I did," Athena said. "It was dreadfully ugly, but it didn't ask to be in a cage. Uncle Poseidon wanted to hunt it, but Father wouldn't buy it. The first sensible thing he's done lately. I'll help you with the cheese."

"Is he still trying to marry you to your uncle?" Nike asked, her hands in a vat of clabbered milk. Nike and her mother made cheese in a little shed beside their house, the walls lined with clay jars and crocks.

"And ill luck to the idea," Athena said. "What

should I do? I'm helpful, but I'm not good at cheese."

"Fetch me the rennet. It's in that crock of salt. Cut me off a little piece."

Athena fished in the crock and drew out the dried rennet. Everything died to make something, even cheese. Rennet was the lining of a kid's fourth stomach, and it was what curdled the milk into cheese. Athena found a knife near the milk crocks and cut off a strip with it. Nike dropped it into the milk and poked it about.

"I hate making cheese," she said, "but at least it's peaceful here today with everyone gone to gawp at the monster. Even Father went, and so of course all the boys who were supposed to be cutting grapes for the pressing went too."

At the start of the summer, Athena would have suggested they run away for the day, but they had done that already, and Pallas was dead, and they seemed to have grown up whether they wanted to or not. So she helped Nike pour the whey off a crock that was ready to be salted and pressed.

"I saw you with Amoni earlier," Nike said. "You had better be careful."

"I have no idea what you mean."

Nike snorted. "Your mother won't let you marry him, even if she won't let your father give you to your uncle. That's what I mean."

"I have no intention of marrying him," Athena said with careful dignity.

"He's nice," Nike admitted. "It must be very satisfactory to have someone like that love you."

"It's not if you can't have them!" Athena snapped. "Not that I want to."

"Oh, I'm sorry." Nike took her hands out of the curds she was turning over. "Maybe I should be happy that all I have to worry about is cheese, and whoever Father finds for me, if he ever does. I may have to wait until one of my brothers marries a woman who can make cheese before he'll let me go be someone else's slave."

"Your oldest brother's wife can't make cheese?" Athena asked, diverted.

"She's dreadful at it. She does try, but it takes a certain skill, which she hasn't got. She gets the house cleaner than anyone I ever saw, though. Even with all my brothers still galumphing through it. I'll give her that."

"I wish I lived in your house." Athena sighed. "There's always something interesting going on, and no one worries about who's going to be king."

"We're too far down the hill for it to matter to us who's king," Nike said. "And what on earth is going on now?" She stuck her head out the shed door.

A faint commotion in the street was growing louder. Athena came to the doorway beside her as a knot of people hurtled past them, screaming.

"It's loose!"

"Catch it!"

"Hide!"

"Run to the temple!"

"Call out the army!"

Athena grabbed a running woman by the arm. "What is it? Stop that and tell me!"

"The monster's loose! That Thing with the Horn on Its Nose from out of the sea! It's got loose and it's rampaging and ravaging and someone has to kill it!"

By this time the streets were thick with citizens and hunters on horseback. She saw Poseidon among them on a black horse. "We turned it back from the city!" he shouted. "Women and children stay inside. We'll circle around below the walls to meet it!"

"You let it out, didn't you?" Athena shouted at him.

He turned to her briefly, looking over his shoulder as his horse reared and pawed the air. "It broke from its cage. I told my brother it was dangerous!"

"You told him to buy it so you could hunt it!" Athena shouted after him. "He wouldn't, so you let it loose!"

No one paid any attention to her. The crowd hurried after Poseidon, mothers carrying children in their arms. They would follow the spectacle, no matter what, to see something killed. Athena saw Arachne, the cloth dyer's daughter, hurrying along with a huge length of wool that she hadn't stopped to put down floating out behind her. The girl who had led the goat at the sacrifices pattered along, towed behind her mother, eyes bright with

excitement. Cecrops, the next-to-eldest of the Areopagus, bowled past them in his chariot. Athena
couldn't imagine Cecrops slaying a monster, especially not with his two younger sisters in the chariot with him. Herse and Aglauros had stayed
unmarried somehow. Athena thought that maybe
she ought to consult them on how. Metis said it
was because they were both so silly that no one
would have them, but Athena had never noticed
that a woman's intelligence meant very much to
prospective husbands. The dumber the better,
Uncle Poseidon had been heard to proclaim. All
it took, he said, was enough brains to lie down
when you were told to.

Athena suspected that most women lay down
when Poseidon told them to because they were
afraid of him, and so were their husbands and
fathers. Pelasgian women hid when they saw him
coming. She had heard her father warn him that
he wouldn't be able to hold on to the kingship if
he pushed the Pelasgians too far. That was what
the amulet was for, she thought, to ingratiate himself with the Pelasgians, who gave their worship
to the old Goddess and her serpent consort. He
planned to give it to her temple, Amoni had said.

She could hear shouting and the rumble of
hooves and wheels on the plain below the city
now. People kept streaming by her. Athena saw
Amoni among them. She called to him and he
pushed his way to her. "The fool let it loose," he
said. "He prodded it with his stick once too often
and it charged him and broke the slats. Theios

told me. He said you've never seen a place clear
out so fast. Then it headed inland and everyone
went charging after it. They claim they turned it
at the gates, but I don't expect it particularly
wanted in. Now it's got to be stopped. I suppose
the army will kill it." His expression was
disgusted.

"Did it hurt anyone?"

"Not so far. But it's bound to."

"Maybe it will be Uncle Poseidon." Athena
closed her eyes and asked the Goddess to make
it so.

"I give up," Nike said. "I will go and see the
monster like everyone else, or Theios will tell me
about it every day for the rest of my life."

They followed the crowd flowing down the hill,
threading their way between the huts and taverns
that sprawled along the road. In the distance they
could see a great cloud of dust and the flash of
spear points. It had gotten in among the wheatfields. Horses and chariots milled in the field
around it, trampling the wheat. As they watched,
the monster burst from the scuffle and began to
gallop again. Athena could see two spears sticking
in its hide. A horde of chariots and mounted riders pursued it. The beast was faster than she
would have thought. A single rider on a black
horse pulled ahead of the pack, drawing back his
bow. He urged the horse forward and let the shaft
fly. It struck the monster in the back of the neck,
between the ears. The monster bellowed, a fearful
sound that set all the horses that weren't already

terrified to dancing in their traces. Then it turned and charged as the rider drew up on it. The horse reared and whinnied in fear, and they went down in a tangle. Athena held her breath. It was Poseidon on the horse; she knew it. The rider rolled free while the horse lay screaming, its belly gashed open. He had somehow held on to his bow and quiver and he stood his ground, nocking another arrow as the beast charged. The shaft flew from his fingers, struck the monster in the neck, and sank up to the fletching. The beast swerved abruptly, bellowed again, and fell sideways, thrashing its tail and its monstrous legs.

"I am disgusted," Athena said to Amoni as he worked at the wax with a small knife. The serpent coiled in his hands, still rough but sinuous, as if it were made of live rock. "He has its head on a pole. It looks so frightened and angry still. I hope it curses him."

"It might," Amoni said. "Things like that sometimes do." He kept his eyes on the wax, but she could see the scornful twist of his mouth.

Athena wondered if they could build their own curse into the amulet and make the Pelasgians hate Poseidon even more than they did already. She didn't speak the thought—Amoni was prideful about his creations and he wouldn't like the idea—but she gazed at the serpent with a fierce concentration, willing the thought into it as it came to life in his hands.

When the wax model was finished, he painted

it with a fine slip of wet clay, building up several layers' thickness before he packed more clay around that and left it to harden. Athena watched it impatiently, and Amoni laughed and said that it wouldn't be dry enough for a day at least.

"Let's take a walk," he suggested. She was pacing with a restless energy, propelled by her anger at her uncle. "Forget about him. I have apples and wine. We'll go where we used to when we were children, and picnic. Just us and Her Feathered Highness." He nodded at Polumetis, messily eating a rat in the rafters.

Something told Athena that wasn't a good idea, but her fury drove her past caution. Everyone else did exactly what they wanted and never counted the consequences; why shouldn't she?

The hills were bathed in a dusty end-of-summer light and heady with the scent of flowers and the warm buzz of bees. The cicadas had all mated and died, leaving their eggs to hatch in the spring and crawl down the tree trunks to bury themselves in the earth for years to come before their own brief moment of giddy flight. Athena spread her cloak on a rock and they sat on it in the shade of a laurel grove, eating apples. She was acutely conscious of Amoni next to her, and the soft whisper of his breath. When he took her hand and lifted it to his lips, she didn't move. She sat, hushed, frozen, every hair on her arms standing up.

"I can't help it if you are the king's daughter," he whispered.

"No," she said. "No, we can't." Everyone else

did what they wanted to. Just once, she would.
He laid a hand tentatively on her breast and all
the bees and the ghosts of the joyous short-lived
cicadas hummed in her blood.

In the heart of the laurel grove the shadows
were thick. Polumetis flew up into them on silent
wings and perched there. The ground beneath the
trees was crackly with dry grass and old leaves.
Amoni spread the cloak out, with the lining fac-
ing up. He ran his hands over her shoulder and
she slid into his arms. He buried his face in her
hair and breathed in her scent. She smelled of
the laurel and the lavender water she washed her
hair in. Her gray eyes had little flickers of fire in
them as he pulled the bronze pins out of the
shoulders of her tunic and let it slip to her feet.
He shed the rough leather jacket and apron he
wore at the forge, and then the wool tunic below
it. Then he knelt and pulled her down with him
onto the cloak. Her lips fastened on his and she
wrapped her arms about him. Whatever inhabited
the cloak rose up out of it and hung above them
like a canopy, enveloping them, shading them
from the outer world.

Afterward they walked hand in hand back to
the city through the warm, dusty twilight, not daring to speak, with Polumetis flying above them.
The owl's round yellow eyes were knowing, but
she was an owl and she kept her comments to
herself.

The next day they tried the mold, heating it over

the fire until the wax melted and ran out. When it had cooled, Amoni cradled it in his hands. His eyes were excited. He stopped the openings at the bottom with bits of clay and braced it with a bronze tripod to hold it steady. Athena held her breath as he melted the gold in the forge furnace and poured it carefully into the mold through a funnel.

When it had cooled, they looked at each other solemnly, hardly daring to break it open. Finally Amoni gritted his teeth and picked up a small hammer.

The snake was perfect, his coils as sinuous as if he were still molten. Every scale was there. He seemed to breathe through the small indentations of his nostrils.

Amoni's smile widened. "If I can do work like this, I will make myself rich," he told her. "Rich enough for your father maybe."

He didn't notice, in his glee, that Athena didn't answer that.

She did think, once or twice, of broaching the matter to Kosmetas. The king was growing older with sudden speed. She could see that now that she paid close attention. His beard had gone nearly all gray, and he walked with a stiffness that surprised her. When had that happened? Kosmetas had seemed to slow further since Poseidon had killed the monster and the Achaeans, at least, were hailing him as a hero. Athena heard angry arguments between them whenever someone came to Kosmetas with a complaint against Poseidon: that he drank at the tavern without paying, or had his way with a girl against her will, or demanded that something that caught his eye be given him as a "gift" whether the owner wished to part with it or not.

"You will never hold them if you make them hate you," Kosmetas said angrily.

"That's what my little niece is for, to woo the Pelasgians," Poseidon said. "So we had better up the wedding date, brother, while you're still aboveground." His voice was cheerfully insulting, and Athena froze in the corridor outside. Would her father stand for that?

Apparently not. Kosmetas roared at Poseidon and Poseidon roared back, but then he came stalking out into the corridor. Athena ducked behind a pillar before he saw her. She knew better than to ask about Amoni now. She was of two minds about Amoni anyway. If she married him, Poseidon might be king. If she were queen and married him afterward, the Areopagus would want to approve it, and argue over his suitability, and consult the Goddess, and then as like as not they would hand all her power over to Amoni. More on her mind was the making of babies, or rather the not making of babies. She consulted Xene the midwife, who frowned at her and tried to pretend she was too busy to talk.

"If your mother heard I spoke to you of such things—"

"Well, she won't hear it from me. Anyway, it's for a friend."

"Bah," Xene said. "Everything is for a 'friend,' especially if the husband might get wind of it. A husband you don't have, I might add."

"I may soon," Athena said. "I may need to know things." It was common knowledge among the women that the midwife dealt in more than bringing babies into the world. There were ways to see that they didn't arrive, or to prevent their starting altogether.

"And if I don't tell you, your 'friend' will do what she will do, I suppose." Xene sighed. "These things are not reliable, you know. They only change the odds."

"I gave the Lady a bowl of milk on my way to talk to you."

"I suggest you help prayer along as much as you can," Xene said dryly. "There are some things that will help." She got out a little cloth bag and began putting pinches of herbs into it from her storebox. The box had many little compartments with round copper lids that lifted off each one. Athena wanted to stay and ask her what each one was, but Xene was brisk. "Your 'friend' should make an infusion from this," she said, "and drink it warm. A dipperful a day for a woman who doesn't want to conceive." She sighed as she tied the end of the bag closed. "A king's daughter has to be more careful than a goatherd's. Now go away before anyone finds you here."

•

"I wish *I* were a goatherd's daughter," Athena muttered.

"I will wish so too if your mother gets wind of this."

Athena smiled at her. "Thank you, Xene."

"I was there when you were born," Xene said. "Your mother damaged her womb in the birth; that's why you have no brothers. Remember that. You may be like her."

"I don't intend to have any," Athena said. "So it won't matter."

"I didn't intend to get old," Xene said. "The ox didn't intend to pull the plow."

She knew every time she slipped away with Amoni that they were taking a chance, but after the first time she yearned for him in ways she hadn't expected. She awoke smiling, thinking of him, of the way his feet looked, long and slender with high, graceful arches, of the way his hair curled at the back of his neck, and the way his eyes were just a little tilted so that he looked like a faun. They found places where no one came and spread her cloak on the ground in the laurel thicket or in the high grass, a whispering curtain all around them. They lay and listened to the beating of each other's hearts, and the shouts of the reapers working at the hay in the autumn, and the high, thin bleating of the new lambs in the spring. Athena knew her freedom to lie with Amoni was limited. She would take it while she could.

V

The *Shearwater*

"I am going away somewhere." Athena's voice was carefully calm.

"Go? Go where?" Amoni looked at her wildly.

"I won't tell you, so when they ask you, you won't know. You can tell them that you think I have run away from the marriage with my uncle. I need to think things through about Pallas, and I need some tricks to put a spoke in my uncle's wheel later, to be away from him so I can think."

Amoni put his head in his hands. "You can't go alone."

"I'm not. Nike's coming with me."

"You would rather have Nike than me," he said miserably.

She bent her head to his and kissed his dark curls gently. "Amoni. I love you. You are dearer to me than anyone. Even more than Pallas was.

But this is something I have to do, and you know
I can't marry you. I will have to just love you."

Nike watched Athena in bemused fascination as
she prepared for their journey. Nothing as mad as
this had ever been proposed to Nike, and she
wasn't certain why she had agreed—perhaps because it *was* mad, and if she didn't go she would
never again have the chance to be mad. That it
was an adventure that could easily kill them was
an idea they considered. Two young women trav-
eling alone were a tempting target; therefore
Athena handed Nike a knife and told her to cut
off her hair.

"I've already done mine," she said. "Look." She
pulled away the mantle she had wrapped about her
head, and Nike gaped. Athena's long, dark hair was
cropped as short as a boy's, and ragged, as if she
had done it with the knife she now offered Nike.

Nike took a hank of her tawny hair in one fist
and looked at the knife for a long moment before
she began to saw through it. The shorn hair
dropped in a pile at her feet. While she hacked at
it, Athena packed a pair of saddlebags with plain
tunics, filched from the laundry, and all the gold
jewelry she could lay her hands on, most of it
hers. She was already wearing a boy's tunic, and
handed a second to Nike, along with a cloth to
bind her breasts.

"Yours are huge," she told Nike. "Wrap it
tightly or you'll never pass."

"Nobody said I had to be a boy," Nike grumbled.

"We'll be like the girls in the ballads, who run away to sea in boys' clothing," Athena said.

Polumetis watched them from just outside Athena's window in the dawn light. Nike had slipped away from her house and walked through the darkness to the palace, scaled a wall as she had done when they were children, and come in through the window, the way in which Athena planned to exit. Below the wall was her father's stable, and his best horses.

"This one is actually Poseidon's," Athena whispered to Nike as she tightened the girth on its saddle. "And he doesn't deserve it after the way he let his mare get killed by that thing he let loose. He had to cut her throat afterward. I wouldn't be his horse for anything."

Nike boosted herself into the saddle. Now she was stealing a horse from Poseidon. She found it impossible to think of anything more dangerously criminal.

They slipped out the stable door into the waking street. Athena had bundled Pallas's cloak into a saddlebag, and wore a plain wool one she had filched from Nurse. Polumetis flew overhead. No one paid them much mind, just two stableboys out to exercise the king's mounts. Nike half expected Amoni to come after them, to try to stop them or go with them, but the forge was silent, and no smoke rose from its roof. They trotted through the

Acropolis gates to the road that wound down its slope to the plain below.

"I bought passage yesterday from the captain of a ship bound for Phoenicia," Athena said. "I told him we are brothers, Evander and Ajax. You're Evander. Try to remember that, and remember which one is you. I paid him to take on the horses too. I don't want to turn them loose to go home or Father will know we've taken a ship. And we may want them. We can sell them, anyway."

"Phoenicia," Nike whispered. It was just a word in her mind, not even a real place, a land so far away that no one knew what sort of people lived there. Athena spoke of it as if they were bound for Eleusis, a day's ride away. Nike had never even been to Eleusis, where the queen went every year to sacrifice to the Goddess.

"Phoenicia is across the sea to the east," Athena said. "The purple dye that Arachne's father uses comes from there, and cedarwood. And glass, and linen cloth. I asked the captain."

All those were luxuries that Nike had no experience of. She tried to picture a mysterious country where everyone dressed in purple and owned glass bottles, but it was beyond her imagining.

The sun was high enough to splash pools of pink and yellow light on the road now, and the land around them was beginning to stir. They could see farm girls working at the hay, and a boy trotting beside his little flock of goats, his pipes in his hand. The melody came to them faintly over the bleating of the goats.

At the harbor their ship, a hulking cargo vessel incongruously called the *Shearwater*, was waiting for the tide. Its captain was a burly man in a blue robe fringed with red, his dark hair covered by a red cap with a jewel in it. His beard was trimmed and oiled and elaborately curled. Polumetis settled on Athena's shoulder and he eyed her dubiously. "You didn't tell me that owl came with you, lad. Some of the men will think it ill luck to have a bird aboard."

"Owls are lucky," Athena said firmly.

"They are that, Captain," a sailor volunteered. "I've docked here before, and they are counted a favorable bird in this land." He bore a box on his shoulder, tied up with rope, and he disappeared down a set of steps into the hold.

"She eats rats," Athena added.

"Very well then. You paid enough for your passage, I suppose. Take the horses belowdecks and you can lay your beds out up here."

Nike poked Athena. "What do they carry on this ship?" she whispered.

"Everything, lad," the captain said proudly. "Ivory, ebony, amber, ostrich eggs. Gold and copper. Tin. Incense. Papyrus from Egypt. Horses. Those are fine ones you brought aboard. I could help you sell them if you wanted to."

"Maybe," Athena said. She was suspicious of anyone so helpful to strangers.

"My name is Ahiram," he said to Nike. "I own this ship and six more like her, sailing out of Tyre to take on copper at Cyprus for the kings of Babylon, ivory from the rajas of the Ganges, and linen cloth from Thebes on the river Nile, even south to the kingdom of Kush for peafowl. If you're wanting to see the world you couldn't do better than come aboard my ship."

"Come. We need to put the horses up." Athena took Nike by the arm.

"What are ostriches?" Nike asked her as they led the horses down the sloping plank into the hold.

"I have no idea." They tethered their mounts in the stalls below where six others were already tied: great black beasts with bowed necks and braided manes. Ahiram dealt in horses as well, he had told Athena. These, from Anatolia, would fetch a good price in his homeland, which he called Canaan. Phoenicia was a catchall Achaean term for the lands to the east, he had said when she paid for their passage. It appeared that its geography was more complex than she had thought, and divided into many rival kingdoms and cities, as the Achaean settlements were. *We always think other people are less complicated than ourselves*, Athena thought.

They stowed their bundled bedding on the upper deck and leaned on the bow to watch the coast recede as the *Shearwater* pulled out of the harbor on the morning tide. The wind filled the huge square sail, and Ahiram shouted orders to the sailor at the tiller. Nike began to look green, but whether it was seasickness or the knowledge of what they had done, Athena wasn't sure. She felt queasy herself, and ravenously hungry at the same time. There was food for a day or so in their bags, and more to be bought when the ship stopped in port, which it would do often. Trading vessels were rarely out of sight of land, their voyage a series of small stops, off-loading and loading goods.

To take her mind from her stomach (if she ate now, she knew it would come back up), she wandered the deck, watching how the sail was set, and quietly observing the sailor at the tiller until he smiled at her and beckoned her over.

"Wanting to see how she's steered, lad?"

Athena nodded and listened intently as he showed her the steering oar and expounded on the setting of sail. She saw Ahiram watching them, smiling indulgently. Her story had been that they were brothers, vintner's sons from Attica, looking for adventure beyond the confines of their father's wine jars. Ahiram had run away to sea himself, when he was a boy, he had said, fingering the elaborate curls of his beard. The life had suited him. It was a fine career for a sharp lad.

At dusk the ship was passing the Cyclades, bound for Naxos. They put into a lee shore and dropped the anchor stone. Polumetis caught a rat that had been living in the grain sacks from which the horses were fed, and ate it headfirst. The sailors, having gotten a close look at her beak and talons, gave her a wide, respectful berth. There was a murmuring as they made their evening prayers to a handful of gods that Athena had never heard of. She tossed a bit of her bread into the wind for the Lady so that she would not feel disrespected among so many foreign gods. It grew cold, and she and Nike wrapped themselves in their cloaks and drew Pallas's goatskin over them both. Tonight it didn't make Nike nervous. Athena felt a warmth emanating from it, and the motion of the ship at anchor on a gentle swell seemed to connect with it, so that they were rocked in some warm womb of their own.

In the morning she splashed her face with fresh-water from the jars in the hold and stretched. She prodded Nike, still wrapped in her cloak. "Are you all right?"

"I felt last night as if I'd eaten Polumetis's rat," Nike said. "It's better this morning."

"Sea legs," Ahiram said, beaming at them. "That's the way. Soon you'll be bounding about like true seamen."

Two of his crew stood on the deck behind him, scratching and peeing over the side into the sea.

"*I* have to pee," Nike hissed at Athena. "I've had to since last night. I'll burst soon."

Athena waited until Ahiram moved on. "Go down in the hold and pee in this jar. It's why I brought it. I'll come with you."

They disappeared into the hold, hiding behind the horses, and then carried their jar back up to dump it surreptitiously overboard.

"I'll never manage," Nike moaned. "What happens when I start to bleed?"

"I didn't think of that," Athena said. "Nobody

ever mentions things like that in stories about girls disguising themselves. We'll just have to hope we're ashore by then."

There were, it seemed, a number of things they hadn't thought out. With each small adjustment, each change in their tale, Ahiram seemed to grow more indulgent and more amused. He scratched his beard and grinned at them as they disappeared into the hold with their jar, or refused to strip and drop overboard to swim with the sailors when the ship lay at anchor in the shallows.

Two weeks into their journey he sat down on the folding chair from which he surveyed his ship and its course, and beckoned to Athena. "Think you're far enough from Attica now, lad?" he asked her.

"Um." She looked at him suspiciously. "I suppose. We want to see foreign lands."

Ahiram chuckled. He adjusted the folds of his gaudy tunic and stroked his beard. "We make a circuitous voyage, you know. And slow. Slow enough for news to catch up sometimes. I hear there is a king's daughter who has vanished from Attica, and some great hue and cry over her."

"Truly?" Athena tried to look innocently interested. "I have seen the king's daughter once. At a festival." She remembered Nike's phrase. "We live too far down the hill, my brother and I, to have dealings with the king."

Ahiram shrugged. "What is an Achaean king's daughter to me? I have drunk wine with the pharaohs at Thebes. Attica is a primitive place. If they have lost a king's daughter, I doubt it will shake the world."

Athena thought of being insulted, but Ahiram was right. She had decided that much just from the beginning of their voyage, listening to the sailors talk of their homelands.

Ahiram sighed. "I am a romantic, though, and not too old to appreciate love. A king's daughter who runs away with a vintner's son—now that is romance."

"I am—" Athena bit the words back, thinking frantically.

"If you were to trust me, mind, I might be able to help. That poor girl won't be able to keep up her disguise for long. She walks like a girl, and she has breasts that any man is going to notice, even bound up."

Athena stifled a laugh, producing a not-very-convincing cough.

"He thinks you're me, and I'm your lover," she announced to Nike, when she had escaped from Ahiram without confessing to anything. She could see him watching them with his usual indulgent expression. "He says you have noticeable breasts."

Nike looked at her chest and sighed. "I know. I think one of the sailors knows, too. The blond one with the curls. He tried to kiss me."

Athena considered. "Maybe we will have to be girls again, if Ahiram will protect us. It depends on what he will want for it." In her experience men always wanted something for that.

"We can protect ourselves," Nike said, one hand on the bronze knife at her belt.

"Company," Ahiram said, looking hurt, when Athena broached the subject—carefully—the next day. "I had a fine wife by my side for forty years, until she died a year gone this summer, and I have married sons and daughters. I am a family man, but none of them likes the sea. If a runaway couple wanted to shelter under my wing, how could I turn them down?"

Athena grinned at him. "You have it backward, I fear." She was wrapped in Pallas's cloak, and the cloak, oddly, seemed to like him. Athena wasn't sure how she knew that, but she did. It was what had made her decide to trust him. That and the fact that Polumetis settled on his head and preened his beard and he only smiled at her.

When she had told him, he laughed, a booming laugh that echoed across the water, and slapped his knee. "Miriam, my wife, always told me I am not as smart as I think I am. I wish I could take this story home to her. She would have laughed." His voice grew sad. "She had a fine laugh, that woman. I married her for that laugh." He gave Athena an avuncular shake of the head. "And you, king's daughter, how did you manage to escape so easily?"

"I must be a favorite among the gods," Athena answered.

Ahiram chuckled. "I know what my Miriam would say. She would say I was not to leave you unprotected, that everything comes to pass for a reason. So. When we make port at Tyre, you will be a young widow and her sister, most unfortunate: your husband was lost overboard in a storm."

"What will your crew say to that?"

"They will say what I tell them to. Most are related to me, and the rest have enough sense to be afraid of me. I shall lend you a house I own. You are carrying enough gold with you to live comfortably in Tyre for a year at the least."

"How do you know that?" Athena demanded.

"I know what comes aboard my ship," Ahiram said. "Lads with rough clothes who pay in gold and have expensive horses and a tame owl bear looking into."

Athena ducked her head, embarrassed. She had been certain that she was a better liar than that.

Ahiram beamed at her. "It's no disgrace to be outfoxed by Ahiram. I was clever before you were born. Besides, I thought you were a boy."

"I am beginning to wish I were," Athena said. "Life would be easier if I were a man."

She retreated to their bedding and lay with her head in Nike's lap, until Ahiram came carrying an armload of bright cloth. "These were my Miriam's," he said. "She liked to sail with me, when our children were grown. I thought to sell them this trip, but I found I hadn't the heart. You wear them, and put away that cloak with the snakes that frightens my sailors. You will be ladies again and brighten my eye." He saw Nike watching him suspiciously, her hand on her belt knife, and added, "I am harmless."

"If he is harmless, a wolf is harmless," Nike said when he had gone, leaving the pile of clothing behind him.

"A wolf makes a good guardian." Athena sat up. While they argued, a sailor came with a striped tent like the fine one that Ahiram slept under, and pitched it on the deck, tying it down to cleats in the planking. "Captain says you are to have this," he told them. His speech was oddly accented, and he stumbled on the Achaean words. He was the blond one with the curls who had tried to kiss Nike, and he eyed her now with elaborate respect.

Miriam's clothes were of patterned wool and fine linen, as bright as the painted gowns on the statue of the Achaean Goddess on the Acropolis. It was plain that she had been spoiled by a wealthy husband. Every edge of her gowns and voluminous shawls was knotted and fringed in red and gold, and her caps jingled with gold disks. When they came hesitantly out of the tent, dressed in her finery, Ahiram beamed at them, but Athena thought he wiped his eyes as well. She had folded Pallas's goatskin cloak away, and hugged a shawl of red and purple, sewn through with gold thread, about her shoulders. Her dark, ragged hair was tucked under a red cap.

"I wish I could thank your wife," she said to Ahiram.

Ahiram sighed. "She lives in Melqart's domain now, and I cannot go and find her as Anat found Baal. When my shade meets her shade I will tell her you thanked her."

"Was she beautiful?" Athena asked him.

"Oh, most beautiful. When she was young I used to call her my gray dove because she had gray eyes like yours. Enough of that, now. It is a fine thing for clothes to have a new life. They are sad, I think, when they are in trunks."

"Then we will try to make these happy," Nike said, relenting because she had never in her life worn anything so fine.

"You are a true friend to come on such a mad voyage as this," Ahiram told her.

"I did want to see the world," Nike said. "I couldn't let Athena go without me."

"The world is vast," Ahiram said. "No one but a sailor can know how vast. Tonight you ladies will dine with me in my tent and I will tell you things to make you wonder at its vastness."

He was true to his word. When they arrived, the front flaps of his tent were folded back, revealing an ebony table and four chairs on graceful legs, which could be folded up on themselves when they were to be stowed away. The table was low and solid against the swell of the sea, and laden with silver dishes, which made Nike gasp. Athena's eyes widened too. Even her father did not eat off silver. They held ripe figs, bought that morning at their last port, a loaf of fresh bread, pastries of pheasant's meat and cheese, and a dish of apples stewed with cinnamon. Small covered sauce dishes surrounded them.

It was dusk, and the *Shearwater* rode at anchor off the island of Naxos, in a little harbor beyond which they could see the last of the sun glinting red off the whitewashed walls of a small village. Ahiram produced a silver ewer of wine and poured it into three silver cups. He raised his cup to Athena and Nike. "To fine company for a lonely sailor."

It was excellent wine. Athena was ravenous now, and when Ahiram motioned toward the dishes on the table, she began to investigate. In two of the small ones were a clear yellow oil, and a small, dark fruit she didn't recognize.

"What are these?"

"Those are olives, the staff of life, oh, barbarian princess," Ahiram said. "Their oil lights my table."

Athena looked up at the silver lamp that hung from a chain fastened on the tent poles. She sniffed. It didn't smell like the tallow lamps she was used to, and it gave off very little smoke. Its yellow glow danced on the silver dishes.

"And it is very good on bread," Ahiram said, pulling a piece off the loaf and dabbing at it with the little brush that sat in the dish of oil. He handed it to her.

Athena bit into it. The taste was light, odd to her tongue. She picked one of the dark fruits from the dish and ate it. It was tart and oily. Her tooth grated on something.

"They have pits," Ahiram said.

Athena spat the pit into her hand and dropped it into an empty dish, which must have been there for the purpose.

"The king at Knossos lights his palace with this oil," Ahiram told her. "And his queen oils her skin with it."

"And why do we know nothing of it?" Athena demanded. Was Attica truly as backward as Ahiram had said?

Ahiram shrugged. "It is expensive, taking a long time to mature. I sell all I can carry to the cities of Egypt. And its cultivation is jealously guarded. I trade in the oil and the fruit, but never the trees."

"It grows on trees?"

"In my homeland, and on Crete as well, where we taught them to cultivate it. A mistake, in my opinion. The secrets of gifts such as these are best kept hidden as the silk weavers of Asu do."

Athena took another thoughtful bite of the bread Ahiram had spread with oil. She wondered who the silk weavers of Asu were, and what silk was, and how many other things there were in the world that she had never heard of.

"It is a wide world," Ahiram said. "I have spent much time in mapping it and I know just the smallest piece, just the lands around the edges of the sea. Of the lands on the other side of it I have no notion."

"The other side of the sea?" Nike asked. Her

mouth was full of pastry, and she had to swallow it and ask again.

"On the other side of the world," Ahiram said.

"How can there be things on the other side of the world? You mean the bottom side? They would fall off."

"We don't know why they don't fall off, but they don't. The world is round, child. Any fool could see that."

"How?" Nike glared at him suspiciously. You *would* fall off.

"When you see a ship sail away, what does it do?"

"It gets smaller with distance. I know that."

"And then it disappears entirely."

"It gets too small to see."

"Aha! Not quite. Watch carefully and you will see that the *bottom* of the ship disappears first. It sails around the curve of the world to where we can't see it. *But* if you climb a mountain, or a high tower, you may see it again from that new angle."

Athena stopped with a bit of bread halfway to her mouth.

"And when you come into port, what do you see? The tops of the mountains first, and *then* the seacoast."

"Then why don't we fall off?"

"Something holds us to the surface. The will of Baal perhaps. That part is a mystery. But you can't fool a sailor."

Later Ahiram stood with them in the bow of

the *Shearwater* and pointed out the stars, the constellations wheeling across the night sky, with the polar star Cynosura constant in its place. He showed them how the paths of the stars and the sun moved through the year and how to measure their distance from the horizon with two fingers held at an arm's length, in order to know where you were on the sea.

Athena drank it all in, as she did the next day when she saw him making something that looked like the marks that Attic merchants used to keep count of their goods, nicking them into a piece of wet clay.

"What is that?"

"A message to my factor on Cyprus. I will send it by courier when we dock there, that I want forty ingots of copper waiting for me in three moons' time."

"You can say all that with marks in clay?"

Ahiram chuckled. "You can say more than that. Wars have been started over things said with marks in clay."

Athena didn't doubt that. Wars were far easier to start than to stop, Kosmetas said.

"You are a curious child," Ahiram said. "So was my Miriam. Forever asking me the why of things." He sighed. "Now all I have is this to remember her by. It doesn't seem very much for a lifetime." He pulled a small gold amulet on a chain from under his tunic and showed it to her. It was a little woman with bare breasts, wearing a pleated skirt low on her wide hips, and a conical headdress. She held sheaves of wheat in both hands. "She is Astarte, queen of heaven. Asherah-yam, Our Lady of the Sea. She was made by the lost-wax process, and she stood on the household altar all the years I was married. Now I carry her with me to remind me."

Lost wax. That is what I taught Amoni, Athena thought. So it wasn't new. "You make an image in wax and then coat the wax with clay and melt the wax out of the mold, don't you?" she asked Ahiram, to be sure.

"Yes. It takes a great deal of skill."

"I thought that up," she said. "I taught it to— Well, to a boy I know. I thought it was new."

"It is very old," Ahiram said. "But you had never seen it done? You thought of it by yourself?"

"Yes."

"Amazing. And what did he make with it?"

"An amulet of the World Serpent, consort of the Lady. For my uncle."

"In our heavens we also have a serpent, Lotan, who fought with Baal for supremacy. Perhaps they are the same."

"My mother says that all gods are the same," Athena said. "They are all pieces of the same thing, appearing in different forms. That the Lady and the World Serpent fit like two halves of a puzzle, and give birth to the world. That is the mystery."

"Your mother is very wise."

"My mother wants me to be queen."

Ahiram raised his eyebrows at her.

"And your father?"

"My father wants to marry me to my uncle and make him king."

"I can see how that can be a very awkward situation."

"Exactly." Athena drew the red-and-purple shawl about her shoulders, its fringes fluttering in the salt breeze. She looked about her for Nike, and saw her across the *Shearwater*'s bow, talking to the sailor with the blond curls.

"Your young friend has my sailors in an uproar," Ahiram said. "You they are a little afraid of."

Amoni had never been afraid of her.

"It is the cloak," Ahiram said. "That is a thing of power even if you have packed it away. It watches over you, I think."

"It was my friend's," Athena said. She found herself telling Ahiram about Pallas, a thing she never spoke of. "Since she died, I've thought that she's still with me somehow. I sewed all those things to it, but she . . . I think she picked them out for me. And when Mother talks to me about being queen, sometimes I think she's right and that frightens me, and at the same time I'm *glad* they're all afraid of me, because that makes it easier."

"You wear a great weight on your shoulders," Ahiram said solemnly, when she had finished. For a moment, under his Miriam's red-and-purple shawl, he thought he saw the folded wings.

VI

❧

Ahiram of Tyre

The great city of Tyre lay on a rocky island close inshore to the Canaanite coast, reachable only by boat, its white walls a splendid fortress rising from the sea. Inside, the buildings crowded close together, six stories tall, leaning over the narrow streets, their topmost towers crowned with balconies. Houses and shops spread over the coastline opposite as well, as if the island had overflowed and the tide carried the spillage ashore.

Athena gaped at all of it as Ahiram led them along the dock, past stone warehouses full of grain and olive oil, while dockworkers in short kilts of white linen loaded and unloaded bales and boxes of goods from the ships that crowded the harbor. Great cedar logs on rollers rumbled past them along the dockside, and Polumetis retreated to the crook of Athena's elbow, under the folds of her shawl. The arable land along the coast here was narrow, Ahiram said, and Tyre imported much of its wheat, sending out in exchange cedars from the forests inland, as well as worked metals, textiles, and olives and their oil. The sound of many languages rose above the crowded streets like a babble of birds, and the Tyrians themselves looked like peacocks to Athena. Attic clothing was mostly white or brown, or the unbleached color of the natural wool. Tyrians' tunics and shawls fluttered with ribbons and colored fringes, every available handspan of cloth dyed in bright stripes of red and yellow, green and purple and blue, and further embellished by gold braid and scarlet thread. The men wore conical hats or rounded caps, their beards trimmed and curled like Ahiram's. The women's caps were jeweled or covered by floating translucent veils, and the most elegant of them had small boys beside them to hold fringed parasols above their heads.

The workshops beyond the docks were a blaze of noise. Athena saw rugmakers' wares hung from lines and spread along the edges of the streets, shelves of glass cups and rows of red pottery lamps, vases painted with palm leaves and lotus flowers. The chimney in the perfume maker's shop emitted a cloud of thick, sweet smoke. Athena's nose caught another brief, malodorous scent that vanished again as the wind shifted.

"The dye works," Ahiram said, wrinkling his own nose. He produced a litter from somewhere and bundled Athena and Nike into it. He walked beside them through the city streets and up a slight rise to a residential quarter of tall, narrow houses painted in bright colors. It was quieter here than at the docks, the streets shaded with palms whose fronds whispered in the sea breeze. The house to which Ahiram brought them was a pale sunny yellow, like the yolk of eggs, with a pair of bronze doors flanked by plaster columns in the shape of palm trees. The rooms of the lower floor opened onto a courtyard where a gnarled tree with gray-green leaves grew amid herbs and trellised grapevines. The tree—an olive, said Ahiram—bore small oval fruits like grapes, green and shiny, in clusters among its boughs.

Inside, the floors were tiled in bright colors and covered with soft carpets. Among the other luxuries were a bathtub, painted bright blue, with leaping fish, and a system of ceiling fans, pulled by a servant, that stirred the air.

On the second floor, the kitchen occupied most of the space, and on the third and fourth, bedchambers. Above that were smaller chambers where servants slept. At the very top was a tiny tower room with a balcony, where his wife had liked to sit and spin or embroider, and look out across the city and the sea. Her bedchamber on the third floor was hung with red and blue tapestries and floored with tiles with yellow birds on them.

"This was my Miriam's room, and you shall have it," Ahiram said to Athena. A bronze bed with scarlet coverlets stood in the center of the chamber, beside a dressing table laden with pots of ivory and glass and silver.

"This is your own house," Athena said.

Ahiram looked embarrassed. "I had thought to give you one that I keep to rent out, you see, in the cloth dyers' quarter, but . . ." He smiled. "This one is much finer, and there are servants to look after you. And I . . . well, I should like the company. I grow lonely without my Miriam, with no one to tell my tales to."

Ahiram's tales were magical. Even Nike lowered her guard for the wonders he spoke of. In her own chamber, next to Athena's, was a bowl painted with a design of palmettes and lions that Ahiram told her was made of the egg of an ostrich, the bird that had puzzled her aboard the *Shearwater*.

"It is a most marvelous bird," said Ahiram. "It lives in the south, and is taller than a man. It cannot fly, but it runs faster than a horse. It has but two toes on each foot, with which it can kick very hard indeed. I have seen one lift a man into a tree."

Nike folded her arms. "You are making that up."

Ahiram handed her a polished silver mirror, backed with ivory. The creature carved into the ivory backing was very like his description. "Those are its feathers in that fan," he said, pointing to a cluster of curling black and white plumes fastened in a silver socket at the end of an ebony handle. The small page who held it waved it so that the feathers fluttered.

Ahiram spoke of other exotic beasts—the hippopotamus that lived in Egypt to the south, and the rhinoceros of Africa, which from his description Athena thought must be Poseidon's monster. He told them of the crocodile, which was a lizard as long as the height of two men and which the Egyptians worshiped as a god. More enthralling yet to Athena was the writing in which Ahiram inscribed words in his own language in tablets of clay. She pestered him to teach them to her, and when he said that they would make no sense if she did not speak his language, she set herself to learn it, practicing on the servants who appeared to see to any need she so much as whispered into the air in Ahiram's house.

Athena's curiosity was boundless. With Ahiram's page as an escort, she toured the dockside workshops, fixing her interest on the sand-core casting that produced glass bottles; on the pottery factory where the potters built their cups and vases on flat, spinning wheels; on the dye liquefying in its malodorous vats beside the shell heaps on the shore. The beautiful purple dye that came from Tyre was, it seemed, achieved by letting murex snails rot in vats until the secretion that produced the color was liquefied out. The darker, richer tones required exposure to the sun. In the evenings, she asked Ahiram about all these things, about who had invented them and why no one in Attica knew of them.

"Because they are barbarians in your Attica, my dear," he said indulgently. She thought of Uncle Poseidon and the rhinoceros, and silently agreed.

Athena settled into a comfortable routine. At night she burned the oil in a lamp in her chamber and sat practicing her letters in clay by its light.

Polumetis found herself a roost in a hole in the olive tree and a supply of mice in the pantry. Athena scolded her when she ate a small yellow songbird from Ahiram's garden, but the owl looked unrepentant. The plants in the garden drew Athena's attention. Some she had never seen. The fruits that ripened on the pomegranate tree were scarlet globes with little crowns at their base. Another tree bore sweet white blossoms and then hard, round, green fruit that slowly swelled to the size of her fist. When winter came, Ahiram's gardener tied mats of straw around it.

The sailor with the blond curls, whose name was Aqhat, had declined to sign on for another voyage and inveigled from Ahiram instead a place in Ahiram's counting house, tallying the cargo that came and went. He too sat in the garden in the evenings, trying to learn Achaean from Nike, or teach her Canaanite. Ahiram himself delayed his next sailing and then sent the ship without him while the servants whispered about that behind their hands.

When the spring nights had begun to soften, Athena sat in the twilit garden and listened to Ahiram's marvelous tales. Aqhat joined them to court Nike after the counting house was closed, and even Polumetis fell in love with a foreign owl who moved into the hole in the olive tree with her.

"Did you know that the men of the desert consider owls a bird of ill omen?" Ahiram asked Athena. "Her eggs are held to make their hair fall out."

"Superstitious nonsense." Athena took note of how much she sounded like her mother, Metis.

"A man must blame it on something," Ahiram said cheerfully.

Athena watched Nike and Aqhat sitting by the cistern, among the lavender. They talked so quietly she couldn't hear, but every so often one of them would stand up and pace the garden paths, waving their arms about and muttering, and she knew what they spoke of. She had dragged Nike halfway across the world to fall in love, and thereby done her no favor. *I am a bad omen all by myself*, she thought dolefully, thinking of Pallas as well.

Ahiram rose and went to a tree at the end of the garden. The round green fruit on it had begun to turn pale gold, and then the bright color of the sunset. He picked one and brought it back to Athena.

"Elsewhere they say that owls are the souls of those who die unavenged," Ahiram said, peeling the thick skin from the fruit with his fingernails.

"That seems more likely," Athena said. "She's small but she's fierce." She yawned.

"Like Anat," Ahiram said. "I will tell you a

tale about her," he offered, "if you will stay awake."

"Tell me," Athena said sleepily. She knew he just wanted her to stay by him in the garden, but the perfume of the herbs was pleasant.

Ahiram settled in the chair beside her. Servants had lit torches along the paths and the light flickered on the heavy gold collar at his throat and on the round fruit in his hands. "Anat is the Maiden, the sister of Baal. Once when Baal was killed by Death, Anat went into the Underworld to look for him. She traveled a long way, through deep passages in the earth, until she found the place where Death was holding him. Then Anat overcame Death himself, cutting him down with a sickle, and used his entrails to resurrect her brother." He paused, pulling a segment from the fruit in his hands. "Here, eat this."

Athena took it. It was a gold crescent, like a fat waxing moon, surrounded by a translucent membrane. She bit into it cautiously. The juice was warm and sweet, the pulp watery. "What is it?"

"It is a naranj," Ahiram said. "It comes from Asu, and they are very rare and must be protected from the cold in the winter." He handed her another piece. "When Anat had killed Death, she would have killed all the other gods as well, for allowing Baal to go into danger, but Baal restrained her and taught her the ways of peace. She is very fierce, even so, like your Polumetis. She rides naked on a lion, bearing serpents and a lotus."

Ahiram's gods all had stories about them, Athena noted, whereas the gods of her land simply were. It was puzzling.

"We are an old people," Ahiram said, when she told him that. "We have been here a long time, and stories accrete. They pile up like shell mounds. Perhaps your people have lost their stories in their travels, and must make new ones."

Athena licked her fingers. He handed her another section of the naranj. "Perhaps you will make them, with your owl and your friend. Perhaps you are the beginning of a story." He looked sorrowful, as if he wished he hadn't said that. "Or perhaps not," he offered. "It isn't comfortable to be a story."

If she went home she would be a story. Athena knew that much. She felt as if she had somehow grown in sections, like the naranj. They separated too easily, and one might become lost, eaten by someone. She also knew that when it was time to leave, Ahiram would ask her to stay.

On a particularly fine day, Ahiram took them in one of his small boats to the coast of the mainland, where he kept a stable. The horses they had stolen from Poseidon were there, but Ahiram hitched tamer steeds to a wagon and bundled them all into it—Athena, Nike, and enough servants to wait on them hand and foot all day. The wagon was painted a bright, clear blue, like the sea, with red wheels, and pale green latticework panels that slid back and forth along the sides. At Ahiram's command, the driver took a road that led away from the settlements of the coast, past swaying groves of date palms, and fields of almond trees in bloom, the air around them thick with bees. Vineyards clung to every slope, and Athena saw orchards of the gnarled trees she recognized now as olives. At a sedate pace, they made their way into the lowlands of the mountains that rose to the east of the coastal plain, through myrtle and rhododendron, stands of sycamore figs and maritime pine, evergreen oaks, tamarisks, and acacias, alien as dream trees, oddly familiar and yet strange, like everything in this land. Above them Athena could see the slopes covered in dark green, the towering trees that Ahiram said were cedars.

"The riches of my land." He waved a hand expansively past the lattice panels. "A man should not brag, but I, Ahiram of Tyre, own half that mountainside."

Nike looked at the slopes of cedars and down at the pale green slope of her lap, clad in brocade that had been Miriam's. Aqhat was rising in the counting house; he had a knack for numbers. If they stayed she could go on wearing clothes like this. She could marry Aqhat, who would buy her a house in Tyre, and she would have at least one servant and he would never expect her to make cheese. She watched Athena out of the corner of her eye and saw Athena watching her.

"He will ask you to marry him," Nike said in Pelasgian. "We could live here."

"You could live here even if I don't," Athena said.

"Let you go home without me?" Nike stared at her. "I have known you longer than I have known Aqhat, or an easy life. No."

And that, of course, made it harder. What Athena chose, she chose for Nike as well.

Soon afterward Nike's words rang true, and Ahiram asked Athena to stay.

"You have brought joy into my house that had been gone since my Miriam died," he said to her. "If you marry me, I will make sure that you never want for anything." He paused. "And you will be a rich widow while you are still young."

"I don't want to be a rich widow!" Athena said.

Ahiram smiled. "I am somewhat older than you, and it is better than being a poor one."

Athena took his hand. He was kind, and very gentle; he would love her and she would have leisure to learn things: the writing that she was only beginning to grasp; the mechanics of the potter's wheel; how to sail a ship by the stars. She thought of never seeing home again and her stomach turned over, making her sway in her chair.

You have to go home. The voice was quite clear in her ear. Whether it was her own, or her mother's, or maybe the Lady's, or even Pallas's, didn't matter. It spoke a truth she felt in her bones. "I can't," she told him. She had learned to breathe here. Now she had to go home.

"Is it some young lover that calls you back?" Ahiram asked her sadly.

Athena shook her head. "It's . . . it's the land, I think. What you said about being a story. I am already. My mother saw to that. I think I have to go back and see it to its finish or the story won't be there later. For whoever comes next."

"That's very philosophical," Ahiram said.

"I'm not sure I understand it," Athena said. "But I have to go. You haven't let me pay for anything. I will leave you those horses, and give you the jewelry I came with for my passage home." She looked down the garden to where Nike and Aqhat were arguing fiercely under the olive tree. "If she stays, I want some of it to be her bride price."

"She won't stay," Ahiram said. "What do you think they are quarreling over? No one who loves you wishes to let you go, it seems."

Athena thought of Amoni. He had let her go. He had had to. Would he let her come back?

Ahiram didn't ask her again, knowing the answer wouldn't change. He arranged her passage on the *Plover*, a ship bound as nearly directly as possible for Attica, and refused to take the gold she tried to give him. "Our Lady of the Sea guard you, my dear," he said. "If you change your mind, remember I am here. I won't wed again, I think. Women like you and my Miriam are too hard to find, and I was never one to settle for less."

She boarded the ship and took a last wistful glance at the bustle of the docks and the workshops. Nike walked beside her, mouth downturned and silent. They wore the plainest of the clothes Ahiram had given them, Athena with Pallas's cloak about her, and Polumetis on her shoulder, despite the wary looks the sailors threw their way.

The sailors were casting off the lines that tethered the *Plover* to the dock when Nike spun around, drawn by a shout. Aqhat stood on the dock. "Tell these fools to let me aboard!"

Athena grabbed the captain of the *Plover* by the shoulder. "Let the plank back down!"

"And who's paid his passage, tell me that?" the captain demanded.

"I can pay my own passage!" Aqhat called. "Ahiram gave me the silver! Now let me aboard or you'll answer to him!" Nike was leaning over the bow, reaching for his hand as if she could pull him across the gap of water.

"This isn't Ahiram's ship," the captain grumbled. "Not that he doesn't own nearly every other ship on the sea, but this one happens to be mine, and by Asherah he doesn't order me about." He folded his arms across his chest.

Athena stared him in the eye. "You won't turn down good silver, *will* you?" she asked him.

"But if you've got silver I suppose you can come aboard." The captain looked mildly startled at his own words, but he growled at the crew to let the boarding plank back down. "And jump to it; I won't miss the tide for some lovelorn fool of a clerk."

The plank thunked down on the dock and Aqhat crossed it. He was carrying a small bag over one shoulder. Nike leaped on his neck and hung onto him as he handed a piece of silver to the captain. They pulled the plank back aboard and two sailors at oars backed the *Plover* out into the harbor. They raised the sail and it bellied in the wind as she set her course westward, the carved, gilded figure of Asherah-yam, Our Lady of the Sea, bending from the prow.

VII

❧

Homecoming

For the duration of the voyage, Athena paced the deck, as if by will she could push the ship onward. *Hurry now,* a voice said in her ear. She didn't think Nike heard it. Nike heard only the voice of Aqhat, learning to speak Achaean, and the small Pelasgian love words she taught him. Athena couldn't be angry at him—how could anyone be angry at a man who had left a place like Tyre to sail into the unknown with a woman who barely spoke his language, and another woman who was going home to trouble?

Despite her protests, the captain put into port at every island and harbor, off-loading one thing, loading another, gauging the space in his hold, drinking some tavern dry at night while Athena paced and fretted.

"I undertook to get the lot of you to Attica, my lady," he said finally, "not to race there come storm or contrary wind, and against my purse. We'll make port in Attica when we make port in Attica."

The wind declined to cooperate. It becalmed. It blew the wrong direction.

"Can't you row?" Athena demanded.

"With two oars?" the captain snorted. "You can't row a cargo ship, my lady, or you displace your cargo with crew, and then where are you? Best to sit in port till the wind shifts. It will, soon enough."

The wind declined to shift for days. Finally, when Athena was distraught enough to swim, the voice in her head urging her onward in a steady hiss that might have been the waves and wasn't, the wind changed. They were anchored off Siphnos in the Cyclades, and the captain made a nearly straight run for Attica, succumbing to the urge he had fought off the entire voyage, which was to get Athena off his ship.

They docked amid the usual crowd that came down to the harbor to see a ship come in, and there were gasps from the onlookers as Athena disembarked. Nike followed her, with Aqhat. No one barred their way, but the people in the crowd looked at Athena with grave wonder as she passed, and she heard a low voice say, "Her mother's called her home; that's what it will be."

They caught a ride with a carter taking a load of copper ingots up the track to the city, and Athena thought of Amoni. She sat silently on the carter's load and felt her heart catch at each new turn of the track, each familiar tree. The news went ahead of them, and when the cart rattled through the city gates, a troop of her father's soldiers was there. They didn't stop her, but turned smartly in formation, and escorted her through the streets while the carter watched them nervously. At the palace courtyard she climbed down, shaking her head at Nike and Aqhat.

"Go home and let them see you are safe. My father will have a lot to say to me. Enough to take till evening, I imagine."

It was Metis instead who met her in the great hall, snatched Athena into her arms, and then glared fiercely around her at the clerks and soldiers and councilors, the elderly ones red faced and breathing hard as if they had come running at the news. "An announcement will be made," she said, and swept Athena from the hall.

It took a long time to explain to Metis where she had been, while Polumetis inspected their old quarters and the scattered sticks of her nest. She had left the foreign owl as easily as she had left this one. She was Athena's owl, not theirs.

"Where is Father?" Athena asked nervously.

Metis compressed her lips and looked for a long while at her hands, covered with gold rings. "Ill," she said finally.

"Ill? How ill?"

"He is in his last days, and Poseidon struts about the palace as if he is king already," Metis said. "You are come home in good time."

"Where is Poseidon?" Athena snapped her head around as if he might be behind her.

"He rode out hunting this morning. He'll have had the news by now, though, and be riding home."

"The whole city will have the news. They looked at me on the dock as if I had returned with two heads. I want to see Father first."

Kosmetas lay on his bed in the king's chambers, which were not nearly as fine as the house of Ahiram of Tyre. His face was nearly as gray as his beard. It shocked Athena how gaunt he had grown, and how rough the cloth of his tunic and bedclothes. His eyes widened at sight of his daughter.

"I had thought you dead," he said. His voice crackled like dead leaves, with a faint whistle in it.

"No, I have sailed to Tyre and back, and I am old enough now not to be afraid of my uncle."

"Was that why you ran away?"

"You would have married me to him."

"I still will," Kosmetas wheezed. His hands plucked at the sheepskins that lay bundled over him. The rings on the fingers were loose and slid against his knuckles.

"No," Athena said. "Not now." She kept her voice gentle because she did think he was dying.

". . . make you," Kosmetas said.

"No," Athena said again. On impulse she bent and kissed his forehead. She couldn't ever remember having kissed him before, but she had changed, and he would soon learn how much.

She left his chamber to speak with Metis again. "I must tell Cecrops," Metis said abruptly. "Cecrops has no love for Poseidon now."

"What is between Cecrops and Poseidon?" Athena asked.

"Cecrops leads the Areopagus now, since Gelon died. Poseidon has said he will disband it when he rules."

"He's a fool!"

"He is arrogant," Metis said. "Cecrops called him to task for riding his horse through the market drunk and upsetting the baker's stall and ruining the bread. Cecrops wanted him to pay, and Poseidon just laughed and called it a tax."

When they called upon Cecrops, now head of the Areopagus, he gave Metis a long, calculating look, and one very like it to Athena. Cecrops was Achaean. It was in his blood that there should be an Achaean king, not a half-Pelasgian queen whose mother he didn't trust. It was clear that this sentiment warred with his dislike of Poseidon.

But he nodded at Athena as if he had decided something. If Father was dying, the rumors about her return would go on swift feet. *Amoni. I have to see Amoni.* What she would say to him, she didn't know, but she had to face him.

The whole town knew where she was headed before she got to the forge. Amoni knew too; she could tell. He was leaning on his anvil, dressed in his working clothes, a heavy shirt and apron of leather. He looked older, his face more defined somehow, the bones and planes of his cheeks and chin more angular.

"I did as you told me," was all he said to her when he saw her standing in the doorway. "I said you'd gone to get away from your uncle. I don't know why you came back now." His mouth was a thin, compressed line when he wasn't speaking, as if it held something in, trapped behind his teeth.

"Same reason," she said.

Amoni's mouth twisted.

Athena came closer and leaned her head against his cheek. His leather shirt was stiff and smelled of sweat and hot metal. His hand on her shoulder was rough; the calloused fingers snagged and caught on her tunic. "You are taller. I used to look you in the eye."

"I grew a handspan after you left. Trying to reach across the water to you maybe. I have made more amulets with the wax trick you thought of. I am a wealthy man now."

"It wasn't new," she said sadly. "I thought it was new, but the artisans in Tyre have made things that way since time long back. We are just backward."

"That's what you learned while you were gone? That we are backward in Attica?"

She nodded.

"I could have told you that."

Athena chuckled. "I suppose so. You always saw deeper into the water than any of us. I saw wonders, though, Amoni. If you are really wealthy, you should go and see them for yourself. Strange animals, and houses seven stories high with little balconies at the top, and gilt roofs. Palm trees."

"Why would I want to leave? You just came home."

"I am tied to this place. You aren't."

"Maybe I am tied to you."

"Don't be."

Amoni just shook his head, his hand still on her shoulder. He was angry, but there was no arguing with him. Amoni had always been a boy who knew what he knew. As a man, clearly, he still knew it.

Everyone else knew too, or thought they did. Generally the things they knew were mutually contradictory, but the return of the king's daughter, and of the vintner's daughter with a foreign husband provided meat for speculation to all.

"The queen has had her in hiding."

"The king began to sicken when she left. Now that she has come back he will be well. It is magic."

"That foreign one, with the pale hair, he is a magician from Tyre. I heard it from the ship's captain himself."

"I heard he came aboard the ship in the night and no one knew from where. Out of the sky."

"He's maybe not human, do you think? A man who could do that?"

Athena went every day to sit at her father's bedside, since he was too ill to stop her. She was eighteen now. It was odd to feel grown-up as he sank into the childhood of his last illness. She cleaned his face with a wet cloth and held his cup to his lips.

The Areopagus met in his chambers, Cecrops complaining that it was not proper, but it was that or meet without him. No one was sure how much of what was said the king understood. The queen and Poseidon sat to either side of his bed, and Athena thought they sometimes pulled him between them, stretching him like a skein of wool. Poseidon had given Athena a furious look on the first night of her return and spat on the floor just nearly at her feet. After that he had gotten a grip on his temper and begun to be jovial with her, patting her backside in a friendly play that set Athena's teeth on edge. He told her in a low voice over the wine cups after dinner that he was prepared to wed her, despite her insolence, and allow her to be his queen. Athena pulled a little bronze knife out of her girdle and threatened him with it, and now he pretended she wasn't there. He was waiting for Kosmetas to die.

Oddly, Kosmetas didn't die. His breath still rasped in his throat, and his skin was like crumbled leaves, but he didn't die. Speculation surrounded that fact, too.

"It's the girl come home, didn't I tell you?"

"It's that foreign wizard. She's brought him back to keep the king alive."

"It's not natural, in my opinion. I asked that foreigner to bring my goat back and he wouldn't do it. She got into some poisonweed, and he could easily have brought her back."

"Aye, well, kings aren't goats, then, are they?"

"It's the same, isn't it? They die or they don't. That was my best doe."

"I heard the vintner brought three pigeons home for the pot and he turned them into rabbits."

"Well, I don't believe that. What would you do with all the feathers?"

"I've seen him making spells. He marks them down in little bits of clay. I won't cross his path."

"They think Aqhat will put the evil eye on them," Nike complained.

"I should think that would be useful," Athena said. "No one will cheat you at the butcher's stall, and you'll get little presents."

"Aqhat doesn't understand. Father tried to teach him to prune the grapes, and Tryphon wouldn't let him touch them." Tryphon owned four hectares of grapes. "He and Father had an argument over it, and Aqhat just came home." Ahiram had given Aqhat silver for a bride price as well as his passage, and thus Aqhat had been welcomed by the vintner's family.

"Aqhat doesn't want to be a vintner anyway," Athena said. "I'll try to find him a place among Father's clerks. He can teach them to set things down as they do in Tyre."

Unfortunately Kosmetas's clerks didn't want to set things down as they did in Tyre, and they thought Aqhat's marks were spells, too. The head clerk complained to Poseidon, who waved him away with a gesture that told him to do as he pleased. So Aqhat had to learn the Attic system, and came home and complained of stupid foreigners to Nike.

Still, there was no denying that even without the benefit of spells, Kosmetas was rallying. The physician stroked his beard and tried to look as if he had personally effected the cure, but in truth he had no idea why the king got better.

He still had a rasp in his throat, and his digestion was unreliable, but Kosmetas's strength came back somewhat so that he could be carried on a litter to the rock where the Areopagus properly met, and could sit for a while at council, although he tired easily. Metis thought he wouldn't live through the winter, but he did, wrapped in blankets, his arms quivering whenever he tried to raise them. She ordered coals burned constantly, in bronze braziers all around the judicial chamber and the king's bedchamber, so that the palace was stuffy and smelled of old smoke and everyone's eyes watered. Metis watched by her husband constantly, giving him potions and drafts supplied by the physician. He swallowed them obediently. Some part of the king still looked out through Kosmetas's eyes, but some other piece of him was gone, flown on ahead to whatever awaited him in the realm of the dead.

Athena wondered whether her mother was keeping him alive until his daughter could reestablish herself with the people of the city. If there was any magic at work in his survival, Athena thought it more likely to be her mother's and the Lady's. She had no idea how her mother actually felt about her father. Did she love him? Had she ever? Athena knew Metis had been married to Kosmetas to cement the Pelasgians' loyalty, as Kosmetas wanted to marry Athena to Poseidon. What came of a match like that? Love? Murder? Indifference? And what became of a stubborn woman like her?

VIII

❧

Witchcraft and Tapestries

In late spring, Athena wore Pallas's cloak to the meeting of the Areopagus. She had never done so before, but it seemed right now, with her father so frail and Poseidon lounging in his chair as if the crown sat on his head already. No one else would challenge him. Kosmetas was well enough to be propped in the high seat, bundled in sheepskins and horsehide rugs, even though the air was clean and balmy. It smelled of new, wet leaves, and the promise of summer hay.

Poseidon stiffened when he saw Athena step into the ring of stone seats, Polumetis riding on her shoulder. The cloak hung about her like a shield. "Take that off," he said.

Athena looked at him gravely and sat down.

"I said, take that off."

"No."

Poseidon half stood, rising from his seat to stab

an accusing finger at her. "It is magic. That is not allowed at the councils of the Areopagus."

"And who are you to speak for the Areopagus?" Metis demanded. Kosmetas was silent in his chair.

"I will be king when my brother is dead," Poseidon said bluntly.

The old men of the Areopagus murmured disapprovingly at that, but no one disputed it.

"He is not dead yet," Athena said to Poseidon. "And nothing is sure in life except that you will die, too, one day." Her gray eyes pinned Poseidon against his seat. "Later or sooner."

"It is not the business of the Areopagus to decide such matters while yet the old king lives," Cecrops said. He cast Poseidon a look of dislike. "And if the king's daughter's cloak holds power, it will not hold less for being in her lap rather than on her shoulders." He pounded the end of his staff once on the ground, the sign that a matter had been decided.

Poseidon sat back down abruptly, furious, lips compressed.

"What business is there to come before this council?" Cecrops asked before anyone could start the argument again.

Tryphon stood. He coughed importantly. "There is the matter of the spring sacrifices." As the newest member, he was in charge of these. "Last year the goats were supplied by Nikolaos, the unguent boiler, and the boar by myself." Tryphon waited for them to note his generosity and piety. "Donors for this year's offerings have not yet been named."

"I volunteer you again," Poseidon said lazily.

Tryphon coughed again behind his hand. "I was going to point out that you yourself have not provided the offerings as yet."

Poseidon smiled. "My house is the royal house. We have given much to the Goddess. Would you have us take on this duty as well, which properly belongs to the citizenry?"

Athena stood. Polumetis shifted on her shoulder, ruffling her feathers. Athena could feel the tips of her talons through the goatskin. "If my uncle cannot part with a boar for the sacrifice, then I will, to honor my father's house. Put my name down."

"This is a men's sacrifice!" Poseidon snapped. "That would defile it."

Cecrops scratched his head, fluffing out the cloud of white hair that crowned it. "The sacrifice must be offered by men," he said. "I don't believe there are rules about who can provide the animal for it."

"Providing it *is* offering it," another one said. "Isn't it?" He scratched his own head.

They argued the issue while the sun traveled a good way across the morning sky, and Kosmetas sat silently in his chair. Athena watched Poseidon with amusement. It was too easy to prick his temper and his pride. It was probably dangerous as well.

*   *   *

They decided ultimately that Athena could provide the boar as long as she handed it over to Tryphon at a distance of more than a hundred paces from the temple. Athena agreed. The mysteries of the Goddess were unfathomable, but they included rules that could not be broken safely. She thought of Ahiram's Lady of the Sea, Asherahyam. Were they the same, as Metis said? They must be, if the Lady created the world. It was all one world. Round, too, according to Ahiram. She wouldn't tell that to the Areopagus; they would think she was mad.

She considered hunting a boar, but Metis advised against it, brushing out her hair in the queen's chamber by lamplight. The tallow lamps smoked and spat, and Athena thought of Ahiram's oil lamps.

"Pay for your boar, and let some man hunt it down. You cannot take them too far back to the old ways too fast, or they will balk."

"I don't want to take them back to the old ways," Athena protested. The old ways seemed to her dark and slightly sinister.

"Do you want your uncle to be king?" Metis snapped the brush through her long dark hair, and Athena thought that sparks cracked out of it.

"No!" But there must be another way than that. Some middle way? "When your people ruled, did the women hunt?" she asked Metis.

"The queen hunted," Metis said.

Athena wasn't sure she wanted to know what the queen hunted. The king maybe, at the end of his seventh year? "Why did you marry Father?" she asked abruptly instead.

Metis stopped, brush in hand, and looked at her. The brush had an ivory back and boar's bristles. The ivory was carved in an image of the Goddess, a bare-breasted figure with great, wide hips and a crown of poppies. When she was small, Athena used to make crowns for herself of the poppies that grew on the hillside, but they always wilted in the sun. The Goddess's were stiff, ever blooming.

"I didn't marry," Metis said. "I was given."

"I know that. But what did you think about it?"

"What did it matter what I thought about it?"

"What did you think of him?"

Metis's lips twitched into a smile. "I thought he had a very nice body. I was gratified."

"Did you love him?"

"No. I was in love with the pig boy. I was only twelve." She began to brush her hair again. "My mother and my aunts dressed me for my wedding. They gave me a vial of poison with which I was supposed to kill my husband."

Athena stared at her.

"They thought their people would rise up and throw off the Achaean rule if I did that, and make me queen."

"Why didn't you?" Athena whispered.

"Because the priestesses told me not to. I don't know why. They know things."

And would you have killed him if they had said to?

Athena didn't ask her mother that. That definitely wasn't a question she wanted the answer to.

Metis laid down the brush. "Some pattern would have been displaced if I had done it. Lately I begin to think you are the core the pattern winds around."

That sat heavily on Athena's shoulders, but the more she thought about it, the more she felt it was true. Pallas and Amoni and Ahiram all seemed to be stepping-stones she had walked on to come here, to a place beside her father's deathbed.

"Some in the Areopagus favor you over Poseidon," Metis said quietly. "They will not say so just now, for fear of him, but you have perhaps three in your camp. There will be more if the king lives a few months longer."

Kosmetas lived another whole year, but by the end of it people began to speak in earnest of witchcraft.

"Have you seen him?" they whispered. "There is nothing behind his eyes."

"It's the queen. She's keeping him alive to keep Poseidon from the throne. Those Pelasgian women are all witches."

"He can walk but it takes two men to hold him up."

"My sister saw her go to the priestesses in the old temple with a bowl. She said it had blood in it."

"Your sister had best not spy on the priestesses; she'll come away with two heads on her neck."

"They turned a man into a black ram once. I saw him."

"It's the king's daughter and that cloak, if you ask me. At night the snakes come off it alive, and do her bidding. I heard she spread it over him and he got up and walked, and when she took it off, he fell down a pile of bones."

This last rumor Athena heard from Amoni, who was halfway between amusement and fear over it. At least they had given up blaming unexplained phenomena on poor Aqhat, who had slipped now into village anonymity and fathered two children on Nike, while he worked his way up among the king's clerks. Nike had her wish and bought cheese from the cheesemonger's for her table.

"If there is too much talk of witchcraft they will frighten themselves into doing something stupid," Amoni said. "Poseidon is egging them on."

"Poseidon is too busy just now chasing after another fool of a girl," Athena said with disgust. "Arachne. She'll be sorry. He isn't kind to women when he's tired of them."

"She's one of the ones yammering about witchcraft," Amoni said. "Her family is Achaean. They'll support him if it comes to a dispute over the throne. Especially if they think he'll be grateful enough to marry their daughter."

"She should know better. He won't make a cloth dyer's daughter queen."

"She makes beautiful tapestries, though," Amoni said.

Athena snorted. "Maybe you should marry her."

"Jealous?"

Athena thought about that. "Probably," she admitted. "Jealous of Arachne that all she has to think about is her weaving. I haven't touched a loom in months, between caring for Father and listening to the Areopagus natter about how many oxen are permitted to be kept inside the city walls, or how early a rooster is allowed to crow."

"She's not as good as you are," Amoni said loyally.

"She's probably better," Athena said, irritable at that thought.

"Come away and forget them for a while," Amoni said cajolingly. "You don't have to care for your father; you just feel guilty if you don't. He used to smack you every time he saw you, and he wants you to marry your uncle."

He leaned against her, maneuvering her into the shadows behind the furnace. His lips brushed the top of her head. Polumetis fluttered off her shoulder into the rafters and turned round, yellow eyes down at them.

"This isn't a good idea," Athena whispered, but she knew that this time she was going to give in to him. It happened only every few moons. Amoni tried every time they were alone, but only once in a while did longing get the better of her, along with the faint, wild hope that it would all be taken out of her hands.

But the Lady sent no pregnancies, or none that lasted past the second month. If there were babies, they were babies that never grew.

Athena lay in Amoni's arms in the bed in his house behind the forge, while Polumetis roosted there above the furnace, waiting for them. It was a dangerous and scandalous thing, going to his house, and she should have been talked about as Arachne was, but no one seemed to notice. Athena walked shrouded in Pallas's cloak and everyone gave her wary respect, and never seemed to remember where it was they had seen her go.

"You're not putting anything over on me, you know," Poseidon said, glaring at her, but the truth was that he had sent men to track her and found they couldn't.

"I have no idea what you mean," Athena said airily.

Poseidon's lips compressed because he didn't either. He merely knew that when he couldn't see her, she was bound to be doing something he didn't like, and he complained of it to Arachne.

"She should stick to her loom," Arachne said, lips pursed. "It ill becomes a woman to meddle in political matters as she does."

"That one!" Arachne's mother said. "Her skill at the loom can't match yours, my dear."

"No," Arachne said, preening a bit. She was a tall girl, with light brown hair in ringlets and a long nose. "But she is passable. Passable."

The cloth dyer beamed at her. It was his daughter's luminous weavings that had attracted the king's brother to her, and here he was sitting at table with them, drinking the cloth dyer's wine and complimenting his wife and daughters on their skill and their looks. Poseidon's gold hair glinted in the sputtering light of a tallow lamp, its wick fizzing and sizzling. The cloth dyer envisioned a future in which they all sat at a table in the palace, around dishes of roast pheasant and compotes of oysters and fish eggs, while a servant poured wine from a silver ewer, and a girl with very little on danced while a boy played the double flute. The cloth dyer could see it all in his head.

Arachne's mother simpered at Poseidon. "I have heard she brags of her tapestries. That ill becomes a king's daughter, too, to lord it over us common folk. I am sure my daughter has the greater skill, but you won't hear her say so. She is far too modest."

"Quite," Poseidon said, ignoring the fact that she *had* just said so. "You have brought your daughters up well." He took a sip of the cloth dyer's wine and winced. "Better brought up, I fear, than my sister-in-law's. Some of the old ways are . . . well, shall I say dubious, and the queen clings to them, I'm afraid. Like mother, like daughter, alas."

"Oh, dear," Arachne's mother said, not exactly following him, but sure that whatever he meant, it was something not quite nice.

"Not what you would want, encouraging the women to behave improperly." He picked a

boiled egg from a dish and cracked it. His pale
hands had gold freckles on them, like a spattering
of pale dirt.

"Certainly not." Arachne's mother nodded
vigorously.

"I heard she said unkind things about poor Arachne," the eldest sister said. "You ought to make
it plain to her we won't stand for that." Her sister's mouth was small and pursed, as if she hadn't
decided she liked the flavor of life.

"Women need productive pastimes to occupy
their minds," Poseidon told her, and she nodded.
"Otherwise they think unsuitable thoughts," he
said.

The sisters clearly wished to fend off unsuitable
thoughts. Poseidon took on a sober, contemplative
expression. He took another gingerly sip of the
cloth dyer's wine, and smiled as at a sudden inspi-
ration. "I will sponsor a competition for the young
women of the city. A weaving competition. I will
award a prize. We'll encourage the feminine arts,
eh?" He winked at Arachne.

"Arachne is bound to win," her mother said.

"Now, now, you can't prejudice the judges
ahead of time," Poseidon said jovially. "I shall
announce it today! We will hold it in the agora,
and any unmarried maiden may enter."

"I have no interest in my uncle's attempt to
make his latest floozy look good," Athena said
with immense dignity when her mother informed
her of the event.

"Arachne isn't a floozy, poor thing," Metis said.

"No, I suppose not. She'd be happier if she were. Poseidon's not going to marry her."

"No, but before she finds that out, he's going to win her family's allegiance with this contest, because he knows she'll take the prize. He's putting up a gold statue of that beast he killed. To commemorate the event."

Athena snorted.

"The theme is heroes and heroic events," Metis added.

Athena rolled her eyes. "Who is to judge it?"

"A committee of wellborn ladies. He hasn't said who. Whoever will vote for Arachne, I expect. And you *will* enter."

"Mother, why?"

"Because it will look spiteful if you don't. Better to lose graciously."

"I won't lose graciously! If I have to enter I will outweave that long-nosed viper. Don't think I won't!"

"That will be pleasant, but how you conduct yourself will be more important."

"Mmm."

Poseidon sent runners through the city to announce his contest, and commissioned from Amoni the statue that was to be the prize. The day that young ladies were to present themselves as candidates took on a festival air. The statue had been set up on a pedestal in the agora for the citizenry to admire (and remember Poseidon's heroism in

defeating its original), while food sellers with
baskets of fresh figs, trays of pastries, and jugs
of cold goat's milk worked their way through
the crowd.

Athena looked at the statue with disgust. It was
a foot long and it glowered at them with small
piggy eyes from behind its horn. She had to admit
Amoni had done a good job of it from memory.
"It's called a rhinoceros," she told him. "Ahiram
told me about them. I wish it had killed my uncle.
Who would want a statue of that?"

"Most people want a statue of anything as long
as it's made out of gold," Amoni said.

"Bah. And watch Arachne; she looks like she
thinks she's being fitted for the queen's crown."

Arachne stood beside Poseidon as he handed
out clay tokens to the girls who came forward to
enter. Athena, who had gotten hers first, tossed it
derisively in her hand. Arachne was wearing new
earrings, she noted. She bobbed her head occasionally, to set them swinging.

"She'll get her comeuppance," Amoni said.
"When she does, I'll try not to feel sorry for her."

"Why?"

"It seems to be important to you."

Athena looked ashamed. "I don't like her, but
I'll feel sorry for her, too. Watch my uncle; he's
not even looking at her while she stands there
simpering at him. He's watching little Medusa."

Amoni shifted his gaze. A girl with rose-gold
curls was receiving her clay token from Poseidon.
Amoni could see Poseidon's eyes lick down the

front of her dress. "She's turned into a beauty," Amoni said uneasily.

"And worse luck for her if my uncle has noticed it. She can't be more than fourteen. I remember the year she led the goat in the spring sacrifice."

"I heard her father has made a match for her with a mill owner from Eleusis."

"Then he had better keep a guard on her," Athena said bitterly. "Anything my uncle looks at, he spoils."

They watched Medusa claim her token and trot down the steps from the dais that Poseidon had planted in the center of the agora. Poseidon's eyes followed her. When the tokens were all claimed, he stepped down.

Arachne remained on the dais, talking with her sister and a few other girls. She had a peculiarly carrying voice. "Of course she entered," she said to her sister. "You would think she'd show respect for the king and stay by his bedside, but that one never did care what people thought. Poseidon tells me things; she's such an embarrassment to him. It's the customs she learned from her mother, I expect. I mean—with no disrespect to the queen, of course—the Pelasgians have funny ways. Their women are never truly . . . well, womanly."

"Ladylike, you mean," her sister said. "Letting that bird sit on her shoulder. That's not clean. And walking about in that horror of a cloak, which no respectable man would allow his wife to wear."

"Well, you'll notice that she's not a wife," Arachne said. "Not that she maybe shouldn't be."

She raised her eyebrows and the other girls giggled.

"Do you think she gets all sooty?" one of them asked, and they dissolved in laughter.

"I'm going to see how funny she finds me now," Athena said, starting across the agora.

"No, you aren't." Amoni caught her arm and pulled her back.

"Let me go!"

"Stop it. Use your head. You'll just make a scandal and prove their point if you go and start pulling hair with her."

"I wasn't going to pull her hair," Athena said with disgust. "I was going to hit her."

Arachne saw them arguing and snickered loudly.

Athena advanced on Arachne, while Amoni tried to follow her. The crowd still milling in the agora widened a space around Athena and watched with interest. "You are an uneducated cow," Athena informed her.

"I spend my time in womanly pursuits," Arachne said primly. "At my loom and my distaff. Mother thinks it unnecessary and coarsening to the spirit for young ladies to go to school with boys."

"Bah! You are just stupid," Athena informed her as Amoni caught up to her. "No tutor would take you. As soon try to teach music to a cabbage. I can weave better and faster than you on your best day. I wouldn't use your tapestries for horse blankets."

Arachne smiled. "Do you really think you can beat me in this contest?"

"I know it!" A voice in the back of Athena's mind nudged her and she ignored it. "I'll show you, too!"

"Then I expect you had better practice," Arachne retorted. "You have a month until the contest. That should be time enough to learn not to catch your fingers in the shuttles." The girls around her snickered, but they watched Athena cautiously. They came from Achaean families and practiced being condescending to the Pelasgians daily, but Athena was the Achaean king's daughter, and he wasn't dead yet. One of their mothers pushed her way out of the crowd and took her daughter by the arm with a disapproving shake of her head.

Amoni managed to draw Athena away. "This is what comes of letting you run wild in your youth—brawling with another girl in the agora! Tut!" He grinned at her.

Athena took a deep breath. "I will beat that little cow at her own game if it kills me."

"Didn't your mother say something about winning the people to your side with gracious behavior?"

"Mmm. What should I weave?"

"This is a political contest, yes? Arachne's job is to make a fool of you, and make your uncle look like a kindly ruler when we both know he's a jackal. Right?"

"That seems to cover it."

"Then you want a subject that links you to Attica, to the city, to the royal house. That makes it clear you are the true heir of both the king and the queen. The Achaeans' queen as well as the Pelasgians'. That you have their welfare at heart, while your uncle wants only the power that goes with the throne."

"All perfectly simple to convey in a tapestry," Athena retorted. "Why not ask me to have it send out for a loaf of bread and a jug of wine and a fresh cheese while I'm at it? And predict next year's weather?"

"I'll work on it," Amoni said.

Athena gave her consideration to the subject of her tapestry, and settled finally on a thoroughly fictionalized depiction of the founding of the city, in which an Achaean king could be seen offering a green branch to a Pelasgian king, while in the background gods and citizens celebrated the wedding feast of their son and daughter.

"You left out the part where the Achaeans slaughtered the Pelasgians and threw the Pelasgian king's children off the Acropolis," Amoni said, when she showed him the sketch. Nike had come to see it too, and sat in the palace garden nursing her youngest.

Athena chuckled. "That part didn't seem tactful. This is the way it *should* have happened." The actual battle had been so long ago that it was legend now, things that had happened before anyone living had even been born. You could joke about things that old, things that hadn't happened to, or by the hand of, people you actually knew. Those old wounds were a dark muttering among the disgruntled, though, and could be used to foment real ill will when the victors were cruel or capricious. Thus the Goddess in her Achaean incarnation hovered above the painted wedding, wings outspread. An owl perched in her open palm.

"The owl might be a bit much," Amoni suggested.

"You said to make it clear. And anyway, owls are lucky; they've always belonged to the Lady. That's not necessarily my owl."

"Is that you in the wedding?" Nike asked her.

"Certainly not. That is a symbolic wedding, the wedding of the Achaean people with the Pelasgians, whose children are the citizens of Attica now."

"Very nice."

"I'm still laying out the thread for it. It's going to be dreadfully complicated; I don't see how that little slut can match it."

"She's not a slut," Amoni said mildly.

"Anyone who sleeps with my uncle is a slut."

"She isn't just sleeping with him; she expects him to marry her," Nike said.

Athena sighed. "All right. I know that. I wish I could warn her, but she'd just think I'm jealous."

"I expect that would trouble you even more if you didn't actually dislike her," Amoni commented.

"All right, I expect it would. What do your spies

tell you she's going to weave?" she inquired of Nike.

Nike pulled the baby from her breast with a little popping sound and switched him to the other side. "Well, she won't talk to me. But Eleni at the tavern told Aqhat that her mother told Eleni that it shows Poseidon's descent from the gods in the marriage of the Goddess and a bull." That was a legend the royal family had clung to for generations. Any true king claimed to be descended from at least one god.

"I expect my uncle picked that theme out. He might as well *be* a bull for all the care he takes. He doesn't think he has to worry about whether the Pelasgians like him or not."

"He doesn't," Nike said. "Most of us are poor and none of us are powerful."

"There is a Pelasgian in the Areopagus," Athena said.

"Out of nine," Nike retorted. "And he has an Achaean mother."

"Oh. I suppose he does. I swear if I am queen it won't be like that."

Nike and Amoni looked at her solemnly. This was the first time that either of them could remember Athena speaking as if being queen might be a possibility; as if she wanted that.

"You said you would never marry your uncle," Nike reminded her.

"Nor will I," Athena said slowly. "If I am queen, I will be queen."

IX

The Gorgon

It was very quiet in the Lady's temple. The black-robed priestesses were gone—at home in their cave, Medusa supposed, doing whatever they did there. She couldn't imagine them cooking onions or a pot of eels on the stove, the way her mother did, but they must eat. She straightened the veil over her hair so that she looked properly modest, and approached the stone that was the Lady a little hesitantly. The stone beside the altar was old and dark with offerings of blood and tallow, hardly a human figure at all, but it emanated power. Medusa stopped before it and set her bowl of meal on the altar.

"I've come to ask your blessing on my wedding," she told the Lady. "Mother says he is a good man, but I haven't met him, and I'm a little afraid. Father says he has money and we're lucky I'm so pretty."

The stone regarded her enigmatically in the silence. Medusa could hear the faint rustle of mice in the dark recesses of the temple, and the flutter and chirp of birds in the smoke-darkened rafters. The sacred snake who lived in the cave with the priestesses fed on them between offerings. Medusa set an egg on its end in the meal for him. Maybe the babies in the rafters would live to fledge if he ate the egg.

"I'm to be married next week," she said to the Goddess, "and go to live in Eleusis. I'm afraid of that too. Tomorrow I put my toys away. Mother says I have to give them to you. I can't take them with me because I'll be a grown lady now."

The snake stirred in his cave. She thought she caught the dry rustle of scales on stone. She cocked her head and the veil slipped from her rose-gold hair. Her gown was a wisp of white smoke in the shadows. Outside, something saw her and slipped into the dimness beyond the portico.

Medusa put her hands on the altar, stroking the cool, dark stone, sooty with the leavings of burned offerings. She wondered what the priestesses did with the toys that girls left. Every girl about to be married brought her childhood to the Goddess and laid it on her altar. There must have been hundreds of toys left here over the years. Were they in some cavern storeroom? Did the black-robed priestesses play with them? She imagined them chasing a ball down the dark corridors, drawing a wooden boat on wheels behind them.

She giggled. A different rustle caught her ear. There was the scrape of a footstep. She turned her head around too late.

He wrapped his arms around her before she could scream. One hand clamped across her mouth. The faint light from the portico outside caught his pale hair and the glint of teeth.

"You're too pretty to go off to Eleusis without giving me a kiss." He was laughing.

She struggled in his grip but he pushed her down on the stone floor. She felt his hand under her gown, closing on her flesh, prying her thighs apart. She tried to bite him and he slapped her across the face.

"Be still! Your mill owner won't mind if I try you out a bit." His voice was slurred, and she could smell the wine on his breath. "Nobody expects a Pelasgian to be a virgin."

She whimpered, and he said, "If you make any noise, I'll strangle you."

He climbed on top of her and his hands forced her legs apart. Her gown was up around her waist. She felt a stabbing pain that made her gag, and she wondered why the priestesses couldn't hear.

The pain spread across her belly until she wanted to scream. The stone floor bruised her buttocks and shoulders as he slammed her down on it again and again. The birds in the rafters fluttered out into the sunlight and were gone. The scream choked in her throat. She went rigid and still, and spiraled out of herself into the air above him, and then into the sky, and then over the rocky headland to the east, until she was stretched so thin on the air that she was invisible.

When Medusa didn't come home in the late-afternoon shadows, her mother went looking for her. The dark priestesses were at the temple, scouring the altar.

"She was here, but she left," the youngest one told her.

"Where did she go?"

"I don't know." The girl rubbed her face with the back of her hand, and the oldest priestess shook her head at her, grim lipped.

"She has been gone since noon," she said.

"Gone where?"

The old priestess shook her head again. "She left. Better maybe if you don't look for her."

"Why? What has happened to my daughter?" Medusa's mother began to take the priestess by the shoulders and shake her. The priestess's eyes snapped and she lowered her hands, wilting.

"That one came. The king's brother. He found her alone here."

"Alone? No one is ever alone here. You are always here."

"We were in the back." The old priestess looked uncomfortable. Uneasy. "We didn't hear."

"Then how do you know?" her mother demanded.

"We found her later."

"We are afraid of him!" the youngest priestess blurted out.

Medusa's mother went pale. "Where is she now?"

"We don't know," the young priestess said while the elder glared at her. "It can't hurt to tell her," she sobbed.

The old priestess snapped her a look that said she would get a beating later, but the young one plunged on. She wasn't any older than Medusa, the mother saw. "We found her on the floor. There was blood on the altar; he had had her up there too. She was alive but she didn't speak. We tried to ask her what happened but she opened her mouth and nothing came out. Then she got up and she ran out of the temple and we don't know where she's gone. Maybe she has gone home," she added hopefully.

"If she had come home, I wouldn't be here," her mother said. She fled from the temple, both hands to her mouth, looking wildly around her in the street. She stopped in the middle of it, screaming, *"Where is my daughter?"*

Heads popped out of doorways and shops, and Eleni from the tavern ran to put her arm around her.

"Where is Medusa? Have you seen her?"

Heads shook quietly. A few ducked back inside their doors, while Medusa's mother called after them.

"I didn't see her," the butcher said flatly, and began to shutter his shop for the night.

No one could say where the girl had gone, or would say. Rumors galloped through the city and then settled, shrugging their shoulders. Poseidon, laughing, said he had only given the girl a kiss in the temple and come away. He was lounging in the tavern, his feet on the table, and he called to Eleni to bring him more wine, and pinched her backside when she did. Likely the girl had run off with some man. It was clear she wasn't an innocent, he said—she had beckoned him into the temple with her and rubbed herself against him.

Eleni shot him a poisonous look, but no one called him a liar. People who did that found themselves with houses that were set on fire, or back taxes were suddenly discovered to be owed, or palace guards came to their doors and took someone away. They decided that very likely the girl was dead, and so there was no point in looking for her. Families began not to let their daughters go about unescorted, but no one, not even Medusa's parents, thought to bring the case before the king. The king was on his deathbed or worse, and a case brought before him would only go to Poseidon, or the Areopagus, who would argue for decades and decide nothing. They couldn't punish royalty. A citizenry could only rely on the royal family to bring its own to heel, and there was no one to do so.

"He is evil," Athena said between her teeth, setting the threads into her loom.

Nike sighed. "She's not the first girl to be

caught by that one. Most just dust themselves off and chalk it up to experience."

"She was a baby!"

"So was I," Nike said.

"Nike!"

"I didn't tell you. There was no point. You would just have made an enemy of him sooner. Mother knew. I think it's why they didn't press me to marry; they were afraid the man wouldn't want me. Aqhat didn't mind." She smiled. "I haven't told him who it was, or he would try to kill your uncle, and I would rather have Aqhat."

Athena dropped her skeins of wool into their basket and stared at Nike. She was older. Athena hadn't thought of other people getting older, or knowing more, just herself. Nike had three babies, the youngest of them kicking his legs in her lap. Her face was that of someone who knew what she wanted, and what was important and what was not.

"Not all of us can get away with what you did," Nike told her. "For most of us it's a matter of trying to stay respectable so the neighbors don't throw rocks at us. If we can find a bit of love and comfort in the meantime, we'll take it, and never mind what goes on at the palace. Or comes *from* the palace, for that matter. For most of us that's the price of being ruled, and we pay it because we have no say. When things get too bad, then there's revolution, or the people invite some other invader in to settle the previous one. But until we get to that point we take what happens and get on with our real lives. We might be at that point now," she added thoughtfully.

Why on earth couldn't they elect Nike to the Areopagus, Athena thought, instead of Tryphon, who was so superstitious he wouldn't put his shoes on in the morning without an elaborate ritual, or Perseus, the youngest member, who was nearly as hotheaded as Poseidon. The only qualifications they had were between their legs, and Perseus's, like Poseidon's, would probably get him in trouble. Nike thought about things since she had been across the sea and seen the world. Aqhat had seen even more of it than she had, and told her about its history at night in their bed. But Nike was a woman and Aqhat a foreigner, so they would never be eligible.

Polumetis landed on the back of Nike's chair and preened the baby's fine, pale hair. The baby giggled.

"Don't you have eggs to sit on?" Nike asked her. "This is my egg." And the moment passed, the serious moment in which Nike had told Athena something she hadn't known, something fearful, as casually as she nursed her baby.

Athena stood, pacing about the loom in her chamber. The blue fish cavorting on her wall smiled at her. They had been painted by an artist from Knossos, someone who knew things too, who had seen the king's palace there. *If we had stayed in Tyre, I could have gone to Knossos*, she thought. What was it worth, to keep Attica and her city out of Poseidon's hands? And why was she playing silly girl games with a loom? She threw the heddle down on the floor with a clatter and Polumetis rose into the air in a soft whir of wings.

Nike picked it up again.

The first wild rumors came down off the headland at the midsummer moon. A goat boy came home with his tunic in tatters and his neck and hand bleeding. Something had tracked him. He had heard its footsteps just before it had leaped on him from above and bitten his neck. The thing had shrieked like a wild animal and he had fought it off, but it had gotten one of his goat kids. He had seen it run off on two legs. He swore to that, downing cup after cup of wine in the tavern, telling and retelling the tale, first to a crowd from the docks and then to the grape cutters from the vineyards, along with Nike's brother Akakios, and Rhoecus the leather merchant.

"I heard something howling up there last night," one of the dockworkers said. "Near scared me out of my sandals. You could hear it clear down by the warehouses. I wouldn't go up there alone."

"My sister found a rabbit's carcass by the spring," a grape cutter volunteered. "It had been torn open with something's teeth, but it didn't look like a wolf had done it. A wolf would have eaten it all, anyway."

"It's a chimera, most likely," Akakios volunteered. "They have a lion's head, but the hinder part's a serpent, and it only drinks the blood."

"Have you ever seen one o' those?" Rhoecus looked dubious.

"No, but I haven't seen the sacred egg either, and I believe in it. Chimeras have a goat's head in the middle, besides, and that one eats hay."

"I'll believe in what I see," Rhoecus said, "and I don't believe the thing had two legs."

"And I believe Akakios has been listening to his sister and that foreign husband of hers," said Rhoecus's apprentice. "That chimera thing sounds foreign to me."

"Wasn't a chimer-whatsis," Photios the goat boy said. "It had on clothes."

"What kind of clothes?"

"Scraps of 'em. Rags, I guess. But it was clothes." His hand felt the bloody chewed places on his neck.

She watched them. They couldn't see her, so she was safe, but she could see them. One of them carried a cloth bag, swinging it from his hand. She could see that there was something heavy in the bottom of it. After a while they would go to sleep in the sun while the goats grazed, and there would be food in the bag. Maybe cheese and fresh figs. Her mouth watered with the memory of figs. She would just take the food. She wouldn't hurt them. They weren't the one who had done it; she had to remember that, and not hurt them, the way she had hurt the other one. It was hard to remember when she was so hungry and so frightened at the same time. She had bashed the kid's head in with a rock and tried to make a fire to cook it but the flame wouldn't come; someone like her hadn't had to do that before. She had drunk the blood when it pooled in her hand. The rabbit had clogged her mouth with sodden fur, and raw it had made her gag. There would be real food in that basket, the kind of food someone like her had eaten once. She crouched on the rocks, hands between her bloody feet, watching them from beneath a tangled mane of dirty hair.

"There's something up there," the younger goatherd said, looking uneasily over his shoulder. "I can feel it."

"Well, there's two of us to one of it," his companion said.

"It's stalking us. If it's the monster that attacked Photios, it won't matter how many of us there are, maybe."

"I don't believe in monsters."

"Maybe it's a lion. If it's a lion it won't matter that there are two of us either."

"All right! We'll move the goats." The second boy got up, exasperated, and began to chivvy their charges down the meadow. Now he could feel something on the back of his neck, too, and he cuffed his companion for making him fanciful.

The watcher in the rocks followed them—carefully, because if they heard her she wouldn't get anything to eat. She was hungry. The same rage that had flooded through her before began to cloud her mind.

"There, now, see any monsters here?"

"No." The midsummer sun was hot enough to make the air shimmer on the rocks above them. A hawk circled in the blue sky, riding the thermals. The air was pungent with the smell of goats. Their bleating carried faintly down the meadow as they grazed, switching their tails, the kids burrowing beneath the does' bellies to get at the teats.

The first goatherd took out his pipes and began to play, a soft lilting melody like water running over stones. The second one, calmed, drowsed beside him.

The watcher in the rocks bit her fist in frustration. They were too big. She was hungry. If they caught her it would happen again. Her fist closed around a rock. She would wait until dusk. She shifted back and forth on her heels, waiting.

As the sun sank, the stones on the hillside threw long shadows like giant elongated eggs. They were bodies for the Goddess, as the stone in the temple was, dark stone bodies that old, raw, dark power lived in. She could feel it come up through the ground into her feet. She ached with it, masking the growling in her stomach with another, fiercer hunger.

The thing came out of the shadows shrieking, a high eldritch howl that raised the hair on their necks in the few seconds before it was on them, clawing and swinging the sharp stone. They beat it off, flailing at it with their arms, but it caught one of them by the hand and sank its teeth into the arm down to the bone. He screamed and the thing let go and grabbed the bag that had held their midday meal. It was empty now. The thing stuck a clawed hand into it and then threw it down and ran wailing into the rocks.

The two of them ran for the goats, shouting, driving them before them at a gallop down the dusty track.

After that the rumors of the monster in the hills grew, until it had three heads, wings, and claws like a bear. It had come up to the edge of the city at night and stolen a piglet: A grape cutter had found the remains scattered among the vineyard terraces. It had taken a cooling loaf of bread from an oven and thrown sheep dung at the walls of the house. It had cut a milk goat loose from its tether and had tried to snatch a child, who had run howling for his mother, with long claw marks raking down his arm. It had stolen a pot of hot coals and burned itself on them, leaving the shattered pot in the road. A grave digger had seen it by moonlight capering among the barrows on the hillside.

Athena listened to them all and went to her mother.

"When you pin them down, they say it goes on two feet and has shreds of clothing," she informed her. "And it seems to have found a knife."

Metis nodded, her head bent over an embroidery hoop. A line of scarlet spirals bordered the cloth that fell from the hoop. She stuck her needle, threaded with bloodred thread, into the pattern and brought it out again. "Madness is a way to escape the inescapable," she said. "The Lady sends it to those who can find no other way out."

Athena sat down at her mother's feet and put her arms around her knees. "You think it's her, too."

"I do. I have small belief in monsters."

"Unless you count my uncle."

"It has been my experience that monsters generally turn out to be human," Metis said.

"What can we do for her?"

"I doubt there is anything. You could try to capture the poor thing and drag her back to the town, to be made sport of for a freak."

"No. That would be horrible. But we can't just leave her out there."

"Probably not forever, no," Metis said. "But pray that we can."

"Why?"

"Think, child. It's afraid. It's vengeful. It's hungry. Those things will merge."

"It? You said you thought it was her."

"Medusa? She isn't that girl anymore. She has become what we have made her."

That thought seemed too dreadful for Athena to contemplate. Whatever Uncle Poseidon made of people would be horrible. Metis had said "we."

Were they all responsible for Uncle Poseidon? Because he was in the family? Because she had thought about letting him rule this place when her father died? Simply because he was human and they were too? The animals and their wants seemed clearer and simpler to Athena than people just now. Polumetis wanted mice and a hollow tree to hatch her eggs in. At times she wanted to mate. She had no use for gold collars or purple clothes or lapis lazuli earrings, or for power over other owls. When it was her time to mate she did, and when she didn't, the male owl wasn't interested in her either. That last trait seemed to Athena a better way than the one the gods had devised for humans.

"Do you think her parents know?" she asked her mother.

"If they don't, would you wish to be the one to tell them?"

"They are already mourning her as dead," Athena said.

"Then let them."

"They have sent back her bride price to the miller in Eleusis. They couldn't afford to. They had spent most of it on clothes for her for the marriage. Someone ought to make Uncle Poseidon pay them for that at least."

Metis set two careful stitches with the scarlet thread. "That kind of debt often gets paid in ways no one is expecting, but it does get paid sooner or later. Leave your uncle to the Lady."

"If the Lady were going to do anything about him she would have protected that child from him," Athena said rebelliously.

"The Lady owns death as well as life. You know that. They are part of the great dance. The Lady owns madness too."

"They were in her temple!"

"I expect that will annoy her," Metis said.

"The only person who has suffered is Medusa!"

Metis set down her stitching. "Learn, child. It is not the function of the Lady to make the world fair, and she is not a force we can control. We can only give her our sacrifices and ask, but we cannot demand. When the hawk prays for dinner, the mouse prays for escape. The Lady is the power of the water that eats away the stone, the force that pushes a green shoot up through the earth, but she is also the breath of the volcano. When a child is born she is there, and when a wolf tears a kid she is there too. If you live to rule this city you will get some taste of that."

"If I live?" Athena looked up at her, startled.

"As soon as he is king, your uncle will come for you. Didn't you know that?"

She had, of course. But she had turned her face away from the thought when it had fluttered against her cheek. She had come home to keep Poseidon from the throne, and she would pay the price of failure if she couldn't.

The sun felt like a molten bowl of bronze in late summer, baking the air until anyone who ventured into the hills might see monsters. But the leavings of what the goatherds began to call the gorgon were real enough. Gorgons were creatures of legend, covered with impenetrable scales, with hair of living snakes, and hands made of bronze. Shepherds began to swear they had seen her with the snakes writhing about her face, and eyes of fire, just before she dropped shrieking on them from the rocks, knife flashing. Her breath was like rotted eggs, they said, and she was stronger than any man. Her mouth was covered with sores, and the bites she inflicted grew inflamed, and putrefied. If anyone had once known her as human, there was nothing left now to recognize.

The king, too, grew unrecognizable, shrinking into his skin as suddenly as if whatever had kept him alive had dissipated, run out of him like water from a jug.

"It won't be long," Metis told Athena. "There is nothing more that will hold off death. You will have to fight your uncle for it." She paused and listened to the commotion in the street. Someone had brought the mangled corpse of a dog in. It had been killed with a knife, but eaten with bare teeth. "That poor creature in the hills may fight on your side," Metis said, "and then you will truly understand the dance of the Lady."

Athena didn't know yet what her mother meant.

Where the gorgon was, the hills were eerily silent. No bird stirred and the small animals cowered in their burrows. Where she had been were the shreds of a rabbit or a turtle shell torn open with her claws. Travelers between the towns felt her eyes on them, heard the faint dry whisper of her footsteps stalking them. When they turned around, necks prickling, there was nothing, only the rustle of tinder-dry grass and a faint acrid odor in the dusty air. At night the city barred the gates against the thing, and latecomers caught outside them pounded on the wooden bars in terror.

Her first kill was a tinker from Eleusis.

They found him on the road outside the gates in the morning, with his throat torn out by teeth, his blood soaking the ground. His donkey stood trembling in a nearby thicket, its lead caught in briars. The packs on its back were askew, their covers ripped open, and the sheets of tin, the awls and pincers scattered among the brambles.

A troop of the palace guard sent out to search the countryside found nothing, except tracks that disappeared into rocky ground that held no footprints, and had far too many hiding places.

Poseidon, supervising the setting up of the village maidens' looms in the agora for his contest, stationed guardsmen at the gates and assured the citizenry that all was well: Tinkers were a chancy lot, and who knew what enemies he might have made?

"This lies at your door," Athena said to him between her teeth as he stood smiling, watching her loom being erected, the strung warp threads glimmering in the dusty sun. "What are you going to do?"

"I suppose the Areopagus will consider the matter. Since the king cannot." He grinned. "Perhaps the time has come to name my brother's heir. Your mother has staved that off long enough. Just now, it's not my business."

Athena narrowed her eyes at him. "It was your business from the beginning!" she snapped.

"I have no idea what you mean." The sea breeze ruffled his gold curls, and his blue eyes glinted. If you weren't looking carefully, you would say he seemed a charming fellow, an affectionate uncle. "There are some things it's safer for a pretty girl not to think about," he said. "One would think one would be safe in a temple, wouldn't one? But life's unpredictable. You may find nowhere is safe if you concern yourself with men's business. I wouldn't want anything to happen to *you*."

Try it and die, she thought. She glared at him. He laughed and turned away to inspect Arachne's loom. Arachne beamed at him and blushed modestly when he brushed his fingertip along her shoulder.

He just threatened me with what Medusa got, Athena thought, stunned. If she were Arachne, she would be terrified. Arachne was too stupid.

The madness that drove the thing in the hills was building. Athena could almost feel it crouching out there, fear and hunger and vengefulness coalescing in it, building to one raw, anguished force, as her mother had said it would. The morning of the weaving contest, the three children of the wheelwright, two girls and a boy, went out to pick flowers for their mother, to lessen the chance that she might smack them for the fact, as yet undiscovered, that they had eaten three of the honeycakes set aside to sell to the crowd that would come to watch. It was barely dawn, with a pink streak just lighting the sky, but it was already hot. The wheelwright lived outside the city gates, in the sprawl of huts below the Acropolis, where they barred their doors at night. But the bar across the door wasn't hard to lift if two of them pushed on it, and the children slipped outside into the pale morning.

Cornflowers covered the ground where the road to Eleusis wound past the slow rise of the foothills. They were filling their arms with them when the gorgon came around an outcropping of rock, and snatched at them with blistered hands, weeping, eyes glazed with madness.

The two eldest, the girls, ran home screaming, the ground behind them strewn with blue flowers. The parents found their brother dead not far away among the cornflowers, his torn throat thick with his own blood.

X

The Dance of the Lady

The preparations in the agora stopped as word went through the city. Athena sat down on the bench before her loom and put her face in her hands. She felt a touch on her shoulder and looked up. It was Amoni, his blue eyes spilling with tears.

"Cecrops has called out the Areopagus," he said. "You had best go. They're meeting on the rock. They won't bother your father this time."

She stood. She couldn't see Poseidon. Her mother came hurrying from the palace, face grim. She held Athena's cloak in her hands and pushed it at her. "Wear this. You know what has to be done."

Athena's stomach churned. She put the cloak on and felt its odd power envelop her, but it didn't quiet her stomach.

"Don't look sick," Metis said. "You can't afford to."

Athena thought of asking how she was to stop it, but the answer came to her before she spoke. *Give it to the Lady.* Give the Lady her nausea as she gave her the bowl of meal or the goat or the drop of blood from the tip of her finger, rubbed into ancient stone.

At the thought, the nausea subsided, replaced with an odd sensation of clarity, as if the daylight were more transparent than it had been a moment ago, the colors on her loom truer, the blue bowl of the sky a high, hard shell enclosing them in some great egg.

Athena settled the cloak on her shoulders and held her arm up. Polumetis fluttered down on silent wings, and her talons gripped the leather wristguard. She nodded once at Amoni and set out toward the Areopagus rock, with Metis behind her.

The Areopagus were shuffling among their stone chairs, eyes wide with shock, mouths pursed in distress. The king's seat was empty, and Athena looked at it thoughtfully. As she did, Poseidon arrived, sauntering and smiling, as if nothing much were amiss. He headed for the high seat, but stopped when he saw Athena.

"Sit down!" she snapped at him. "My father isn't dead yet."

He opened his mouth to protest, but Cecrops rose from his own chair, leaning on his cane, and said, "The spirit of the king sits in the high seat. There is no need for anyone else to do so."

Poseidon sat, and gave Athena an evil look. She sat too, drawing the goatskin cloak around her, feeling the ghosts in the snakeskins rise up and look out at the world with grave bright eyes.

Cecrops was still standing. His hand shook on his cane. "What the monster that plagues us may be, I do not know," he said. "But now it has taken life, and must be stopped."

"How?" someone demanded. "The thing's a monster."

"If it's a gorgon you can't look it in the face," Tryphon said. "They'll turn you to stone if you look them in the face."

"A hero has to go and kill it." That was Perseus, youngest member of the Areopagus. He stood, eyes bright with excitement, leaning on his spear as if he were ready to set out.

"It's not a gorgon," Athena said.

"How do you know what it is?" Tryphon demanded.

"Because if you get to the bottom of the wild tales, they say it wears clothes and goes on two legs. Nothing goes on two legs but humans."

"It isn't human!" Perseus said indignantly. "Photios the goatherd said it had fangs as long as his hand and stank of corpses."

"It had better be killed then," Poseidon said. He smiled at Perseus. "We'll go together."

There was a stiff silence. Cecrops opened his mouth to speak and Poseidon looked at him. Cecrops hesitated.

Athena stood. The folds of the cloak moved about

her calves although there was no breeze. "That is an evil idea. The thing out there was human until you made her into a monster. Stay here and judge your silly contest. I will go with Perseus."

The Areopagus shuffled their feet and murmured. Athena had spoken the thing they were afraid to say. They might be saying it to the next king, and it was never wise to criticize a king to his face.

"It's a gorgon," Tryphon said uncomfortably.

"Bah!" Athena stamped her foot, disturbing Polumetis, who flapped into the air indignantly. "There was no gorgon in the hills until that poor girl ran away."

"Likely it ate her," Tryphon suggested.

"And began wearing her clothes."

"Well, now we don't know that," Perseus said. He wanted a monster.

Cecrops watched them sadly. Athena thought he knew what it was. He looked at Metis but she didn't speak. Her eyes were on her daughter. "Are we agreed that it must be killed? Whatever it is?" Cecrops asked.

There was a murmur of assent at that.

"Then let Perseus go after it," he suggested to them.

"Just him alone?"

"Would it be better to send a troop of soldiers with him?"

"If the thing hears a troop of soldiers coming, it's bound to hide."

"Best to send one man in."

"It will be dangerous. Job for a hero, as young Perseus says."

"I will go with him," Athena said again. She stared at Poseidon, daring him to challenge her.

"Not a job for a girl," Perseus said uncomfortably.

"Perseus." She stood waiting until he looked at her. The folds of the cloak moved in the invisible wind that seemed to touch only Athena. The snakes' eyes were bright along its hem. He thought he saw them move.

"Yes, lady," he said as if she had given him some order.

"I will go with you because that thing in the hills was a human woman once, and it is not right that she be hunted down by men."

"A lot of fuss over nothing," Poseidon said disgustedly. "Everyone knows women get hysterical when their wombs wander about in their body— ask any physician. There's only one cure for it. This one ought to be married."

"So you can cure me the way you cured Medusa?" Athena asked him. "In the Goddess's temple? If I had done that I would be afraid."

"I told you I didn't harm the little slut!" His eyes snapped with anger.

"Tell that to the Lady," Athena said. Her gray eyes darkened, and for a moment he thought he saw the snakes on her cloak swing their flat heads around to watch him.

He stepped back a pace and the illusion went away. The Lady in the Pelasgian temple was nothing but an old stone. The Achaean Goddess had a proper statue that you could give public attention to and not bother about otherwise. It was time that old temple was torn down, he thought. When he was king . . .

"Is it the will of the Areopagus that the king's daughter be allowed to go with Perseus to hunt down this creature?" Cecrops asked.

Athena bristled, but Polumetis pecked at her ear with her beak. It would be unwise to defy the Areopagus, to make decisions without their consent. A king held his power, her father had told her before he grew sick, by allowing the people to consent to being governed by him. It was possible for a ruler to do otherwise, he had said, but that ruler had to look behind him all his reign. *Poseidon will have to look behind him*, she thought, *if he is king*.

Metis stood and spoke for the first time. "The Lady, by whatever name you call her, holds her monsters, those who are afflicted with her madness, in her hand. One of hers, one of us, must be there at this one's ending, if you do not want its spirit to walk in the hills when the body is gone."

That was an idea that made them all distinctly uneasy. There was another general muttering, and then a murmur of consent. "Let the king's daughter go with Perseus to send the gorgon's soul to the Underworld once he has killed it," Tryphon said. "You can't be too careful with these things."

They all nodded, comforted by the polite fiction that Metis had devised for them—the double layer to its naming that allowed them still to think of it as a monster, and not to be forced to that other knowledge.

The looms still stood set up in their frames in the agora, but no one was attending to them. Arachne stood beside hers, sulkily furious. "A lot of fuss over a child and a tinker," she said to her friends. "And they'll postpone the contest while she goes running about in the hills with a spear, like a hoyden."

"You could demand they hold it anyway," one of her friends said. "It isn't as if she *had* to go."

"And have it said she could have beaten me if she'd been here?" Arachne snorted. "No, thank you. I'll wait until she comes back. If that thing doesn't eat her."

"Well, *I* think it's unwomanly," the other friend said.

"Of course it is. Poseidon will put a leash on her when he's king. It isn't fitting for a member of the royal family to go about like that. She may have to be locked up." Arachne looked satisfied at that notion.

The first friend hesitated. She had heard that Poseidon still wanted to marry the king's daughter, to make the kingship certain. It wouldn't do to say that to Arachne. "Well, I hope the monster does eat her," she said loyally.

Amoni listened to them nattering and ground his teeth. He hadn't been allowed to see Athena since she had gone to the Areopagus. She and Perseus were gathering their weapons and gear.

They would ride rather than drive a chariot into the rocky uplands. A crowd had gathered in the agora to see them off. Food sellers were hawking the same wares they had planned to sell at the weaving contest. Except for the wheelwright's wife, who was bathing the body of her child and wrapping his torn throat in white cloth. Amoni wanted to take Arachne by the arm and drag her down the steep street to the wheelwright's hut. To push her long nose into tragedy and wake her.

A murmur rose from the crowd and began to swell. Athena and Perseus rode out of the alley behind the king's stable. Perseus sat a big bay gelding with the easy air of one who has no doubts. His bronze helmet and breastplate shone, and a gray hunting dog trotted at the gelding's heels. Athena rode beside him in a boy's tunic, on a red roan mare with long legs and a wild eye. She held the reins easily in one hand, but her own eyes were troubled, and the cloak whipped about her bare legs as if it were angry. She carried a spear in her other hand. A quiver of arrows and a bow were slung from her back. Amoni didn't see Polumetis.

They trotted across the square while people stood back to make room for them. Amoni saw Medusa's parents in the crowd, their faces blank, shuttered like a house closed up for the night. The two riders threaded their way between the looms standing abandoned in the agora, their warp threads like transparent curtains into some other, half-finished world. When they reined their horses onto the steep road that dropped to the city gates at the foot of the Acropolis, he turned away and went back to the forge.

Something fluttered in the shadows under the roof, and Amoni looked up, startled. Polumetis perched on one foot on a rafter, clutching a mouse in her talons. She opened her beak, swallowed it neatly, and regarded him with round gold eyes.

"She left you with me, did she?" he said.

Polumetis appeared to nod. The mouse's tail dangled from her beak.

Amoni sighed. "She does that, doesn't she? You. Me." No one, no matter how beloved, could go with Athena to some of the places she chose to go.

Nike saw them ride by, as she sat with her small son in her lap. For a moment she was ready to put him down and take up her old hunting spear. Go with Athena wherever she was going. But she didn't. The baby grabbed at her hair and she tickled him. You couldn't be a mother and have adventures. That was a choice Nike had made, and she wouldn't unmake it if she could.

Medusa's parents left the crowd in the agora and went to their house, halfway down the hillside. They closed the door and bolted it, and her mother picked up her spinning. Her father got into their bed and turned his face to the wall to wait. Someone had left a piece of silver in a bag hung from his door latch. He knew it wasn't Poseidon.

The sun was blazing. It glinted blindingly off Perseus's armor, limning him in white and gold,

dazzling the eye. The bay horse pranced, tossing
his head. Perseus's cloak was bright blue and it
rippled out behind him like the sea on a bright
day. His eyes were bright, too, excited.

"We will track it from where it killed the child,"
he said to Athena. "My hound can nose it out
when the tracks fade."

Athena nodded but she didn't speak to him. She
felt encapsulated in the cloak, prisoner of some
force she could perhaps direct but not escape.
Tears streamed down her face.

It was easy to see where to begin. Broken flowers littered the road, their bright blue fading as
they wilted. In the meadow where the children
had picked them, a wide swath had been trodden
down as if some great beast had thrashed in the
grass. Blood had soaked the ground where the
child had lain, and more blood spattered the trampled grass where the monster had fled. They
climbed past the vineyard terraces and the Hill of
Tombs, into the rocky, unstable ground above.
The horses picked their way carefully among loose
stone and rubble, between uplifted boulders, leavings of an old earthquake. The ground heaved
often in Attica, reshaping itself at will.

They followed the trail of blood for a way, inter-
spersed with occasional prints of a bare foot.

"I told you it was human," Athena said finally.

Perseus shifted his shoulders uncomfortably.
"They can take any shape," he said. "So I've heard."

Athena could see the sweat running down his
neck below the helmet's face guard. "You will die

of heatstroke in that armor if you ride in it all
day," she told him.

"One has to be prepared," Perseus said with
dignity.

The way grew stonier. There was no more blood
or footprints to be seen. His hound had its nose
to the ground now, plunging through the brush,
sniffing, quartering back and forth, with an occasional satisfied bark that said it had found the
scent again. The sun burned hotter, until she
began to be afraid that Perseus really would suffo-
cate in his helmet and breastplate. At noon she
persuaded him to stop in the thin shade of a tamarisk and eat. Perseus set his helmet beside him on
the ground, but he kept the breastplate on.

Athena dropped the heavy cloak from her
shoulders and let the sea breeze cool her. The
dried tears on her face made her skin feel stiff.
They had come a long way, wandering as their
quarry must have done, until now they sat on the
headland not far from the spring. She tipped her
waterskin up and drank, swallowing greedily, letting the water run down her chin. "We can refill
these at the spring," she said when she had had
enough. She splashed a handful on her face, shook
a few drops onto her head, and pulled the thong
from her hair, shaking it out. She reknotted her
hair and tied it up again, envying Perseus's short
locks. When she had shorn her hair like a boy's
she had had the oddest sense of freedom, of some
weight lifted that was more than just the weight
of the hair itself.

Perseus was eating a cheese and a boiled egg, cracking the shell against his breastplate, which made her smile. He caught her and gave a shamefaced grin. "You'd be surprised the things that armor's good for, besides fighting in," he confided. "You can make soup in the helmet."

Athena looked faintly revolted.

"Well, I would wash it out first," he said.

She chuckled. He looked even younger than he had on the Areopagus rock, but she had begun to like him. He wasn't like Poseidon; he was just young, and no one had ever suggested to him that women were human.

They ate while the horses nosed at the thin leaves of the tamarisk and the dry grass that blew on the headland. Perseus tossed a ball of bread and cheese to the hound, and it caught it with a clomp of its jaws.

"What was it like," he asked Athena, "going to foreign places?"

She looked up, startled.

"Well, I heard when you came home that you'd been in Tyre and lived among the Phoenicians there," he said. "It's all just rumors still, you know, but I thought how wonderful that would be, to see foreign places."

"It was," she said softly.

"Why did you come back? I'm not sure I would have."

"This is my place," Athena said. "It owns me. Kingship is like that. It gives your children to the land and they have no choice."

"Oh." Perseus was silent for a moment, working that out.

"Heroes, on the other hand," she said kindly, "may come and go."

"I sometimes think of setting forth," he confessed. "The way they do in the stories. Take a ship across the sea and have adventures."

"What sort of adventures?"

His eyes shone. "Saving maidens, defeating monsters, doing heroic tasks."

"Aren't you supposed to marry the maiden once you've saved her? Maybe you shouldn't save but one."

"You're making fun of me," he said.

"Not really. The world needs heroes. I always wonder, when those stories are over, what it was like afterward, though. Was he happy married to the maiden? Did they get along? Did he miss wandering and fighting monsters?" Or was one monster enough for him when he finally saw it clearly, looked in its eyes and knew it?

"I never thought of that," Perseus said. "The stories always end when he gets the kingdom and the king's daughter." He paused, looking at her shrewdly. "Then he gets tied to the land, doesn't he?"

Athena smiled gravely. "These are things to ponder before you set sail, I should think."

"Ha! I'll keep that in mind." He began to stow the half-eaten loaf of bread back into his pack with the cheese, rewrapped in its thin cloth. He drained the last of his own waterskin. "We had best refill these and be on our way. We don't want to give it too much lead on us."

"I think it sleeps in the day," Athena said. "When it can. It will have gone to ground." Easier to say "it" than to think what they were about to do. Maybe it really would be a gorgon, she told herself. Maybe she was wrong. Maybe the monsters of legend existed. Maybe stones would fly upward off the hillside.

They mounted and rode to the spring, which bubbled up through the earth under a grove of stunted trees, into a catchbasin of rock so old that no one knew who had set it there. The Stone People maybe. They let the horses drink their fill and then sank their waterskins beneath the surface, watching the bubbles rise up as they filled, arms buried to the elbows in cool water. Athena had put off the cloak and tied it behind her saddle and now she felt the sea breeze lift the hair on her arms and wondered if Pallas's ghost haunted the place. She knelt and stared into the basin to see if anything looked back at her. Only her own face, distorted in the ripples that spread from the disturbance of their hands.

Finally she sat back, splashed her face again, and stood. If Pallas came to the spring it would be because she had been happy here in her girlhood. She wouldn't be a danger to travelers, just a playful presence, laughing and dancing on the wind. Maybe she could comfort the other one.

They mounted and rode on across the headland, following Perseus's hound, who followed its nose.

Its great paws made no sound, but the clop of hooves that followed it would warn her if she wasn't asleep. Athena thought she might be. There would be waking, strung tight as a bow with fear and fury and hunger, a state like raw, flayed flesh; and sleeping, the kindly darkness of oblivion, of not-being. That would be all, nothing in between. It was the in-between parts that made you human.

They began to climb away from the sea into another tumble of stones heaved sideways by old earthquakes, as if the bones of the lower hills had been lifted up through the headland to its surface. She and Pallas, Nike, and Amoni had played here as children, hiding from one another in the little caves made by the jumbled rock. They had learned to make their explorations cautiously, as the caves often hid vipers.

The hound barked ahead of them, a sharp yip of excitement. They rounded an outcropping of stone and Perseus drew rein and held up a hand. At first Athena thought the cave was only a shadow on the rocks, a vertical line marked by an upright plinth taller than her head, outlined black against the sun. But the hound began to sniff harder at the gap between the stones and then to yelp. Perseus shushed it with a quick command and it sat down among the loose stones, eyes intent on the dark opening.

Athena squinted her eyes against the glare of the sun. The ground was dusty white, reflecting its rays in a shimmer of heat. Among the stones outside the cave was a litter of bones, none of them old. The sun had barely bleached them, and scraps of meat still clung to some. Athena recognized a rabbit's skull and the hindquarters of a goat. She scanned them quickly in fear of finding something human. Athena could feel an answering quiver of fear in the roan mare's flanks. The mare stood stiffly under her rider's weight, nostrils flared, her eyes wild, ears swiveling for sounds among the rocks.

The air had been full of gulls moments ago. Now the birds were gone, the blue sky blank above the currents where they had wheeled and called.

"It will be denned in there," Perseus said quietly, pointing his spear at the cleft in the rocks. In the silence they heard the faint scrape of movement inside the cave. The hair rose along the dog's backbone, and Perseus dismounted and gripped his spear, shield at the ready.

Outside, one bare footprint showed in the dry earth. They heard its owner scrabbling more loudly inside the cave.

"Only one of us can enter at a time," Perseus said. "I will go first. You can follow," he offered.

"You will be in danger as you go in," Athena said. "That passage is narrow and you don't know how long it is."

"I will have my spear. If it's narrow, it can't come around the spear."

They heard one more rattle of stones inside the hill and then silence. Athena took her cloak from where she had tied it behind her saddle and fastened it about her shoulders. What they had to do had to be done in the Lady's name, not theirs, if it was not to follow them home again. Perseus settled his helmet on his head. He sidled through the cleft in the rocks and she watched him disappear, whistling the hound to his heels. No other sound came out. She dismounted and followed them, leaving the roan mare's reins to trail on the ground as Perseus had done. The horses were well trained and would stand as if tethered, although Athena could see the mare didn't like it.

She stood a moment looking into the blackness of the cleft, her own spear gripped in her right hand, which to her annoyance began to twitch, the muscle jumping under her thumb. She was flexing her fingers to loosen it when the thing dropped screaming onto her back from the rocks above her.

Athena fell, flailing, with its foul breath in her face and its teeth tearing at her throat. She writhed in its grip and they rolled over and over in the scraps of hide and desiccating bones that littered the ground outside its cave. They rolled toward where the horses stood, and the red mare reared and backed away, snorting. All Athena could see of her enemy was a tangle of wild hair and the flash of a bronze blade. Its claws dug into her ribs and raked her thighs. The cloak tangled about them both. She could hear Perseus shouting inside the cave. Athena heaved her attacker away from her, fumbling for her own belt knife. The thing was still screaming, a horrible, high-pitched shriek that went on and on endlessly and wordlessly, a howl of despair in a voice no longer human. Athena rolled momentarily from its grasp and saw Perseus above them, spear drawn back as he fumbled for a clean strike. The thing hurled itself at her again and they rolled past his feet.

Athena got her hands around its throat and pushed it from her long enough to see its face. Wild blank eyes stared back at her, and the lips, covered in sores, were drawn back over bloody teeth. The long hair was a matt of burrs and blood, tangled locks writhing like snakes about the grimacing face. The bones felt thin and as if they would snap in Athena's hands, but the arms were remarkably powerful, with the hideous strength of madness.

"Don't look at it!" Perseus shouted at her, dancing about them, trying to find an opening for his spear.

Athena ignored him, and the shrieking thing pinned her to the ground again, struggling to get at her throat. The red mare was dancing, neighing, her hooves a dangerous clatter in the rocks. Her mouth was foam flecked. The knife flashed above Athena. She grabbed the hand that gripped it, and twisted. Still screaming, the apparition dropped the knife and tried to sink sharp teeth into her shoulder. Athena kicked hard. The form she grappled with was nearly naked, clothed in just the shreds of what might once have been a gown, girdled at the waist now with a ragged length of rope made from a piece of raw rabbit skin. Bare breasts hung above the girdle, white skin and pale nipples covered in dirt and dried blood.

They rolled over once again, and Athena managed to pin her adversary to the ground, kneeling above the heaving form, fingers dug into the skeletal arms. She sat back and then stood with a lurch, pulling its body up with her. She felt the cloak envelop them both, and watched as the girl appeared behind the monster's face, rose-gold hair a glowing aureole superimposed on the writhing filthy tangles. Over the dirt and sores was the true face of the maiden, pale and clean with friendly, hopeful eyes. The shrieking howl changed its tone, coming between ragged gasps, and Athena realized that the thing she held was sobbing now. And then she was gone and the gorgon was in her place again, malevolent in her ignorance of anything save need—hunger, anger, anguish within what was left of a human form.

She flung herself at Athena again, teeth bared, claws outstretched, and Perseus drove his spear through her from the back. Athena saw it come through the breastbone and the wild eyes go wide. Blood spurted from her mouth. She stood fixed on the spear, and then Perseus drew it back and she slumped and flung her arms out as if in an embrace. Athena caught her as she fell and laid her in the dirt among the bones. The fingers moved once, and a last shuddering breath sighed past her lips.

Death comes in threes. The thought caught in her throat. This was the third death. It had been waiting for her here all this time. When Pallas died this one had been a child, the chosen one selected to lead the sacrifice to the Goddess. In old times she would have been the sacrifice. Had the Lady taken her now for that reason? Would it have been better if she had gone to the Lady before Poseidon took her? No one had asked the girl what she had wanted, not even her parents or the mill owner from Eleusis.

Perseus gripped Athena's shoulder. "Come away. Don't look at it."

Athena shook her head. She felt dizzy. Her heart pounded in her chest, and she saw that her arm dripped blood where teeth had sunk through the flesh. "We are here to look at it," she said, while the landscape wavered and shimmered in front of her. She sat down abruptly in the dirt beside the dead girl. "We are here to look at her. To see what monsters are made from."

The hound came around his legs and nosed at the body. Then it sat on its haunches and howled.

"It knows," Athena said. She looked at the horses, still ground-tethered. The red mare had quieted and watched them with grave dark eyes.

Perseus pulled his helmet off and looked at the girl on the ground. Her face was plain now, still dirt-streaked and pocked with sores, but there was no monster left beneath the dirt and blood. "I knew her," he said softly. His voice was perplexed.

Athena stroked the tangled, matted hair. Blood ran down the filthy chin, already coagulating in the heat. A fly buzzed inquiringly over the face, and Athena brushed it away angrily.

"What do we do with her?" Perseus asked. It was one thing to slay a monster and leave it for the carrion birds, or carry its head triumphantly back. But if your monster metamorphosed in death into the body of a girl? What did you do then?

Athena thought of Medusa's parents, thought of bringing her bloody, ravaged body back to them to bury on the Hill of Tombs. They would take the sight of it to their own graves, along with the hisses and whispers of everyone who saw it, or told the story amid drunken, careless laughter in the taverns. They would wear their daughter's fate like a punishment because they had been too poor for a man like Poseidon to pay any mind to. If it were her own mother, Athena knew what she would do. Metis had always looked things in the face. But Medusa's mother? How could she make that choice for her? Better maybe the small lie, the slight twist of fact to suit truth.

"We have killed the gorgon," she said sadly. "Young Medusa was among its victims." She lifted one limp hand and found a thin silver ring on the forefinger. She slid it off. "We will tell her mother that. What have you got to dig with?"

"My knife?" Perseus said. "A spoon in my saddlebags. I hadn't thought to bury it."

"No, of course not." Athena looked around them. A clean breeze blew up off the water, and the gulls had come back, wheeling and crying in the sky. The gap in the rocks looked cool and inviting now, not sinister but a place to sleep out of the sun. "How far back does the passage go?" she asked him.

"Not far. There's a little cave beyond it. That's where she was living. There must be another way out, too, that she used. I didn't look. I turned around as soon as I heard you scream."

"That wasn't me screaming."

"No, of course not," he said.

"It might have been, if I had had the breath," she conceded. "You wouldn't think to look at her how strong she was."

"My granny went mad," Perseus offered. "She was a little thing, but two men couldn't hold her." He stopped thoughtfully. "My grandpa locked her up in a shed."

"How did it happen?"

Perseus shrugged. "It was a long time ago. I was just little. She was Pelasgian, I think. My father told me the old man killed her first husband and their baby, in order to marry her himself. She started dreaming about them when she got old. They got realer to her than he was."

Had the woman ever been real to him? Athena wondered. All she knew was that Medusa hadn't been real to Poseidon, and she herself wasn't either. She was pretty sure they were both real to Perseus by now, though.

"We'll put her in the cave," she said. They would let her sleep in the arms of the Lady. Athena knew now what her mother had meant about the Lady being in all things: the birth and the death and the murder. *If I am queen I will have to do this again*, she thought. Not this exactly, but something this hard. She must be willing to take that fearful responsibility if she asked the people to give the throne to her. She would have to be willing to give herself to them in exchange.

In order to remember that equation, she took out her belt knife and grasped the still head by the hair. The knife slid through the matted tangle next to the scalp and it came away in her hand in a piece, long snakes of what had once been hair, glued into a knot with blood and dirt. Athena held it up and stared at it as if it had been the head itself. Then she took out the pin that closed her tunic at the shoulder. She tied the shoulder ends in a knot to keep the tunic up, and jabbed the bronze pin through the mass of hair and into the leather of her cloak, so that the trophy hung just between her breasts when the cloak was pulled closed.

She stood. Her bare legs were streaked with Medusa's blood. The knot of snaky hair seemed to Perseus to have a face behind it. He backed away uneasily, thinking it watched him.

"That thing is dreadful," he said. "How can you wear it?"

"It's an aegis," Athena said. "A shield."

"Against what?"

"Against forgetting. These are the things I mustn't forget."

"I'd be just as happy to forget them if it was me," Perseus said.

"That's another thing about kingship," Athena said. "Kings aren't allowed to forget. Think about that before you marry your princess."

Perseus smiled. "I haven't won her yet. Maybe I won't, after all. Not if she wears something like that."

"They all wear something," Athena said. Some mark of the land on them.

Perseus picked up the dead girl and cradled her in his arms for a moment. She hardly weighed anything now. "I can't carry her through the passage," he said. "It's too narrow. You'll have to take her feet."

Athena nodded. She took the bone-thin ankles in her hands and walked after him as he inched backward into the cleft in the stones. It was dark. The only light that followed them slanted through the cleft over Athena's shoulder.

"Just a bit more," Perseus said. Then she felt the stone slide away from her shoulders on either side. "Lay her down here. I'll get a light."

She stood in the darkness breathing the dank smell of the cave. After a few moments her eyes could make out a faint light near the ceiling of jagged rock. It faded as the flare of a torch filled the chamber. You could count on a hero to bring a little pot of slowburner in his saddlebags, Athena thought, and wick and tallow for a torch. Maybe he would make a hero after all. Perseus held the torch high over his head, wrapped around a length of green sapling (he must have had a hatchet as well). More bones littered the cave floor along with a little pile of assorted odd items: a bronze knife with a nick in the blade, a cracked clay spindle, a child's red ball, a scrap of blue cloth that might once have been a veil, a basket with its top rim unraveling. They looked as if she had found them in the midden, broken relics of a life she remembered leading once. Athena knelt beside the body and arranged it with the hands laid across the bare chest. She folded the fingers around the red ball and spread the blue veil over her while Perseus watched.

"Give me the knife."

Perseus handed it to her silently. She dug a small female shape—wide hips, bare breasts, crowned head—into the cave floor and scratched another on the wall above Medusa's head. She dipped her forefinger in the congealing blood and traced the outlines with it.

Perseus looked away. This was the Goddess's business, not something it would be healthy for men to watch.

Athena pricked her own finger, and pressed a print into the cave wall above the figure of the Lady. She sang the Spring Hymn because she knew no other ritual. The mysterious, half-understood words echoed hollowly in the cave: *That which dies will rise up again. In the wheat, in the vine, in the tree.*

Perseus waited while she finished, distracting himself by lifting the torch to inspect the walls and roof. He found the opening Athena had seen in the low ceiling. It was narrow, but someone like Medusa could have jumped, caught the lip, and lifted herself into it. Perseus measured his shoulders against the opening. He couldn't.

"Lift me," Athena said.

He put his hands gingerly around her waist and boosted her into the narrow gap. The torch, propped against the wall, fell to the floor and went out, and he swore.

"I can see the surface," Athena said. "It's just a short shaft; she must have wriggled up it like a lizard. It's amazing. There's a young cypress growing at the lip. It won't be hard to find."

He let her down again into the darkness, and they eased their way out. The daylight outside was blinding white. They covered their eyes, squinting into it.

Together they piled stones into the cleft in the rock, filling it to the roof, until their hands were bloodied with the work. The horses and the hound watched them quietly, as if giving respect to human ritual. The opening above they inspected and left alone. Nothing that ate carrion would go down it except the roots of the cypress, and the insect people into whose jaws everyone came; and if Medusa's soul wanted to wander, a stone on top of the shaft wouldn't stop her.

XI

The Hill of Tombs

Perseus and Athena rode back to the city in the dusk, the air cooling around them as the sun set. They stopped at the spring and washed as well as they could. Perseus scrubbed and scrubbed at his hands until he caught Athena watching him with an understanding half smile, and then he dried them on his tunic, embarrassed. She washed her legs and arms, and bent her face over the pool to soak her long dark hair in the cold water. She pulled her face back dripping and looked into the pool again, still half expecting to see Pallas just over her shoulder. Perseus gave her the same understanding half smile she had given him, startling her. This one would be a hero after all, she decided. He saw things that people didn't intend to show him—the way out of the maze, or past the sleeping monster, or into the dragon's lair; the secret intentions of the heart.

"She was your friend," he said to her now. "The girl who fell from the cliff here. I was just little but I remember it. No one's mother would let them out alone for a long time."

"I had known her since I was four," Athena said slowly. "I don't remember not knowing her. She was a part of me. This"—she gestured at the cloak lying folded beside the pool—"was hers. I began to sew things to it after she died. I don't know quite why. Sometimes I think she lives in it. Or something does."

"Something does," Perseus agreed. He squatted on his heels beside the pool and touched the tip of his finger to it. "Grief, maybe. It will have soaked up something in the cave back there, too."

She nodded at him with respect. "You are clever." *There is more to you than I thought.*

"I am cleverer than I was this morning," he admitted.

"That's all we are ever given, probably," Athena said. She stood and shook her long wet hair out, and then twisted it to wring the water from it. She knotted it and pinned it with the bronze pins she had laid beside the pool. It felt cool and heavy on her head. The night was nearly full dark now, with a fingernail of a moon hanging in the sky, against a spattering of stars. She slipped Pallas's cloak about her, and felt Medusa settle on her shoulders as well. Both girls were no more than a whisper of breeze in her ear, voices barely heard but not diminishing. She thought their faint presence might stay with her now, and

the notion was oddly comforting. They belonged
to the land here now. Their bones were part of its
bones, bone into rock, like the ancient fish they
had found occasionally on the headland, mysterious bodies imprinted in stone. The fish and the
girls had died to take on that form, but they
would show Athena how she must do it living.

They mounted and set the horses' heads inland.

They knew something was wrong before they
came to the lower gates. The city heaved and
moved with a restless humming that made Athena
think of a hive of bees. Torchlight came and went
along the walls, and a high, thin keening rose
above the city, vibrating in the air like a kithara's
string. Athena knew what it was: the voices of the
priestesses in their temples, singing a king into
the next world.

"Death has come for my father," she said.

She could see the thoughts chase themselves
across Perseus's face: Now there would have to
be a new king, and unless someone were very
clever, it would be Poseidon. And the Areopagus
was uneasy with that choice.

The soldiers at the gates flung them wide as
they entered and watched Athena ride past, their
faces unreadable. Athena's face too was masked
as she rode up the torchlit street. The shadows of
people coming and going flickered on the stone
walls. They were restless, clustered in groups
about the tavern door, or trading furious whispers
in the shadows of the looms that still stood in the

agora. *This will be the end of my uncle's ridiculous contest*, Athena thought with satisfaction.

"Have you killed it?" someone shouted to her from the crowd. Others pushed fearfully around them, their faces pleading. The king was dead. A monster on the loose as well was more than they could bear.

"The gorgon is dead," Perseus said, loudly enough for the murmuring crowd in the agora to hear. "The king's daughter wears its scalp on her aegis."

They pressed closer at that, staring, half-curious, half-fearful.

"The earth fell in on it," Perseus went on, "and it lies buried in the mountain with the bones of its victims. It will come here no more." The high chanting of the priestesses from the temples vibrated in the air around him. The faces in the agora were wild with fear and excitement. At a king's death anything might happen.

Athena saw Amoni on the edge of the crowd and nodded to him gravely. He lifted a hand, and Polumetis fluttered from his wrist to light on her shoulder. She nodded to him again and reined the mare about in the agora and down the lane where Medusa's family lived. That was the first thing she must do, whatever came after.

The mother came to the door when Athena knocked, and gasped when she saw who it was. Athena ducked through the low doorway at her whispered invitation, leaving the red mare in the street with Polumetis perched on the saddle. The father was sitting at a table, a wine cup between his hands, turning it around and around. Athena felt for the ring she had tied into the hem of her tunic and undid the knot. She held it out on the palm of her hand.

"I am sorry," she said. "Your daughter is dead. But she is at rest, and the monster who killed her has been done away with. I found this to bring back to you."

The father looked up slowly. "It was a gorgon after all? That killed my daughter?" She could see the will to believe it in his eyes.

"We slew it, Perseus and I," Athena said. "I am sorry we could not save her." This was the little lie, the skewing of the facts that made life bearable afterward.

The mother closed her hand around the ring, and tears slid from her eyes.

"She is at peace," Athena said again. "I promise you." The mother knew. But she would let her husband have the comfort of the lie.

"Thank you, lady." Medusa's mother put the ring into the pocket of her apron. She stroked her husband's head gently, an absent gesture of comfort, as if to soothe a fretful child.

When Athena came out of the lane into the agora again, Arachne was there with her friends, fuming beside her loom in the torchlit night. The wailing of the priestesses set Athena's teeth on edge, but Arachne seemed immune to it. "Ha!" she spat as Athena rode by. "I heard you had come back. You should be grateful the king's death has canceled the contest. Now you won't be shown up for an unwomanly fraud!''

Her friends looked uneasy at that, but Arachne stood her ground. She could afford to insult the king's daughter: She herself would be queen shortly and the king's daughter locked up. An expression of malign satisfaction crossed her face.

Athena drew rein. The red mare halted and stood, ears swiveling at the crowd, and at the unfamiliar presence of the owl. Athena swung her leg over the mare's back, disturbing Polumetis briefly, and dropped lightly to the ground. The cloak closed around her, and she felt it move as if of its own accord. The hem whispered and the snakes' dark eyes opened. She advanced on Arachne. As she came, the knot of matted hair pinned to the cloak's breast began to move, to resolve itself into separate tendrils, twining about each other. Even Arachne saw that.

Arachne took a step back. The gorgon's hair lifted up flat, triangular heads, and their dark quick tongues flicked out hungrily. "Fool," Athena said. Her voice was as old and dark as the serpents. "You play with shuttles and thread, and make silly pictures without seeing what is under your nose. Know this: What is under your nose is more dangerous than anything you have dreamed of."

"You can't speak to me like that," Arachne said. There was a high edge of fright in her voice. "I will tell your uncle."

"My uncle will soon have other things to think

of than you, if you are lucky," Athena said. She pointed a finger at Arachne, and the finger became a serpent. Arachne cowered back and shrank against the loom's frame. The dark shadow of the loom dwarfed her in the torchlight. Her own shadow pressed long-fingered hands to her face. Her back humped and shrank. Everyone saw that.

Arachne began to weep, and her friends edged away from her. Athena stood pointing at her until Arachne had shrunk into herself utterly, and was only a dark, amorphous blob in the torchlight. Her long hands and legs scuttled against the ground, trying to hide beneath her loom.

Athena seemed to be taller than the loom. Even Amoni, watching in the shadows, felt uneasy in her presence. She towered over the quivering girl. "Be still and stick to your weaving, or one day you will find yourself hanging from your own threads," she said. Her voice seemed to come up from the earth under their feet. "Next time be careful who you trifle with."

Athena turned on her heel, and the crowd parted to make way for her. She leaped lightly to the red mare's back and held out her hand. The owl lit on it and regarded them with round yellow eyes, seeing everything. Then she was gone.

Arachne, quivering, crept out from under the loom. She was sobbing incoherently, her fingers pressed to her mouth.

"Did you see?" The crowd backed away from Arachne, too.

Arachne's mother pushed through them and

took her daughter in her arms, lifting her into the torchlight. "Stop that!" Arachne's face was screwed up into something unrecognizable.

"She turned her into a spider! Right in front of us. I saw it."

"Nonsense!" Arachne's mother said, but Arachne's friends had fled into the crowd. Arachne felt boneless in her arms, as if terror had dissolved her. She was hiccupping now, trying to talk. "She . . . I was . . . Everything was . . ." She wrapped her arms around herself, feeling her own body, patting at it. "I was . . ."

"Hush! You were nothing of the sort. Now come along home. I'll send your father to take your loom down." She led Arachne away and the crowd stared after them, wild-eyed.

The rumor didn't even take until morning to spread through the city. The king's daughter had turned Arachne into a spider. The listeners shuddered. Where were they keeping it? The king's daughter had relented and let her resume her old form with a warning.

"I saw it. You could see her legs growing out, and her face . . . Well, it was something awful."

"Her mother pretended it didn't happen, but I wouldn't want that in *my* house!"

"Horrible! And you know, once someone's been bewitched, they'll take the shape on again sometime, when you aren't expecting it."

"Without warning, like."

"I heard it from Rhoecus, who saw it with his

own eyes. They say the mother won't let her out of the house now, for fear she'll turn again."

"Well, I believe it. I wouldn't cross the king's daughter, and her just back from killing the gorgon."

"I expect she thought Poseidon would protect her."

There was a general snort of derision at that. Poseidon was unlikely to protect anyone but himself.

Even Amoni, who had been there, thought the tale might be true. And he found it interesting how everyone, despite being afraid of Poseidon, had no trouble in naming him. But Athena's name was rarely spoken. She was "the king's daughter," as if her name alone held some power it was better not to trifle with.

The burial of a king was not something that could be accomplished quickly. Kosmetas's body lay in state in the great hall of the palace for one full day, arranged on a scarlet bed under a tasseled gold-and-purple coverlet. His thin white hair and beard had been washed and oiled, his forehead encircled by his golden diadem. His skin was waxy, his face pinched and skeletal. The body had been rubbed with spices and other mysterious things that the physician said would deter decay and the smell of death. Athena could smell death anyway. He had smelled of it before he had died, before she had left to hunt the gorgon, but she had become so used to that, she had not thought that he would actually die. Her father had smelled of death, of the Underworld reaching up through the earth for him, for a long time.

The queen and her maids and the royal daughter stood beside the bier, wailing and tearing their gowns in ritual mourning. Metis had taken Athena by the hand as she entered the palace, handed her over to the maids to be bathed and combed, and then taken her with no sleep to the bier in the great hall to mourn her father. Athena felt her eyes closing as she chanted the prayers. She could say them in her sleep by now, and was.

Poseidon came to pay his respects, with one wary eye on Athena. He had heard the tale of her enchantment of Arachne. It didn't matter whether he believed it or not, if the people did. He said suitable prayers and went away again, importantly, to order the trappings of a state funeral. Mourning was left to women.

The Areopagus ordered the streets swept and the way to the Hill of Tombs strewn with rue and laurel leaves. The bier would be drawn on a wagon draped with purple cloth and fitted with gold mountings. The tomb, dug more than a year ago, had been excavated into the hillside where Kosmetas's father and grandfather lay, their chambers outfitted, as his would be, with goods for the afterlife: jars of wine and meal, mounds of figs and apples, theirs now desiccated with the decades, and pots of honey that would never spoil. The honey, which did not decay, would endure when the kings were dust. Twelve goats, twelve oxen, and six black rams would be sacrificed to the gods at the tomb, and six horses would be killed to pull his chariot in the Underworld. Small furnishings of gold would accompany him as well: tiny chairs, tables, beds, and couches made by Amoni to furnish his netherworld palace. "I don't know," Amoni had said when Athena asked him. "Maybe we are smaller in the next world. Or the furniture gets bigger."

Athena suspected he was joking. Amoni gave careful respect to the powers of the gods, but very little to the rituals devised by men to influence them. Poseidon had ordered the golden furnishings months ago, to demonstrate his open hand and his position as the presumptive heir.

The Areopagus bustled about the tomb chamber arranging all these things. The succession was not openly discussed. That would be unsuitable until the old king had been properly honored. Instead, there were quiet murmurings, feelings out of sentiment and inclination.

"There are the people to consider," Cecrops said quietly. He spoke of them as if they were an unruly beast, best tamed cautiously with both whips and food.

"Has anyone spoken with the Old Ones?" That appellation for the Pelasgians indicated a respect they were not often given. They were the ones who lived "too far down the hill," but they were numerous and they had long memories.

"Does anyone doubt what they would say?"

That was Perseus, and the elders turned to frown at him. He was unnervingly prone to speak incautiously since he had killed the gorgon. It was as if looking at the thing had turned him not to stone but to someone with a stone's sense of danger. If he spoke too freely the words would go back on the wind to Poseidon.

The mourning women stood by the bier all day, and at nightfall Athena, released by Metis, fell into her bed and slept. In her dreams she walked on the headland with the two dead girls while Nike and Amoni called to her to come back. In the morning the maids shook her awake and dressed her in her best gown. They fastened her gold collar about her throat, set all her bracelets on her arms, and hung gold and lapis lazuli drops from her ears. Her hands were heavy with rings. They dressed her dark hair into an elaborate knot on her head, from which sprouted an improbable array of ringlets curled with hot tongs. On top of that they set a diadem of beaten gold supporting tiny gold leaves on quivering stems that rustled as she moved. They held the mirror out.

"That isn't mine," Athena said.

"The queen sent it to you."

Mother would set something like a crown on her head for the effect. "Very well." Athena regarded her image in the mirror and settled Pallas's cloak on her shoulders, folded back so that her finery showed. The gorgon's head rested on her right shoulder. She touched her left shoulder and Polumetis swooped silently down to perch there.

Metis, Poseidon, and Cecrops awaited her in the great hall by the bier, with the Areopagus arrayed behind them.

"You look ridiculous." Poseidon snorted, glancing sideways at her. "Honor your father and take that thing off, and put your pet in her cage. You aren't a child."

"I am not your child," Athena said. "Nor your wife. If you find honor lacking here, you'd best look for it yourself."

Poseidon spun around, snarling, his veneer of cheerful friendliness split open. "You had best keep a civil tongue in your head. You may find I can make you *very* unhappy."

Cecrops coughed. "The citizens are waiting to bury their king," he said.

Poseidon turned back to the bier. He nodded at the waiting soldiers, and they lifted the dead king to their shoulders and carried him in solemn procession to the gilded wagon. The family followed, in a little cloud of dark lightning that was nearly visible, with the Areopagus behind them. As they passed the temples of the Goddess, old and new, the priestesses fell into step before and behind them. People stood along the street to watch them pass. Athena saw Amoni, and Nike and Aqhat with their children. Medusa's parents stood in their doorway, eyes grave. The sound of flutes and the chanting of the priestesses rose and fell along the road all the way to the Hill of Tombs. The burial place of the kings rose above the rest, the older tombs with stone doorways cut into the hillside as if they slept in little houses. Those were said to be the graves of the Pelasgian queens, so old that no one now knew their names. Achaean kings were buried in underground chambers with domed tops like bee skeps. Kosmetas's stood open, steps leading down into the darkness, out of which Athena could see the faint flare of a torch. She followed the soldiers who lifted the bier from the wagon and carried it into the earth.

One wall of the tomb chamber was painted with scenes of the king's hunting. The torch flare made the horses' legs seem to move, in endless pursuit of a lion. All through his illness, artists had been painting him into the next world. On the opposite wall he rode to war, face hidden behind his helmet and spear raised. In between he sat in judgment. He looked wise, one hand uplifted, the other extended toward a supplicant. On the last wall, his wife and daughter bore him gifts. Athena recognized herself, a stylized maiden with dark-rimmed eyes and a stately manner.

The bier was set down in the center of the chamber, the golden furniture and jars and bowls of food arrayed around it. Six soldiers unhitched the horses from the wagon and led them into the tomb, clattering awkwardly on the rock-cut stairs. Athena was glad to see that her favorite, the red mare, was not among them.

The soldiers, the Areopagus, and the king's family climbed out of the tomb into the daylight, leaving the black-robed votaries of the old temple and the pale priestesses of the new to make the sacrifice. Afterward, the goats, the oxen, and the rams were killed outside the tomb, the flesh cut away for the funeral feast, and the bones burned. A cloud of black, greasy smoke rose over the Hill of Tombs, making Athena gag. She had not had enough sleep and the day looked askew to her, the sun too bright and the ground uncertain under her feet. She leaned against her mother, and Metis took her hand.

The old doors of the dead queens swam in her vision. What would happen if she opened those doors? Would the queens rise up in their bones and speak to her? Tell her how to govern this land? Tell her how to defeat her uncle? Athena wondered where their kings slept, those men who had been royal pets, given every luxury and the body of the queen for seven years, before they were sent to the Goddess to water the crops with their blood. How many Corn Kings would a queen see sacrificed in her reign? Did she choose husbands she could love for those seven years? Men she hated? Were they only stud horses to get her with child? Metis said the king must be a perfect man, unblemished and strong, a warrior, or the Goddess would be insulted when they gave him to her.

If Athena were willing to do that, she knew, the Pelasgians would rise up to make her queen, and there might be enough of them to do it. Poseidon was thoroughly hated. But the Areopagus would never agree, and Athena's stomach turned over at the thought of the ritual marriage. Not even if she could start with Poseidon.

She looked carefully at the crowd of citizens gathered for the burial of their king. Their eyes, she noted with interest, shifted from her to Poseidon and back. They were the living embodiment of the land, and they might be as unstable as the Attic earth, which could rock underfoot with no warning. Cecrops knew that. She could see him assessing them as well. Herse and Aglauros were with him and she saw Amoni slip through the crowd until he stood near her, his eyes on her.

Metis frowned. She began to say something to Athena, but Athena's eyes had closed now, and she stood weaving on her feet.

Athena sat glassy eyed through the funeral feast that followed, at which the palace fed the populace with the meat of the sacrifices and other animals slaughtered for the occasion. Servants passed through the throng with trays of figs and wine, and flute players and dancers cavorted to entertain them. When Metis finally let her go, she fell into bed again and slept the day around, rising only when Metis came herself to tell her that the Areopagus was meeting.

She came to the Areopagus rock in a plain gown, without the gold diadem Metis had made her wear to the burial, but with the cloak, her aegis, about her, and Polumetis on her shoulder. The Areopagus were gathered already, milling among the stone seats, no one ready to sit down, as if sitting down might commit them to something. Poseidon stood before the high seat, smiling, rocking back and forth a bit on his heels, waiting for them.

Metis swept past him with Athena in her wake. They took chairs in the front row and looked expectantly at Cecrops. Cecrops coughed. Poseidon settled himself on the high seat, hands on his knees.

"That is not your place," Metis said levelly. "Not yet."

The Areopagus sat down abruptly as Poseidon leaned forward. They didn't look acquiescent, though. "It is as the queen says," Cecrops said levelly. "The kingship has not yet been decided."

"Of course." Poseidon smiled benevolently, but he didn't stand. Everyone knew that the smile meant that when it was decided, when he was king, he would remember who had voted against him.

Metis rose.

"Let the queen speak," Cecrops said.

"When I was given to be married to the king," she said, "it was for the sake of this land, that there should be an heir who came of the old blood of the land and the new blood both, who could command the love and loyalty of each. That heir sits beside me, not on the high seat."

Tryphon looked shocked. "A woman?" He peered at Athena as if she had developed a tail or some other unorthodox organ.

Poseidon snorted. "A girl? Let her marry the king then. Are we to go back to barbarism? To the murder of kings? To old dark ways that would disgrace a civilized people?"

"*Who* has disgraced a civilized people?" Athena demanded angrily, and Metis frowned at her.

"The old ways should not have been strayed from," Metis said. "The Lady has not been given her due, and as a result ill times have befallen us, when monsters roam the hills. We have left the old true ways and come into the time of the gorgon."

The Areopagus waited expectantly to see what Poseidon would say to that. The king's brother couldn't deny the existence of the gorgon without admitting to its actual nature, which most of them suspected.

Cecrops stroked his white beard while Poseidon glared at Metis.

Perseus's lip twitched in spite of the solemnity of the morning. He would never vote for a return to the days of the Corn King, but it was satisfactory to see Poseidon squirm.

Athena stood. Polumetis shifted from foot to foot on her shoulder and ruffled up her feathers. "Hush." Athena stroked her back. "Let my uncle tell us why he should be the king. That my grandfather got a bastard on a kitchen wench late in his life seems to me to be small enough reason."

Their eyes widened at that, and Poseidon narrowed his. "A ruler should have his people's welfare foremost at heart. To prove it I will say this: Let my niece show that she can give more to our people than I can! I have already given the gold for a new roof on the temple of the Goddess, and a public square to enlarge the market." He held out one hand, ticking off each new item on his fingers. "A shrine to the gods of the sea at the harbor, to bring our fishermen safely home each night. A new granary at the docks. What can this girl give you that will match that?"

"To give gold is easy," Athena said scornfully. "What can you give that cannot be bought with gold?"

"What can you?" Poseidon demanded.

"I can give honor, which you lack. I can give a love for Attica and its people; you can only give them gold. I can give them my life."

"And the lives of kings! Murder!"

"No murder. I will rule alone."

"The Pelasgians will not recognize you if you do," Metis hissed.

"They will if the other choice is my uncle!"

"They won't rise up for any but the Lady."

"I don't want them to rise up. No more death." They argued in whispers while the Areopagus watched them uneasily and Poseidon grinned.

"My niece can't shake off the influence of the Pelasgian witch even now. What do you expect if she wears the crown?"

Athena turned her back on him so that she faced

the Areopagus. "What do you expect if my uncle rules? More taxes levied to fund the things he 'gives' you? More citizens bullied just because he can? More girls left ruined by his hand, just because he can? Think of my father, whom you have just buried, and then think how he will rest in the Underworld while my uncle abuses his kingdom."

Poseidon stood at that and snatched at her arm. She spun around and he found himself holding a fold of the aegis. It was hot to his hand, and he was sure he saw the snakes move. He snatched his fingers back. "This is the witch's daughter! See the cloak she wears? She will bewitch all of you if she is given power. Only I can hold her in check. Give her to me now!"

"If I have power," Athena said, "and I believe now that I do, it comes of the Lady and the World Serpent. I did not ask for it, and it is a fearsome burden at times. No one gives me to any man. My father could not, and you will not."

The Areopagus looked from one to the other of them nervously. When royalty quarreled, things happened in the natural world outside them, because the royal house was tied, as Athena had said, to the land. Even Poseidon, the old king's father's son, was connected to the heart of the earth under their feet. When he lost his temper the hills rumbled.

"This *girl* will lead you in battle when there is war?" Poseidon sneered. "No doubt with all her ladies, carrying spindles!"

"She fought the gorgon," Perseus said softly.

"I will fight you," Athena said to Poseidon. "Give me a spear."

Poseidon was looking at Perseus. Perseus squared his shoulders and looked back levelly.

Cecrops stumped to the head of the Areopagus, leaning on his staff. "It is a grave danger to choose hastily between two claimants," he said. "Errors born that way cannot be undone. And bloodshed between kin of the royal house will stain the land. Who can propose a challenge that does not involve spears?"

An elderly member of the Areopagus sat up with a snort. "Are we considering letting a woman rule unmarried?" he demanded of his neighbor. "Have I been sleeping?"

Poseidon blew his breath out in disgust. "Let her show what she can do for the city that I cannot, as I said."

"You would bow to that decision if her gift were the better?" Cecrops fixed him with a steady gaze from under bushy brows.

"Who would decide?" Poseidon asked with sudden suspicion.

"If it is not clear, the priestesses of the new temple will have the final word."

A thoughtful look crossed over his face, and a flash of cleverness. "Done." He looked pleased, a man who had put one over on someone. "Now it's for the witch's daughter to make good on her word. I doubt she can."

"If you call my mother a witch again, you will be sorry," Athena said to him. "I accept."

Metis began to protest, and Athena hushed her. Metis folded her arms with an expression that said her counsel should have been heeded. "Let Cecrops and the Areopagus rule for a year," Athena said, "and at the end of it we will each give our gift to the city. The one whose gift is best will rule."

Poseidon grinned. "And if you lose?"

"Then I will marry you." *I have him*, Athena thought.

"You are going to make her *queen*?" Arachne's voice rose indignantly. "After all my father has done, putting your case before the merchants and artisans in their clubs?"

"Hush, silly," Poseidon said lazily. "And get me some more of this wine. This one is actually a reasonable vintage."

"After he's brought you the support of every decent Achaean citizen?" Arachne's voice rose still further, and she didn't fetch the wine.

Poseidon began to look annoyed. "Don't screech like that; it makes your face red."

Something in his expression made her lower her voice. She sniffled. "You have betrayed me."

"Nothing of the sort, you silly girl. Before I have to marry her, I'll have her locked up. She's mad as a frog in the full moon, you know."

"Everyone else knows it too." Arachne sniffed. "Going about in that awful cloak, carrying a spear. But what about saying you would marry her?" Arachne returned to her first grievance.

"That was for the Areopagus. It will make my claim stronger in their eyes. And when she goes stark, barking mad and has to be incarcerated, well, that will be a shame. Now are you going to fetch me some wine?"

Arachne had grown a little afraid of Poseidon's anger. She took his cup, the only silver one her household possessed, and went to fill it again. She splashed just a little water in on top of the wine. He didn't like his wine thin. He had cuffed her the last time she had overwatered it.

She thought of herself as queen, when there would be servants to fetch his wine, and anything she wanted as well. And Athena would be locked up, and Arachne would stop having the awful dreams, the ones in which her arms and legs stretched out and grew soft, dark fur and divided in two, while her body swelled into a round mass, bulbous and boneless. She was shivering when she handed him his wine.

He cuffed her gently this time, almost affectionately. "Stop that. I have told you, you have no need to worry."

"What will you give to the city?" she asked him. "A new temple? A statue?" She was still smarting from the cancellation of the weaving competition. She could see the golden statue out the window, still on its stand in the agora. She would have won that statue.

He saw her coveting it. "I shall put my golden monster up on a permanent pedestal," he said, because he knew that Arachne wanted it and it amused him to keep it from her. "So that the citizens will know I will defend them." Its display might encourage people to forget about the other monster, too, or to say they had.

Arachne was silent, and when she didn't ask him anything further, he said, annoyed because he was bursting with his clever idea, "My gift will be nothing that can be bought with gold. They will find out that I can wield the old powers of the earth as well as she can. Ha!"

"What will you do?" she whispered.

"Strike water from a rock. Open the earth. That is *my* birthright. She'll find that out."

XII

❧

The Lady of Olives

The water shimmered. It was like sailing through a length of Ahiram's silk. Athena stood in the bow of the *Lady of Olives* and let the wind ruffle her hair. She had told no one she was sailing until that morning because she didn't trust Poseidon, but when the Tyrian ship had docked and she had heard its name, she had known it was the one to take. She had booked her passage, and a place in the only cabin, and gone back to pack a trunk with all her best clothes, her jewels and finery, even the gold diadem with the rustling leaves that Metis had sent her. Ahiram would see her real self this time.

And this time she sailed alone, except for Polumetis. Nike had said she was mad, and then offered to come all the same. Amoni had said he *was* coming this time. Cecrops had said, "One year. If you don't return in time . . ." His sentence had trailed off at that, but she knew what he meant.

"If I don't return in time it will mean I am dead," she told him.

Cecrops nodded. They both knew what Poseidon would do then.

"I will go with you," Amoni said again.

"No." Ahiram of Tyre wouldn't welcome her in the same way with a lover in tow. She didn't say that.

Now she stood in the bow of the *Lady of Olives*, watching the painted figurehead of Asherah-yam, whose blue robe was the color of the sea. A spray of olive leaves and fruit was painted on the bow at her feet. Athena whispered a prayer to her, the goddess of Tyre. No sound came back to her ears but the swell of the waves and the cry of the gulls overhead, but maybe the Goddess had heard.

Perhaps she had, because the voyage to Tyre was smooth, with a fine wind all the way. The sailors said that the owl, of which they had been suspicious at first, had brought them luck.

There had been no time to send a message ahead of her, so she disembarked with Polumetis on her shoulder and a sailor to trundle her trunk along the streets in a barrow. For propriety's sake she hired a litter to carry her, but she leaned so far out of it to see the tall houses with their tower balconies, and the olive groves turning the coastal hills gray-green across the water, and the bright bolts of cloth in the Street of the Dyers, that they nearly tipped her into the road.

"My lady needs to sit quietly," one of the bearers said, grunting as he righted the litter, and Athena found that she still knew enough of the language to understand him. She laughed and sat quietly, staring with delight at the palm trees swaying overhead and at a woman in a scarlet veil anchored by a cap of pearls and gold disks. The woman's shoes were yellow with red buckles. Athena's cloak, her aegis, was folded in her trunk. She would look like a madwoman from the hills if she wore it here.

She had wondered what she would do if Ahiram was not at home—he might be on a voyage to anywhere, or even have died—but when the litter bearers reached the yellow house and pulled the bell, the bronze doors swung open immediately, and Athena recognized his housekeeper. A smile spread across the woman's dark face, and she called into the house, "Fetch the master! Come and see who is here!"

Ahiram was in residence. He came padding from his study in the plain long tunic he wore at home, a goose quill stuck behind his ear like a strange ornament.

"Athena! No more boys' clothes? You have run away to Tyre to see me!"

"I have." She smiled and gave him her hand.

"You have come back to marry me." He beamed at her.

She thought it was only half a joke. "I have come to buy a potter's wheel," she said, laughing.

"A potter's wheel? And they do not make these where you come from?"

"Not in my uncivilized country. If I take back a potter's wheel to copy and teach our potters to use it, we can produce fine lamps and jars of our own, and have no need to pay for ones from Crete." She had thought that out carefully on the voyage. "I am to be queen, it seems, if I can best my dreadful uncle and give my city a gift that will be more use to it than the new temple he is building."

"Clever girl."

I hope so, she thought guiltily.

Ahiram laughed and held out his arms. "Have you a kiss on the cheek for an old man? Or will I make you a scandal?"

Athena kissed him. "I have been a scandal since I was born. I have been told so. So we won't worry about that."

"Come in, come in, and have that man bring your trunk. You shall have my Miriam's room again. How is young Aqhat and your Nike?" Ahiram snapped his fingers for a servant to help carry the trunk and peppered her with questions as they ascended the stairs. "Three children? And you? Still only this old owl to keep you company?" He winked at Polumetis as if she understood him.

Ahiram's servants bustled around her in a flurry of fresh bedding and sweets and wine. A

plate with a naranj, cut in sections, appeared.
Ahiram smiled as she popped one in her mouth.

"You see, I remember you like those."

Another servant brought clean towels and a
long white tunic like the one Ahiram wore. She
bowed to Athena.

Ahiram said, "There will be a bath ready for
you now, my dear. And then we will have dinner
in my garden and you will tell me all the news."

Athena followed the servant girl downstairs
again to the bath chamber and sank gratefully into
the bright blue tub with its leaping fish. *Bathtubs
and naranjes. Those are what I should bring home,* she
thought, luxuriating in the scented water. Tyre
was a different world, as strange and wonderful
as the rhinoceros, and certainly more beautiful.
She could just give in and come here to live with
Amoni, where people didn't react to wonders by
trying to kill them. And let Poseidon rule
Attica . . . *No.*

In the evening she sat with Ahiram in his garden, watching the sun go down behind the roof-
tops of the island city, while Polumetis rummaged
in her old roost in the olive tree, throwing out
dead leaves and eggshells. Athena wondered if
the foreign owl would come and court her again,
and what had happened to the owlets who
fledged from the eggs she laid there four years
ago. Athena had put on the white tunic Ahiram
had given her, and its loose folds spilled over her
knees like milk where she sat. It was a fine weave,
finer than anything at home, even finer than she

could manage. It wasn't wool, but silk mixed with some plant that Ahiram had told her of. *Cloth from plants,* she thought. A servant set down a glass cup full of nuts. *And glass. Why do we not know how to make these things?*

"We are old here," Ahiram said, when she asked him that. "Your people are younger, I think, and when a people are young they think only of the things that will ensure their survival. Old civilizations have the leisure to contemplate luxuries. And sell them to others."

"My father's palace seems very grand to me at home," she said. "Until I come here and see your house. What kind of palaces do your kings live in, if you have a house like this?"

Ahiram chuckled. "I am richer than some of our kings," he admitted. "If you really want a potter's wheel, I will send for a potter and have you taught to use it properly. How long can you stay before you must sail home and face your dreadful uncle?"

"A little while." She watched the leaves of the olive tree shifting in the evening breeze, mysterious as gray-green fish in the currents of air. The fruit was ripening, turning a deep purpley black. "I have one year to come and go. I sailed at the solstice."

"Ah! Well, then, we have a little time. I will send for a potter. And you must tell me how I may entertain you otherwise."

"Show me things," she said, because she knew

he loved to do that. "Show me sights to take back with me and think about when I am in Attica."

"Ah! Such things I will show you." He looked delighted.

It was clear that Ahiram would not only show Athena any sight she wished to see; he would give her anything she asked for. She had to stop him from presenting her with a chair made of carved ivory that she had admired in a market, or a talking raven that Polumetis would have tried to kill, or a pair of palm trees in monstrous bronze pots.

"I can't take those on a ship," she said, laughing.

They toured the glass works and she watched the glass casters intently. He brought her to the dye works, where she held her nose and picked her way through the piles of shells, peering into the malodorous vats and asking the foreman questions. She watched the potters at their wheels, and practiced with the man Ahiram hired to teach her until she could build a fair pot up from a lump of clay, spinning the wheel with her foot. "My lady has a skill for this," he said grudgingly.

"I will get better," Athena said. She had him take the wheel and its mechanism apart and put it together again, and then supervise her until she could do it. The potter shrugged his shoulders. If the foreign lady wanted to waste her time and money on a clay wheel, it was her affair. Foreigners were all mad.

She practiced her Canaanite speech with Ahiram and the servants as well as the potter, until she could wrap her tongue around the strange words, and then Ahiram showed her again how to write down the marks that pinned that speech to paper, to be deciphered by someone else later. Letters, he called them. You could mark them in clay or in wax, or use the dark, rich ink to draw them onto a flat sheet of papyrus, which was like a skin, but which he said was made of a plant from Egypt. The letters weren't just to count with, or mark down so many sheep or so many jars of wine. You could set down a whole story with them if you wanted to, or tell someone far away what you needed them to do. They enthralled Athena.

"Each makes a sound," Ahiram said.

"Well, then you *could* write in another language with them," Athena said. "A sound is the same in any language; it just means different things."

Ahiram scratched his beard. "I suppose you could. I never thought of that. Clever girl. You are wasted on your barbarian country."

"Write my name."

Ahiram drew a few marks on the papyrus. "Like that, maybe. They don't make all the sounds. Ooh and aah and oh—you have to know how to put those in between."

"Write something else. Pomegranate. Olive. In your language."

He obliged her. "You will spoil your nice gray eyes staring at these little letters. Come, what would you really like to do? This is for scribes and clerks."

"Could we go to the mainland? Could you show me your farms? We didn't see much when I was here before."

"Of course. I will show it all to you. I have houses on the mainland too, you know. I have kept those horses you gave me, sentimental old fool that I am. You can visit them."

Ahiram's blue wagon with the red wheels met them on the shore, and his servants loaded Athena's trunk full of clothes and jewelry into it, along with a hamper of necessities like fish eggs and live oysters in a tub from Ahiram's pantry. Ahiram was jovial and expansive, dressed in a fringed scarlet shawl and blue tunic, with a great gold collar about his neck. His graying curls were crowned with a blue cap embroidered in red and gold. He sat beside Athena in the wagon, the green lattice sides pushed back to catch the fresh breeze and give the best view. The vineyards on the slopes were in harvest now, and she could see scores of workers cutting the grapes and loading them into baskets on a cart. They wore very little under a hot sun, no more than a white loincloth against dark, coppery skin.

"Are these your vineyards?"

"Yes, all of these and some farther up the coast."

She wondered how many servants it took to work all this land. They passed the orchards of almond trees and date palms and then the olive groves she remembered.

"These olives were my Miriam's dowry," Ahiram said. "They were planted by her grandfather's father, and they came with her when she married me. I would have married her without a dowry, but it is always well for each to bring something to a marriage."

"How long do olive trees live?" Athena asked him, looking speculatively at the gray-green branches and the gnarled trunks.

"Hundreds of years," Ahiram said. "Forever maybe. They thrive on bad soil and drought. They take a long time to bear, of course. Olives are for a patient man."

She remembered that he had said that. "Sixteen years, isn't it?"

"You pay attention," he said approvingly.

"Do you grow them from the seeds?" The dark fruits had an oval pit inside that had to be spit out.

"It is possible," Ahiram conceded. "Not from the pits of cured olives—the curing kills the life inside the seed. But from the green fruit. Better is to root cuttings. We have a field on my farm just for rooting young trees."

"You mean the way sometimes a stick will sprout if you drive it into the ground to grow beans on?"

"Exactly."

"My father's gardener grows fig trees that way.

And grapevines, of course. What makes bare
wood grow roots?"

"That is a mystery to me. My arborist tells me
that the life force in the wood seeks earth, and so
it sends out roots if it feels the earth around it."

Athena thought about that. Everything sought
something to keep it fed. The stick felt the water
in the earth, she supposed, and began to look for
it. "I should like to see that," she told Ahiram. "A
whole field full of new trees."

Ahiram smiled indulgently. "Any other woman
would want to see the kitchens and the maids
at their looms. Only my Athena would want to
see trees."

"What about your Miriam?"

"Ah, she was like you. She loved the olive trees.
I used to say she was a tree spirit in disguise, and
when she died she would go back into the trunk
of an olive tree." He sighed. "She would have
liked to do that, I think."

"You must miss her greatly."

Ahiram nodded. Then he brightened. "I will
show you the trees by moonlight. My Miriam
used to love that."

A little farther along, the driver turned the wagon
onto a road that ran between the orchards. It was
spread with shells that crunched under the horses'
feet. Ahead lay a grove of taller trees, and as they
drew closer she could see that the road went into
the grove. At its entrance were two tall sentinel
palms, and then the grove resolved itself into a ring

of trees that she remembered Ahiram having called sycamore figs. They bore a small woody fig that he said tasted bad, but the trees were lovely, dark leafed, stout, and wide-branching. "My children used to climb these when they were small," Ahiram said. He smiled. "Tree sprites all."

The wagon rattled through the trees and the grove opened on the house. It was stone, in two stories, with a vine-covered arbor jutting from one side. The shell road became a circle in front of the house, surrounding a fountain with a dolphin at the center, standing on his nose, tail flipped to the sun. Water jetted up around him and fell away into a blue pool. Three servants came out of the house as the wagon rattled to a halt. They helped the driver heft Athena's trunk from the wagon bed, along with Ahiram's bags and his hamper of provisions. He handed the last over to a fourth man, who appeared to be the cook.

"Ahiram, how many servants do you have, in all?" Athena whispered to him.

Ahiram scratched his head. He shrugged, perhaps embarrassed. "I don't know," he whispered back.

The house was nearly as luxurious as Ahiram's house in Tyre, but more countrified. The furniture was older, worn with being climbed upon by children now grown. The servants brought them dinner in a room with a tree growing through the roof, which fascinated Athena. Afterward as the moon rose, he took her to see the olive trees.

Athena thought it would not surprise her if

spirits lived in them. The night breeze whispered mysteriously through their leaves, and she said another quick little prayer under her breath to Asherah-yam. "Show me how you grow the young ones."

The field where Ahiram's orchard master rooted young trees was not far from the house, behind a stone building that in any other establishment would have been a potting shed. In Ahiram's orchard it was as big as someone's house, dark and dusty and filled with scythes and pruning hooks and rows and rows of empty clay pots. Athena peered curiously through the open door as they passed. Beyond was a field of what looked like knee-high grasses, until they got closer and she saw that it was filled with young trees.

"We take branches," Ahiram said, "and lay them under the earth. After a long while they will sprout new trees. Or it is possible to cut small twigs and root those. And there are ovuli, small swellings that grow from the trunk, that a skillful gardener can cut off and root. They root easily, but it is bad for the parent tree. It is all tedious. Olives are slow. A tree that lives hundreds of years is in no hurry to put out roots. They think about it first, I believe."

Athena knelt and brushed the new stems with her fingertips. They shone black and silver in the moonlight. She prodded carefully at the base of one, feeling how it was rooted.

"Athena."

She looked up.

"I know why you have come. I did not get to

be a rich man by being easily fooled, even by lovely women."

She started to answer him, and then she hung her head.

"Here. Give me your hand and get out of the dirt." She stood up and he smiled at her. "A potter's wheel is a fine notion, and your pottery shops will be revolutionized by it; I can see that. But a gift for a city? No."

"No," she admitted.

"But the olive. The olive is a whole economy in itself, light and food and medicine in one small fruit. Now that is a gift your dreadful uncle cannot match. I had been hoping you would tell me what you wanted. Perhaps I was foolish."

"I was afraid to."

"Ah. I did say I would never sell trees. I remember that."

"You have been a friend to me, and I came to steal from you." Polumetis appeared from somewhere on silent wings and lit on her shoulder. Athena sighed. "But you don't know what my uncle will do if he is allowed to rule. I could stay here happily. I have thought about it. But I can't leave my people to him."

"The land owns you, I can see." Ahiram sighed. "You are a king's daughter after all. You will have to take them at least three-year-old trees. In pots."

"You'll give them to me?" Her heart began to pound in her chest.

"It will happen sooner or later. I have thought about this since the last time you were here, when you were so interested in everything, soaking up every scrap of new knowledge like a sponge. Knowledge should move outward, or the barbarian world will stay ignorant and uncivilized. Even the silk weavers of Asu will find that someone will steal their secret sometime. You will spend the winter with me because the seas will be bad soon, and then I will send you home with your trees."

"Ahiram, I'm grateful." Three-year-old trees, in pots! "I will pray to the Lady that you find your Miriam again."

"I have found her." Ahiram put an arm around her shoulders gently and turned her toward the groves of olive trees beyond the field of cuttings. "When I come here in the moonlight I will see both of you in the trees. Tree sprites, laughing at me from the branches."

Ahiram didn't change his mind over the winter, as she had feared he might. He seemed resigned to her leaving, and said that his grandchildren's grandchildren might be annoyed with him when Attica finally had enough olive trees to cut into Tyre's market, but he would be gone a long time by then. "And who can look into the future anyway? Kings come and go, and the great merchant houses as well, but trees stay. Better we should populate the world with trees than with people like your uncle."

In the spring he booked her passage aboard *Gullwing*, a ship from his fleet. The prow bore great back-folded wings carved on either side, the long feathers painted red and gold. Ahiram sent Athena aboard with a cargo of thirty jars of olive oil and cured olives, as well as ten trees in pots. The jars were stored in the hold with her crated potter's wheel, the trees lashed to the deck and wrapped in fine cloth to keep the salt wind from drying their leaves.

"Take clear water and sprinkle the leaves with your fingers twice a day," Ahiram advised Athena. "Water them only when the soil in the pot is dry to the touch. Keep the salt wind away, but when you ride at anchor take the cloth off and let them have sun."

She listened carefully as he told her how to plant and prune them. "They are like children. They will be a great deal of trouble until they are grown."

Athena tended them like a nursemaid during the long voyage, wistfully remembering Ahiram's house with its bathtubs and feather beds, and plates of naranjes and dates that appeared as if by magic at her side every time she thought of being hungry.

She thought about that as they sailed. She sat in the stern among the olive trees in their pots, watching the coast of Phoenicia, and then the white foam of their wake, recede behind her. *I will never be able to come back,* she thought. If she were not to be queen, she could come here and bring Amoni. Amoni could make a fine living for them here. He was as good as any of the metalworkers of Tyre. And what would she do? *Sit in my court-yard and weave. And eat naranjes.*

The aegis, Pallas's goatskin cloak, still lay at the bottom of her trunk. She had shown it to Ahiram, after he had offered her the olive trees, and he sat with it across his lap for a long time, eyes closed. When he opened them he said finally, "This is a thing of terrible power. No wonder you can't marry."

It was late spring when the *Gullwing* made port. Her prow with its great bird wings nosed up to the dock, and the small crew maneuvered it about with their oars. The trees attracted attention, and when Athena, wrapped in the aegis, stepped ashore, word went quickly inland.

"Trees?" Poseidon chuckled. A grin spread over his face. "Have them brought up to the palace, by all means. I must inspect these wonderful trees."

Athena stood her ground when his soldiers came for them. "No one asked my uncle for aid. Go away. I have sent for my own bearers."

The soldiers looked uneasy. Poseidon's orders were not comfortably disobeyed. The arrival of Cecrops in a chariot, with most of the rest of the Areopagus hurrying after him, gave them some comfort. They saluted Cecrops and withdrew. The trees and the jars of olives and oil, and the crate with the potter's wheel, were off-loaded, and everything but the wheel put in wagons with Cecrops's own servants to guard them.

"Let me offer the hospitality of my house," Cecrops said. His expression said that it would not be wise to sleep at the palace. "Your lady mother has been honoring me with her presence since you sailed."

"Evil times," Metis added to that at dinner, sitting with Athena, Cecrops, and his sisters. "Poseidon thought you wouldn't be back. He's been waiting the year out, and he's not best pleased to see you."

Athena bit the edge of her thumb, picking at a fingernail she had split tending the trees. "Perhaps one of your servants will let slip the word that I failed in my search. All I have brought back are jars of wine and a few rare trees as gifts for the Areopagus, to flatter them."

"Our servants never gossip," Herse said. She looked shocked, then dismayed. "And failed in your search? Oh, lady, how dreadful to hear."

"I expect that can be arranged," Cecrops said. He patted Herse's hand. "We aren't beaten yet, my dear."

Athena thought that Herse was more likely to spread the word than the servants, the silly rabbit. She smiled affectionately at her. "I do have a wondrous thing," she said. "It's a wheel that turns while you build a clay pot, so that it's easy to make it even on all sides. I learned of it in Tyre."

"A wheel to make pots! Imagine!" Aglauros said. She thought hard. "Well, wheels are round, of course."

*   *   *

"A wheel! She *is* mad." Arachne smiled. She felt an immense relief flood over her. Now it would be settled. Poseidon would win, and he would lock the madwoman up as he had promised. Arachne inspected the tips of her fingers. She held them out before her. They didn't change. Sometimes she thought that they were growing longer.

She looked out the window into the square. Surely he would come and see her now. The market was full of people. She looked for the glint of his pale hair and thought she saw him. She patted her curls into place and fixed a smile on her face, not too presuming—he didn't like that—and not too broad, which wasn't ladylike. She waited but no one jingled the bell. She saw him go by then— not Poseidon at all, but Nike's Aqhat. A small boy and girl ran after him. Arachne put her hand across her stomach. She felt sick.

Athena left her trees and jars in Cecrops's keeping and went to see Nike.

"Your uncle hasn't accomplished anything that I can see," Nike said. "He had some men digging up the paving stones at the edge of the agora last fall. Near the fowler's stall where the hillside rises up a bit and there's that big rock?"

Athena nodded, suspicious now.

"He was very mysterious about it, but I don't know that it amounted to anything. Anyway, have you been to see Amoni?" Nike demanded.

"I'm afraid to. I don't know what to say to him."

Nike gave an exasperated sigh. She put her

hands on her hips. Motherhood suited her, Athena thought. She was softer, affectionate with her brood. The youngest, now a bit older than a year, sat paddling in a bowl of water on the floor. Aqhat had built Nike a house with a stone floor. "You've been gone a year. That man loves you. He hasn't courted any other girl."

Athena hung her head, feeling as ashamed as she had in front of Ahiram. It was worse that she would have been angry if Amoni had courted someone else.

"You're going to be queen, aren't you?" Nike said. "I heard a lot of wild talk. People have no sense."

"What else has my uncle done while I've been gone?"

"Made nice girls afraid to go out alone," Nike said. "Taken what he wanted and thought up a new tax to justify it. The Areopagus have barely managed to control him." She paused, rolling dough on her kitchen table. She made Athena think of her mother. Nike's mother. Athena's mother was another proposition. "Aqhat got a look at your trees," Nike said.

"Aqhat needs to be very quiet," Athena said.

Nike nodded. "When is the contest? And why does everything with that man come down to a contest, as if you could settle life by throwing dice?" She smacked the dough with her fist. "He challenged Akakios to a horse race and won his best horse, that he paid nearly everything he had for. For some reason the horse could barely stagger on race day. It's remarkably improved since."

"In a ten-day," Athena said. "That's when the high priestess says the day will be auspicious."

"The priestess of the new temple."

"Yes."

"And then what will you do with Amoni? Assuming you don't lose and have to marry your uncle. He has something up his sleeve, I swear."

"If I have to marry him, I'll have a knife up mine," Athena said.

Nike smiled. "Give him to the Goddess."

Athena's lip twitched. "I don't think the queen is allowed to do that on her own. I think priestesses are supposed to be involved. I must ask Mother."

"The Old Ones have begun to say that's why all this ill fortune has befallen us—because we haven't crowned a Corn King. That will be your mother's doing, I think. My father believes it."

"Will they back me if it's just me?" Athena asked her. "No sacrificial king?"

"I will," Nike said. "For the rest . . . The Achaeans know what your uncle is, but they don't like the idea of being ruled by a woman. They might be happy if you married Amoni."

"No!"

"And the Pelasgians . . . We are not powerful, but we are too many to fight if we are driven to that. I don't know. We had power once. That is hard to pass by, the thought that we might have it again. I think the Old Ones will want a Corn King, to be willing to put a woman on the throne."

Athena felt the hair stand up on her arms. There was old power in the Corn King that could not be denied. Ten days. She would have to be extremely careful for ten days.

On the third day, Amoni came to her where she sat spinning—because it calmed her nerves—in Cecrops's garden. The garden was a small walled space between his house and his stable, and the sisters had been told firmly to let no one in. Amoni came over the wall.

Athena jumped at his footstep, flinging the spindle with its trailing thread into a lettuce bed. She gave him a wild look, as if she wanted to run.

"Were you intending to see me at all?" Amoni demanded. He was another year older, settled firmly now into his adult countenance. His beard was thicker, curled and neatly trimmed, and his hair was faintly dusted with ash from the furnace. He wore his working clothes, a kilt and shirt of heavy leather, much scarred with old burns. He stood on the stone path beside her chair, waiting for an answer.

Athena retrieved the spindle and put it in the basket with her wool. "I . . . I was . . ." She looked up at him and her heart ached. It would be so easy just to marry him, to go to Tyre and live with him. Why did she feel as if some root grew from her feet into the soil of the Acropolis? That her blood flowed underground through its stones before it came back to her?

"Yes? You were?"

"I was afraid to see you because I don't trust myself not to fling myself at you and make awful trouble." She glared at him.

"Well, that's novel. Women rarely find me that attractive."

That was because he gave them no sign that he was interested. That he wanted any woman but her. Athena knew it. She took a long, deep breath. "I can't love you and be queen. Well, that's not right. I can love you and be queen. I can't marry you and be queen."

"It's a hellishly strong force," Amoni said. "Love."

"It is," she conceded.

"Dangerous. Like holding fire in your hand."

"You're angry with me."

"No." His shoulders slumped. "I thought I could convince you I was more important than the throne, but it's not that, is it?"

"It isn't the throne, if that's what you mean. It's not about wanting to be queen. That's Mother."

"No," he said slowly. "It's about the land. Perseus told me what you said to him. He didn't completely understand, but I think I do."

Ahiram was the other one who had understood. Good men, both of them. People like Poseidon saw only the power. "Amoni, it's as if it owns me. It's as bad as love."

"It *is* love in a way, I suppose," he said. He put a hand on her shoulder and she brushed her cheek against it. "Did you know your uncle has ordered the wedding feast already?"

"What?"

"He's given orders at the palace for a feast to be readied for the evening of the contest. I am to

make you a gold fillet for your head, and a gold
necklace in the shape of the World Serpent hung
with gold chain and carnelian drops. Very elegant.
He designed it himself. It looks oddly like a collar
and leash, though."

Athena closed her eyes.

"It isn't a commission I wanted," Amoni said.
"I should give him back his gold and leave here
and marry someone else."

"Will you?"

"No." He stroked her dark hair with his other
hand. "That's why love is so dreadful."

Love was dreadful. Arachne could see that.
There would be a wedding feast and it wouldn't
be hers. She had tried to see him when she heard
the news but the palace guards wouldn't let her
in. He had lied to her, and then her father had
cuffed her and said she was a slut. He hadn't
thought so before—not when he thought Poseidon
would marry her, and he had let him into her
chamber at night. Now he was blaming her, and
talking of sending her away so as not to anger
Poseidon. She looked at the half-finished tapestry
on her loom, the unwoven weft threads piled in
their basket, all separated by color and length. She
had spun it all herself, and it was strong, fine thread,
stronger and finer than anything anyone else could
make. Stronger than promises. Maybe stronger than
love. It would hold a heavy weight. She took a
length from the basket and began to coil it around
her hand.

XIII

❧

The Corn King

Arachne's mother found her hanging from her own threads in horrible fulfillment of Athena's prophecy, in the shadows of the chamber, beside her loom. The neighbors came running as the mother's wailing rose and fell in a long howl of anguish. Her father heard the commotion at the dye works and ignored it, a busy man with other things on his mind, until a terrified foreman pulled him by the arm, and told him it was his wife screaming.

They had cut her down by the time he got there, and the wife ran at him with a kitchen knife in her hand. The neighbors held her until someone got the knife away from her, while she shrieked at her husband, "You let him have her! You said we'd be rich! Now my child is dead!"

Arachne's sisters sat in the corner with their

hands over their faces, afraid to look at her dreadful, dark face.

The auspicious day, named by the priestesses to settle the rule of Attica, dawned clear and already hot. Metis came to the agora with the dark-robed servants of the Lady, meeting in solemn ceremony with those of the Achaean Goddess in their pale mantles, while the Areopagus gathered to give its judgment. Athena wore the aegis, to look as little like a bride as possible, and Polumetis perched on its shoulder, digging her talons into the leather.

Poseidon had decreed that the contest take place in the agora—near the fowler's stall where Nike said he had been digging up the pavement, Athena noted suspiciously. At this side of the market, the hill of the Acropolis rose a bit farther, in a stubby outcropping of rock with a jumble of stones at its base. Snakes tended to like the stones. As a child, Athena had caught a viper there once, and only Amoni's stealing it away from her had kept her from putting it in her uncle's bed. Vipers were unreliable, Amoni had told her solemnly. It might move about and end in Nurse's bed instead, and then how would Athena feel? She saw Amoni now in the crowd that pushed and flowed about the rocks. He stood leaning his shoulder against the warm gray stone, expressionless. She smiled at him hopefully and he nodded at her just a bit.

Poseidon arrived in a chariot drawn by white horses, with a purple cloak flowing from his

shoulders and a gold fillet that wasn't quite a cor-
onet in his hair, a regal counterpoint to his niece—
a tall gray-eyed woman in a goatskin sewn with
snakes. He halted his restive horses just a little too
close to her, as if she weren't there, and smiled at
the waiting crowd. He carried a tall staff in one
hand. Revulsion rose in Athena's throat, and she
swallowed hard. Arachne had been buried in
haste on the Hill of Tombs with the unborn child
still in her. Poseidon had spent no more grief for
her than he had given Medusa. Now he stood
lordly-wise in his chariot, leaning on his staff,
while the horses danced nervously, ears swiveling
to the shifting crowd. He appeared to notice
Athena for the first time. "Ah, there you are. And
where is the offering you have brought to the city?
You haven't kept the Areopagus waiting for a year
for nothing, I trust?"

"It comes," Athena said between her teeth. She
turned her back on him as an oxcart rattled into
the agora. The crowd parted slowly for it. The
branches of the olive trees whispered together.

"Trees!" Poseidon snorted with laughter.

A second cart followed, laden with clay jars.

"And wine to get us drunk enough to think that
trees are valuable!" Poseidon shouted, his voice
thick with amusement, drowning Athena's words.

"May I or may I not speak of the nature of my
gift?" Athena asked the Achaean high priestess
who stood beside Poseidon's chariot.

"You may speak," she announced.

Poseidon subsided, smirking but silent.

Athena hopped into the wagon with the trees. Nike's Aqhat hefted one of the jars onto his shoulder and brought it to her. She held out a bowl and he poured it carefully full of golden oil. When he had stoppered the jar and set it back in the rack on the cart, he brought a second. Athena said nothing as the citizens peered at the bowl in her hand, at the jars and the trees, while a little ripple of speculation ran through them. Out of the second jar Aqhat poured a bowlful of olives, dark and purpley black, and glistening with oil. Athena presented both bowls to the priestesses as Aqhat began to pour small cups full and pass them into the crowd.

"These are the riches of Tyre," Athena said in a voice loud enough to carry across the agora. The murmuring stopped and they listened. "Olives. They are born of trees that take sixteen years to mature, and then live forever. Their oil burns clean, it soothes the skin, and it gives nourishment. This is the gift I bring. Food and light."

The bowls went from hand to hand and people dipped their fingers in.

"The trees thrive in the harshest ground," Athena said. "Their oil gives much nourishment, and in a famine year it often means the difference between life and death in the lands where olives grow."

They licked their fingers and ate the dark olives with wary looks.

"It burns clean. Olive oil lights the world where the Phoenicians live. It lights the city of Tyre."

She held out her hand and Aqhat gave her a clay lamp filled with oil. She lit the wick. "It will light ours. The grape was the first great gift given to the people of Attica by the Goddess. This is the second. With the grape and the olive we will want for nothing." She handed the lamp carefully into the crowd and they sniffed at the flame. "The lamps of the Goddess will burn brighter and cleaner," she said to the priestesses. "And the oil will feed her servants," she added. "The Lady in all her guises will smile at this tree."

"Moonshine!" Poseidon spat out the word. "Wild tales. Who will believe all that?"

Aqhat stood up among the oil jars. "Tyre is my home," he said. "I lived my life by the light of the olives until I came here, where you burn tallow."

"Oh. You. Aren't you a clerk?" Poseidon gave him a cursory glance.

The chief priestess of the Achaean Goddess dipped her finger in the oil and put it to her lips. A little silence gathered about her, an expectant hush. The oxen watched her gravely from wide, dark eyes. Athena wondered if the priestesses had made up their minds already who would win the contest. And if they had, whom they favored. They didn't like Poseidon, but the priestesses of the Achaean Goddess wanted no return to old ways. Perhaps better an evil king for a span until someone more suitable was born. Athena thought the priestesses could arrange that. Priestesses looked a very long way down the road.

"The olive growers of Tyre do not sell these

trees," Athena said. "They sell the oil and fruit only, and they fetch a great price. Nowhere in the lands that border our sea are these trees grown except for Crete. Will we be a land of goatherds burning tallow or a land of gold light whose children never go hungry? There are many wondrous things to come from Tyre, but olive trees are the queen of them."

The councilors of the Areopagus dipped their fingers in the oil and sucked on the olive fruits, spitting the pits into their palms, where they studied them intently, as if they might be a new species of insect. Tryphon put his nose down to a pit and inhaled. The pit went into his nose and he snorted it out again, wheezing. Perseus choked on a laugh, coughing, but it wasn't convincing. Tryphon glared at him.

"Foreign plants." Tryphon snorted again. The pit had scratched his nose.

"It has a pleasant taste. Like nuts." Perseus dipped his finger in the oil again.

"I am told they bathe themselves with it at the king's palace at Knossos," Cecrops said.

"Told by whom?" Poseidon asked scornfully.

"Their lords and ladies perfume their hair and beards with it."

"If that is true, why haven't I heard of this miraculous oil that you can eat and burn and rub in your hair?" Poseidon lifted an eyebrow.

"I do not know," Cecrops said carefully. "Perhaps you pay less attention to the merchants and travelers who visit here."

"I have heard of it," Poseidon said grudgingly. "But a tree that takes sixteen years to bear fruit? A fine gift, that one."

"It is wise to look into the future, lord," the priestess of the Lady of the old temple said. Her eyes were cold. He was not forgiven.

"And what can my uncle offer that is finer?" Athena demanded. "Another temple built with money taxed from the citizens?"

Poseidon looped his horses' reins about the gold finials that ornamented the front of his chariot. "I will bring my gift from the heart of the earth. Let this woman work an equal wonder if she can." He raised his staff. The air seemed to shimmer around him, and the crowd tensed. There was odd blood in the royal family. Look at the niece. And this one—it was already known that when he lost his temper the ground shook. Clearly some great magic was coming.

Poseidon struck the stone beside him and it cracked open like an egg. The crowd gasped as a stream of bright water began to flow from it.

That was what he had been doing, Athena thought. There were underground watercourses in these hills, which fed the springs. She was familiar with most of them from her childhood rambles. Poseidon had tampered with one to bring it to the surface here. He must have known beforehand that it ran beneath the agora. He had an odd and literal connection to the Attic earth. She tried to feel that same link, hear the water deep below her, and trace its path. She knelt and put her fingers to the spout of water that gushed from the rock and flowed away over the paving stones.

The Areopagus and even the priestesses looked at Poseidon with awe. It didn't matter how unattractive or even how evil a form his human side took; the old king's brother was clearly possessed of the royal gift. His blood flowed with the water through the rock of the Acropolis.

"He came here beforehand and cleft the rock to make it loose the trapped water when he struck it," Athena said disgustedly, crouched by the flowing stream, but neither the keepers of the temples nor the crowd listened now. Metis whispered in the chief priestess's ear but the woman waved her away.

"I will build a fountain and a pool here to honor the Goddess who gives us the waters of life," Poseidon said. "This girl can buy trees with gold, but I can bring water from the earth. Remember that!"

Athena put her wet fingers to her lips, and her expression changed. She began to laugh. "It's salt!" She held a cupped hand out to the chief priestess. "Taste it, Mother. It is salty enough to keep mullet in!"

A disturbed murmur went through the crowd. That might be a bad omen.

"It is water from living rock!" Poseidon shouted. "I struck the rock and it came forth!" His horses danced nervously at his voice.

The chief priestess ignored Athena. She bent to the stream of water herself and dipped her fingers in it. She brought them to her mouth. "It is salt."

Athena grinned at her uncle. "What use is a well of salty water, oh wonder worker?"

Poseidon lifted his staff furiously. His face was red with anger. Athena backed away from his horses' hooves. "You lie!" he shouted at her. "You are a lying whore!" The ground began to shake at the words, and the crowd backed away.

"We live on the edge of the sea," Athena said. "Her waters go where they will. It is salt."

"You lie!" Poseidon struck the rock with his staff again, hard enough to snap the wood, as if he could force freshwater from it. The stone cracked under the blow and a piece of it fell away with the shards of the staff. No water came out this time, but something else fell from the rocks with a furious hissing: snakes, a nest of vipers disturbed by the blows. They writhed about the horses' feet while the horses reared and screamed. The crowd scattered and the chief priestess fell, slipping on the wet stone. For a moment the snakes were compacted into a ball like a head of writhing hair. It rolled across the stones, and the white horses flung themselves away from it in terror.

The reins were still lashed to the chariot, and Poseidon grabbed at them frantically now, but they came loose and flew from his hands. The horses surged down the steep street with the long reins snapping behind them until they stepped on them and tore them free. Athena could see Poseidon leaning from the chariot, reaching desperately for the cut ends. Then the chariot careened from view, around a corner where the road ran through the city gates. With no hand on the reins, the horses let their fear drive them. Their hooves thundered on the road. The crowd ran to the edge of the agora, where the Acropolis looked down on the coastal plain. They stared in horror and elbowed one another for the best view. Poseidon's horses flew at full gallop along the harbor road, with Poseidon clinging to the chariot. A cart laden with bright bronze pots was coming up the road, and the sun flashed off the pots into their eyes. They flung up their heads and left the road entirely, galloping toward the headland. Poseidon was a small, dark figure now, swaying in the jouncing car.

The vipers slithered back into their stones. Behind her Athena knew her mother was tending to the priestess, who was old and frail, with brittle bones, but she couldn't take her eyes from the chariot growing smaller in the distance, flying toward the headland like a huge, ungainly bird.

Poseidon could see the ground rushing away beneath him, through the jagged broken floor of the chariot as it bounced and rumbled over the stones. The horses were in full panic now. The foam flew from their mouths, and their white backs were wet with sweat. They didn't know where they were running to, or from what. They simply ran. They would slow eventually. They had to; not even his horses could run at that pace forever. Poseidon clung to the sides of the swaying car. They were going too fast over the rocky ground to jump. He had begun to, but the sight of it falling away beneath his feet stopped him.

The horizon heaved as the car careened. A wheel snapped off with a shriek of splintering wood, but the horses didn't slow. Now the car banged and bounced on one wheel, nearly overturning with each stride. Poseidon's teeth cut through his lip as he was flung against the side of the car. The gold fillet flew off his head, trampled under the horses' hooves. The salt taste of blood filled his mouth. Something wrapped itself around his ankle and he snatched at it, thinking it was the snapped-off rein. It writhed in his hand and he saw he was holding a viper. The snake twisted its length about his arm and struck. Poseidon felt the fangs go in and flailed his arm, trying to shake it off. The viper's slitted eyes held his for a moment. He thought he saw the girl's face behind them, wild rose-gold curls tangling with the writhing body of the snake. She opened her mouth and hissed at him. Her teeth were fanged like the viper's.

Poseidon wrenched the snake from his arm with his other hand, its fangs raking his flesh, and flung it from the chariot. The chariot hit a stone and he staggered and fell again, tangled in the purple cloak. He lay against the side of the car staring at his arm. The punctures of the viper's fangs were dark blue dots that seemed to expand as he watched. His arm was growing numb. How had it gotten in the chariot with him? The other wheel crumpled and the car slid along on its belly. Poseidon staggered to his feet, clutching the rim, and shouted to the horses. They never slowed. The sun blazed into his eyes. The horizon before him shimmered with its heat. He squinted and saw the headland looming at him with the long drop to the rock-fanged shore below it. He shouted again at the horses. Their lathered sides heaved as they flung themselves outward, leaving land behind entirely, and fell into the water, the shattered pieces of the chariots whirling through the air behind them. It was high tide, and Poseidon sank beneath the surf, rolling over and over in the bright, cold blue water as it pulled him from land.

Poseidon's body never came floating back to shore, and nor did his horses. The gods had taken them, Cecrops said, standing on the wet sand where fishermen mending their nets had seen the chariot fall past them.

"He has gone to dwell under the sea," the old priestess announced, after they had carried her to the shore on a litter.

The Areopagus nodded. That seemed a far better place than in the palace, just now. The Acropolis itself had set vipers on him, and if the land rejected him there would be no prosperity while he was king. The land had spoken.

Athena arrived on horseback, the aegis flowing from her shoulders, with Polumetis on her wrist. She sat on the red roan mare and watched the breakers roll in and pull away again, their white foam manes the last sight of Poseidon's horses. The sea breeze lifted her dark hair about her face and whispered in her ear. She saw that the Areopagus were watching her, as was the old priestess. She didn't see Metis. It seemed that she had finally outdistanced her mother.

"The sea has taken my uncle," she said at last. "The land has given you me. Will you have me?"

Cecrops shuffled across the sand and knelt formally before her horse's head. "Will you consent to rule Attica in your father's stead?"

"I consent," she said.

Cecrops and the rest nodded at that. There were more things to be settled, but not here on this wild, wet beach. The Areopagus would meet tomorrow, with a queen in the high seat, and that was time enough. For tonight she would return to her old quarters in the palace, and order her uncle's chambers swept out, his possessions brought to her. She wasn't sure what she would do with his things—gold jewelry and clothes too fine to waste. Give them to Medusa's mother maybe. And Arachne's.

She saw her own mother pushing her way through the Areopagus to her. "Take me up on your saddle," Metis said. "I rode here on a cart with Tryphon, the fool."

Athena extended her hand and her mother leaped up behind her. The roan mare tossed her head at the added weight. Athena smiled. Not many women Metis's age could still do that. She saw Tryphon looking at them disapprovingly.

"I must talk to you," Metis said. "Before you meet with them. We must plan."

Athena looked out at the cold sea and the waves rolling in and out. A single seabird skimmed the water. What would it be like to have bird's wings? Poseidon must have known, for just a moment. She put her heels to the red mare's flanks and they raced along the sand, Metis with her arms about Athena's waist, hair and cloaks flying out behind them, wild as the seabird. She saw Tryphon give them another dark look and laughed, but she said to Metis, "No, Mother."

In the morning the Areopagus came ceremonially to escort her to the council rock. If Metis found her unmalleable, so would the Areopagus, Athena thought with satisfaction. She had lain awake most of the night in her old rooms, watching the painted fish swim around the walls, and she knew what she would say. The exact words came to her clearly as she sat down in the high seat and surveyed them. "There are things to be done," she told them.

Tryphon rose, one finger extended in the air like a tutor giving a lesson.

"No, I shall not marry," Athena said, forestalling him.

Tryphon opened and closed his mouth several times.

Cecrops rose. "It is a matter for some consideration," he said mildly.

"I have considered," Athena said. "If I marry,

the Areopagus will give my power to my husband, just because I am a woman. You say you will not," she added as Cecrops started to answer her, "but it will happen. It will be slow. At first you will consult him on matters in which you wish to influence me. And then on matters that seem to require the masculine viewpoint. There will be children and I will be occupied in my nursery. You will rely more heavily on him. And then he will be the king and I will be the consort. So, no."

Metis rose next. She would have her say if she could. "The Old Ones—"

"No, Mother," Athena said again. "I know what the Old Ones want, but those times are past. I will not marry in that fashion either; there will be no killing of kings. The Lady has taken her last husband. We gave him to her, the vipers and I, and I think she will be content with that."

There was a general murmuring at that, and a nodding of heads, even by the Pelasgian member.

Perseus stood. "What you say may be true," he said. "I have ridden with you and will happily give myself to your rule. I think you have sacrificed much for us. But who will succeed you if you don't marry?"

They all nodded again. That delicate question had been in all their minds, but they had left it to Perseus, who was fearless, to voice it.

"There must be an heir," they said, concurring, now that he had spoken and she hadn't turned him into a stone or a yapping dog.

"Can't have an heir without babies."

"Can't have babies without a husband, stands to reason."

"Well, it has happened. Showers of light and bulls and things. It has happened."

"Unlikely, if you ask me."

"Stop it!" Athena said, trying not to laugh. They would be funny if the matter were not so deadly serious. A war over the succession, just now so narrowly avoided, had to be forestalled at all costs. Such wars ruined kingdoms.

"Cecrops will rule with me," she informed them, setting out what she had thought of in the night. "Not as king but as the eldest and wisest of the Areopagus. After us, we will, in our wisdom, choose an heir."

"What about the Old Ones?" Metis demanded. "The Pelasgians have suffered at your uncle's hands. Give them some redress."

"Very well," Athena said. "I have thought of this also. The Areopagus is to be expanded until a full third part of its members are Pelasgian."

"That's too many," one of them said. "We'll never get anything done."

Athena refrained from saying that they rarely got anything done anyway. They had just made her queen. "Then your ranks may be thinned as the oldest of you die," she told them frankly. "But one in three of you will be Pelasgian until such time as no one can tell Pelasgian from Achaean."

They looked disbelieving of that idea.

"Believe me," she said, "the time will come."

*   *   *

"And now that you are queen," Nike asked her, twisting her thread expertly from the distaff under the spindle's weight, "what will you do?" Aqhat was head of the counting house now, and the other clerks learned from him at Athena's orders to set things down as they did in Tyre. His wife brought her children to play in the palace courtyard as Athena and Nike, Pallas and Amoni, had once played as children.

"I will learn to use my potter's wheel." Athena chuckled. "Do you want Chryseis eating that caterpillar?"

Nike leaped from her chair and retrieved the caterpillar, an exceptionally large green one with orange spots. Chryseis howled.

"In the meantime, I sit in court with Cecrops," Athena went on, "deciding whose pig has been found in the street. There are more claimants for a loose pig than you can imagine."

"What else will you do, between pigs? I heard of your order about the Areopagus." Nike picked up her spindle again. "I don't suppose you could insist that they put women in it."

"The old men's nerves wouldn't stand it," Athena said. She smiled. "I will grow my trees."

She planted nine olive trees in ground that the vintner's crew prepared, as Ahiram had told her to, in a grove on the hill above the grape terraces, and the tenth in the heart of the agora, where it would shade the benches where the old men sat and argued philosophy and whether or not pilchards were bad for the digestion. That one would sink its roots deep into the heart of the Acropolis. She liked to think of it growing when none of them were living, when she had chosen an heir and his children's children ruled. Or didn't rule. You never knew. But the tree would be there.

She had been queen for one month when Amoni came to her in the palace courtyard, by the usual route this time, through the great doors into the council hall, and with the escort of the palace guard. He stood by her seat in the sun.

She looked up at him and smiled. "I wondered when you would come."

"What made you think I would?" He was dressed in his finest today, no burned and scarred leather apron. His tunic was of white wool, bordered with gold thread, and his sandals were soft red leather. Amoni could afford finery. No one had his skill with metal, whether he made a pot or a breastplate or a brooch. He stood watching her gravely, one hand behind his back.

"Because I didn't come to you," she said.

"Witch." He smiled. "I suppose you couldn't, now. You would be a scandal."

"Not at all," she said with dignity. "I can do anything I please. I am queen."

"You said that when you were five," he pointed out. "And you got a smacking."

She laughed. "When I rode Father's horse. I had forgotten."

"I haven't. You nearly ran me over."

"Oh, sit down." She patted the bench next to her. "Someone will bring us something to eat and drink in a moment; we won't have time to be a scandal. I can't sit here for more than a breath before someone brings me food. It's a wonder I'm not fat already."

He sat and she saw that he held a small package in his hand.

"Is that for me?"

"Don't be greedy."

"Very well. I will pretend there is no box in your hand."

"Since you can do anything."

"I don't do that very well," she admitted.

"I approve of what you've done about the Areopagus. We've been careless of our power, I think, we Achaeans."

"Your mother was Pelasgian," she pointed out.

"Ah, but one claims the side that has the power. Here." He unwrapped the cloth from around the box and she saw that it was made of gold, smaller than the palm of her hand, with a hinged lid with an owl atop it.

"This is your uncle's gold. It was supposed to be your bridal crown."

He handed it to her and she opened it. Inside was a ring of gold pierced with leaf-shaped holes around its band, ghost leaves, the souls of olive trees. At its top were three leaves of green peridot and three oval onyx olives. Athena caught her breath.

"Put it on," he said.

She put it to her finger and hesitated.

"Yes, it will bind you to me," he said. "But no one will know that but you." His pale eyes held hers. "I will not live my life without you," he said.

"I can't marry you," she whispered. "I can't give you children. What do you want with me?"

Amoni sat back on the bench and stretched his arms out along its back. "Love is very mysterious," he told her. "Nike keeps recommending nice girls to me. I don't know why I love you and not those nice girls, but I do."

Athena slid the ring onto her finger. The green leaves glimmered against Poseidon's gold. Polumetis landed on her lap and tried the onyx olives with her beak.

A servant girl bustled out of the palace with a tray of nuts and fruit and a silver ewer of wine, horrified that the queen had entertained a guest for so long without refreshment. She set the tray on a small table before them and scurried off.

"Do they always do that?" Amoni inquired.

"This one was late. Sometimes they get here before the guest actually has arrived. To be honest, I think my uncle probably beat them if they didn't. He had a dreadful temper for someone who looked so beautiful."

"Beauty is dangerous," he said, in the way he had once said love was dangerous. "I don't suppose there is any place they don't pop into like that? Would they assume you didn't need any more food if we ate this?"

Athena gave him a long look. "They don't pop

into my private chamber, if that is what you mean."

"Of course not," Amoni said. "That would be a scandal."

Athena burst out laughing, spilling her wine and unsettling Polumetis, who gave them a round yellow look of wounded dignity.

Athena shook her head, her expression sobering now. "Amoni, it doesn't do to tempt the Lady," she whispered.

"Surely the Lady wouldn't take that last thing from you, when you have given up so much." He was serious now.

Athena thought about the Lady of the Pelasgians, in her dark stone. The Achaean Goddess in her painted temple, poised for flight, poised to dance on the wind. Asherah-yam, Our Lady of the Sea and the Olives, watching over her boats. They all spoke to her, whispered that the parts of Athena that were bone and blood, stone and water, of Attica, belonged to the land and not to any man; those were the parts that would not die. Whispered to her that there was another part of her that was the woman who would live one life, and that part she might give as she would.

She slid her hand, the hand with the ring, slowly into Amoni's. The familiar tingle ran through her, through the parts that were not the land but the living woman. She stood, and he stood too, never taking his eyes off hers or his fingers from her hand. "I can't marry you," she said again. "I can only love you."

"That's enough," he said.

As for Poseidon, it wasn't long before people began to build a shrine where his chariot had flown like a huge bird into the sky and then vanished under the waves. Those at the coast who had seen it fall now swore that he had stood at the reins, his hair flaming like a sunset, a thunderbolt in either hand, and driven horses of sea foam down the air into blue water.

The shrine was just a cairn of stones at first, where the fisherfolk left little things—a spray of pink flowers, a seashell, a silver bead—and said their prayers for fair weather or a good catch of tunny. But slowly, as Athena ruled Attica with no man by her side, it began to be said that he had indeed been the last Corn King. His blood had watered the sea as well as the land, they said, and when in summer there was an abundant crop of wheat and rye, and the grapes sweetened in perfect weather until harvest, and the fishing boats brought in a catch that overflowed their nets, the stone cairn gave way to a wooden temple and then to a house of cut stone with painted pillars to support its roof, looking out over the headland to the sea. The old shrine at the harbor also began to be called by his name. They gave him a ram every summer now on the day when he had ridden into the sea.

What the queen thought of that, she never said. But the olive tree in the agora flourished.